Praise for *The Br*

"*The Broken Hearts Club* is very much like the Frankenbiscuit from its own pages—dreamy first love wrapped in a big lie topped with some bad decisions and sprinkled with complications, served with a side of great banter and one incredible best friend. You will not regret ordering."

—Samantha Markum, author of *This May End Badly* and *You Wouldn't Dare*

"With a charming cast, artistic eye, and its perfectly imperfect "love rules," Susan Bishop Crispell's *The Broken Hearts Club* glows rose-gold. Readers will root for Imogen, wish August would slide into their DMs, and crave a Frankenbiscuit long after the last page!"

—K. L. Walther, bestselling author of *The Summer of Broken Rules*

Also by Susan Bishop Crispell

The Holloway Girls

The Broken Hearts Club

SUSAN BISHOP CRISPELL

The characters and events portrayed in this book are fictitious or are used fictitiously. Any similarity to real persons, living or dead, is purely coincidental and not intended by the author.

Published by Sourcebooks Fire, an imprint of Sourcebooks
P.O. Box 4410, Naperville, Illinois 60567–4410
(630) 961-3900
sourcebooks.com

Cataloging-in-Publication data is on file with the Library of Congress.

Printed and bound in Canada.
MBP 10 9 8 7 6 5 4 3 2 1

For Dad & Susan, thank you
for showing me that true love will
always find a way.

Chapter ONE

Love Rule #21: You must be willing to give a part of your heart to gain a piece of someone's in return.

Love makes people do ridiculous things. Take me for example: today I'm celebrating my one-year anniversary with my very *fake* boyfriend.

Don't get me wrong. August is not made up. He's a real seventeen-year-old I spent an afternoon with almost two summers ago while my mom set up his mom through her matchmaking service. He just doesn't happen to know I borrowed his name and a few of his most charming personality traits for personal use.

I don't know if the real August is romantic. But the fake August is off the charts. The *surprise* anniversary gift on my front doorstep—orchestrated between August and my BFF, Gemma, if anyone asks—is going to light up my Insta all day long. The gift is a bouquet of ranunculus flowers, with their fat delicate balls of layered petals that you can't help but smile at, and a black velvet box open to display a rose-gold disc necklace engraved with a camera icon on one side and #mostloved, our relationship hashtag, on the other. It's sweet enough to make a cynic believe in love. At least for a moment.

No one will ever know it's not real.

Gemma's the only one in on my lie. It was her idea, actually, after she saw the photo I snapped of him on the day we met. August's cute in an emo sort of way. In the picture, he's on the dock behind my house, his dark brown hair long enough to fall into his eyes. He wore a beanie that the nearly eighty-five-degree day was way too hot for but that he refused to take off, and a fitted baseball tee that hinted at muscles on his otherwise skinny frame. And he lives across the state in Winston-Salem, which made him the perfect choice when being the perpetually single daughter of a never-fails matchmaker became too much pressure.

So when Gemma looks at the gifts I've staged and says, "Overkill, Mo," I have to stop and gawk at her.

This was the least over-the-top of my ideas. I considered splurging on this killer rose-gold ring inset with an ombré-teal enamel from a jewelry artist in Scotland (which cost more than I make in a month working at Gemma's dads' restaurant) or buying the naming rights to a binary star (until I realized it was a total scam—only the International Astronomical Union can name stars). I also thought about paying a stranger to get a #mostloved tattoo so I could take a photo and pretend it was August, but even I realized that was going too far.

"What are you talking about? This is exactly the right amount of kill," I say.

"If by *kill* you mean desperation," Gemma says. She lifts the necklace from our WELCOME Y'ALL doormat, effectively ruining my ten minutes of tedious setup.

After swatting her hand away, I readjust the box so the early morning light hits it just right. Then I snap a few final shots with my Nikon D500. I've got just enough time to transfer it to my phone with my portable SD-card reader and post a story on Insta before first period.

"I've spent a year trying to sell this relationship. I can't blow it now!"

"Then you might want to lose the flowers that look like a wedding bouquet. Otherwise, it looks like you're trying too hard."

"Not me, Gemma. August. Plus, they're my favorite flowers, so it would be weird if he got me something different."

She makes a production of rolling her eyes. If she weren't so damn good at building sets for the drama club, I'd say she should be the lead in every play. "Fine. But hurry up. I need coffee before class."

"You could've stopped on your way here. I might've even been done by the time you got here if you weren't distracting me with your overkill talk."

She huffs out an exasperated sigh, closing her eyes as if looking at me is too much effort. Her blended teal-and-purple mermaid eyeshadow shimmers with the movement.

I laugh.

She laughs.

We fall right back into the conversation as if the interruption never even happened.

"And deprive you of the opportunity to get a surprise anniversary coffee from August? I wouldn't dare," she says.

Gemma pretends to hate all this fanfare, but I know she loves it. She's as single as I am, so this fake relationship is the most action either of us has seen in way too long. But she refuses to use me to boost her love life. Even when I could tell her with one look if the person she likes feels the same way.

Grinning at her, I say, "Not much of a surprise now, is it?"

She shrugs. "Well, nothing with your boyfriend ever is, so at least it tracks."

"Harsh."

"But no less true. Now make it *snappy*."

Doing as she instructed, I take a few more shots and, with as much drama as I can muster, say, "Snap, snap, snap." One for each click of the shutter.

"Sip, sip, sip," she replies.

Not-so-subtle hint taken, I scoop up the anniversary photo shoot accessories and arrange them back into the tote bag where they've lived for the past two weeks. My fingers linger on the necklace. It's been hard not to break it out early. The gifts from August are part lie perpetuation, part sensible planning since I was going to buy them myself anyway. This way I have the added benefit of seeming like I'm one-half of a perfect relationship.

Gemma speeds up my meticulous process by jamming the

ranunculus into the vase of water sitting on the porch and shoving it at me so water drenches the front of my dress.

"It'll air-dry," she says by way of apology.

"Remind me to keep my surprise anniversary coffee away from you, or I might end up wearing it too."

Gemma glares at me, one eyebrow raised in warning. "Only if you make me late for first period."

"We're going, we're going." I set the tote and flowers on the hallway table, yell goodbye to my mom, who's already in her home office prepping for today's first match-seeking client, and race to the car before Gemma leaves without me. She's done it before, and I had to run three blocks before I caught up to her at a stop sign. She laughed so hard, she started wheezing.

Once I'm safely in the front seat, I connect my SD drive to my phone, then transfer the photos, and after selecting the best one, I pull up the photo caption I drafted during a shift at Yeastie Boys last week and add it to my anniversary post. One year of being #mostloved. Gemma thinks the hashtag is obnoxious and that if August ever found out about our fake relationship, he'd use the embarrassment of it as justification for murdering me on the spot. Thankfully, it's not like he'll ever find out. I made a fake Instagram account for *my* August so I can tag him in my stories and posts without linking back to the *real* August.

Selling a lie like this is all about the details. And I am the queen of details. It's what makes me such a good photographer. I see things others don't notice, and I make them stand out.

Like this picture. Most people would've focused on getting

every item in frame. Giving each part of the gift equal billing. But not me. I picked an angle that put the necklace slightly off center, with the curvy-stemmed flowers coming in from one corner, and it makes the photo a thousand times more interesting. It tells a story instead of being static, flat. A love story. And maybe one day that story will be real. Not with August but with someone who finally sees me as more than a friend.

Gemma's dads own Yeastie Boys Café. It's a breakfast-all-day joint with the best biscuits in the state of North Carolina. The award plaque to prove it hangs on the wall by the register. Gemma and I have been working here since we could see over the counter, though it only became official when we turned fourteen and her dads could legally put us on the payroll.

The small diner-style room sizzles with conversation and bacon cooking in the kitchen. A dozen familiar faces turn our way with some form of "morning, Gemma; morning, Mo." We know all the regulars by name and customary order. Though we're in here so often for a kick of caffeine on our way to school that they'd recognize us even if we didn't work here.

I return every greeting personally. Gemma throws a wave to the room at large, only adding a smile when one of her dads, Lee, shoots her a look.

"One shot," Gemma says to me, dashing behind the counter to collect two to-go mugs from Lee. She pops a kiss onto his cheek as thanks.

I pretend not to get her meaning just to get a rise out of her. "Of espresso? Do you want us to sleep through class?"

"You know full well what I mean. No turning the cup this way and that, trying to find the best light. All the light in here is perfect." She offers up the cup, a note handwritten in black marker on the side facing me.

I love you most.

For a moment I forget it's all made up. That August isn't really my boyfriend and this love note isn't really from him. And my heart goes all warm and fuzzy.

"Wow, that must be some coffee," says a voice behind me.

I don't have to turn around to know it's Ren. But I do. Because I'm apparently a masochist.

Ren Kano. My forever crush. With his easy surfer smile and wavy dark hair that begs for hands to get tangled in it. He's the reason I made up a relationship with August in the first place. To force myself to stop pining for him when he and Lana Abrams were *actual* couple goals. They've been together since freshman year and are basically halfway down the aisle already. All I have to do is look at the rose-gold auras swirling around them when they're together to know it's true love.

The ability to literally see when people are in love is what makes my mom one of the most sought-after matchmakers in the country. It's not as idyllic for the daughter of said matchmaker. Having my crushes treat me like a freak—or worse, ask me to tell them if their crushes feel the same—all but put a nail in my dating coffin. Ren has never done either, but thanks to Lana, he's never going to look at me the way I'm apparently looking at my salted caramel mocha.

A lie is on my tongue before I even think about it. "This is special anniversary coffee. August and I have been together for a year today. Since we don't get to see each other, Gemma's helping him carry out surprises for me. Hence me mooning over my coffee." I turn the cup so he and Lana can see the note that is very much *not* from my boyfriend.

Lana waits until Ren is distracted with ordering their drinks, then says, "You're lucky he goes to this much effort to let you know he loves you. Especially a year in. I think Ren stopped doing stuff like that after the first three months." Her usual love-fueled rose-gold aura is shot through with whirls of teal like patina.

The color of heartbreak.

The shimmer of color against her dark skin is stunning. The watery teal glow is such a stark difference from how I've seen her for the past three plus years that I almost don't recognize her. My fingers itch to snap a picture of her with my phone to make sure I'm not seeing something that's not actually there. But I don't because I have manners.

If I did though, I'd be able to capture her heartbreak aura in the picture. No one other than Mom or me would be able to see it, but it would be there as vibrant swirls of color just as I see it in real life.

My eyes drift to Ren, who is currently colorless. No love, no heartbreak. Whatever he's feeling for Lana in the wake of her comment isn't something I can see. But the tension building between the three of us threatens to suck all the air out of the room. Though I'm the only one who seems to notice.

It's not that I *want* them to break up. I'm not that heartless. But I wouldn't be disappointed if it happened.

Guilt creeps across my skin like a sunburn, and I rush to try and spackle over the cracks in their relationship before they grow too deep to be fixed. "It's just a coffee. At least you get to see Ren every day. He doesn't have to do extra stuff to remind you he's thinking about you."

"Doesn't mean it wouldn't be nice to be reminded every once in a while."

Ren waves at Lee to get him to hold on the orders he just placed. Slipping his arm around Lana's shoulders, Ren pulls her into his side. "Do you want me to have them write something special on your coffee?"

"It's not special if you have to ask me first."

"So that's a no?" There's a subtle bite to his words, a jagged edge smoothed over by a teasing smile.

My fingers cramp from holding my cup so tightly. "If you give me a heads-up before you come in next time I'm working, I've got you covered." Crap. Did I really just volunteer to write a love note for my crush's girlfriend? There's something seriously wrong with me.

Giving my cup a death glare, Lana shakes out of his hold.

"Don't bother, Mo. If he doesn't want to do it on his own, I'm not going to force him. I have to do that enough already." The teal in her aura grows darker until it's a storm cloud raging around her chest, blocking all the brightness and warmth of the love she feels for Ren beneath the hurt.

"What's that supposed to mean?" he asks.

"Exactly what it sounds like. If I didn't make plans for us to do things together or come find you when I know you'll be someplace like here getting coffee before school, our relationship would be nonexistent."

Lee slides their drinks across the counter—sans note—and Ren takes his as if it's a sword he can defend himself with. Brandishing it toward Lana, he says, "If that's how you feel, maybe you should see if Mo's perfect boyfriend has a friend you can date instead."

They both look at me like this is an actual request. Like my response will dictate the future of their relationship. I don't need that kind of pressure. That's why I have a strict no-matchmaking policy in place. The only relationship I want to be in the middle of is my own. "I—"

"You know what? It'd be better than sitting here waiting for you to remember I exist. So, if you want me to find someone else, fine. I'm sure Mo will be more than happy to help me. Don't come crawling back to me when you finally realize what you gave away."

Gemma swoops in to save me before I make things worse. "Her mom's the matchmaker. And we should get to school before we're late. One more time and it's detention for me." Hooking her arm through mine, she steers me away from them before I've gotten a picture of my coffee. The melting whipped cream and chocolaty drink slosh up through the hole in the lid I slapped on it and dribble over the side, leaving a trail of stickiness right through my message.

Happy fake anniversary to me.

Chapter TWO

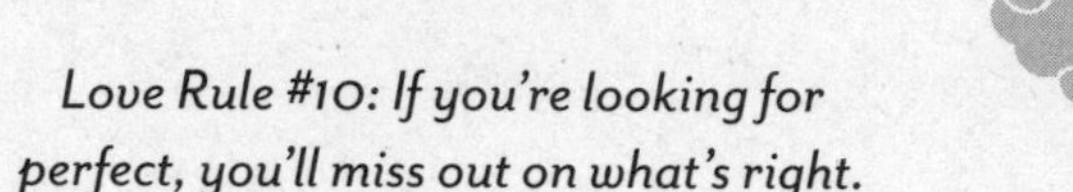

Love Rule #10: If you're looking for perfect, you'll miss out on what's right.

With all my fake anniversary planning and the surprise of Ren and Lana possibly breaking up, I completely forget about my meeting with my adviser during the lunch break. My application for the Kinsey School of Art and Design's summer art intensive is due in thirty-seven days. I have a countdown on my phone. Mrs. Clemente is helping me pick my best shots. The ones that say as much about me as a photographer as about the subject.

When I get to the photography lab on the other side of campus, she's not there. I'm only a couple of minutes late, so I doubt she's already bailed. Though it is lasagna day, and the cafeteria makes better Italian food than Flour + Salt, the fanciest restaurant in town. Nice to know our tuition money goes toward something everyone can benefit from.

I lay my leather portfolio case on the table and unpack the portraits Gemma and I deemed the best. Twelve in all.

The application requires eight, so I have some decisions to make. By the time I've arranged them—and rearranged them—on the desk, Mrs. Clemente dashes into the room, a plate of lasagna sliding across the plastic tray she carries one-handed. "Look at you, all ready to go." She stuffs a forkful of cheesy, saucy noodles in her mouth. "Let me just set this down."

"You can keep eating. I don't mind."

"Oh, no. For the next ten, maybe twelve minutes, you get my full attention. Show me what you got."

My palms go all clammy, like they do whenever Ren comes into the café. I wipe them dry on my thighs and hope Mrs. Clemente doesn't notice. Turns out, she's not even watching me. She's already studying my photos, her eyes squinted slightly in concentration.

Objectively, I know my pictures are good. With a pale gray backdrop and natural light flooding in through floor-to-ceiling windows in the studio, each subject's love glow shines. I shoot them all from the torso up, where their glow is on full display. Mrs. Clemente can't see the swirling cloud of rose gold in each portrait the way I do, but each one is unmistakably a person in love.

My pants are no match for my overactive nervous sweat, and I give up, curling my hands into balls behind my back.

"These are good, Imogen." Her tone is cautious, like she's scared to say more. Like she knows what comes out next is going to destroy me. She doesn't disappoint. "But do they really showcase your talent? Do they show the range and artistic depth you and I both know you're capable of?"

I've wanted to be a photographer since I was little and would fill my mom's phone with picture after picture of every person we met. I didn't care about capturing things or places. Always people. I loved the way most people would stop everything when they saw a camera aimed their way and put on their brightest smile. I used to delete all the pictures where the person wasn't smiling, thinking it was a bad shot. But now I see the beauty in different expressions. The story being told through their eyes, the set of their jaw, the tilt of their head. And it's my job to make sure that story gets heard.

"But I do portrait photography. These are my best ones," I say.

"And they are beautiful. As a portfolio though, it's a little one-note. They're too similar. You want to wow the summer program's admission panel, and I'm afraid this won't stand out. I think you keep this one," she points to a portrait of Delaney Richards, one of my mom's frequent clients. As much as Delaney wants to find true love, the closest she's come to it is falling for the idea of her perfect man. So far, Mom hasn't found him. "And this one." Mrs. Clemente taps the portrait of Gabe, Gemma's other dad. He agreed to be part of my portfolio in exchange for me working extra shifts when one of the other servers called in sick for a week. "Maybe one other. For the rest of the submission, let's try something new. Something that really sets you apart and allows your talent to shine. Think you can do that?"

No. The word screams in my head. But I refuse to give voice to it. I just have to show Mrs. Clemente she's wrong about my work.

"I have other pictures, from class projects and just random shots I've taken of nature and places around town."

"That's a good start. I'm going to push you to think outside your comfort zone though. The goal is to make sure each piece makes a statement. That it says something to the viewer. You take stunning photographs of people because that's what you love. Now we just need to find something other than people that you're just as passionate about. It could be landscapes or pets or a different format like underwater photography. Whatever gets you excited. I know you can do this, Imogen."

The thing is, I *love* love. That's why my portraits are so good. I can see the moment love takes hold and sets someone's heart on fire. Ask the right questions, get them to tell a story, and they literally glow. The photographs practically take themselves.

But I can't magic an inanimate object into the perfect shot. And I can't make her see what I see. The swirling mist of rose gold that ripples around the images. The thickness and brightness and movement that is unique to each person. When I look at my photos, I see the love pouring off them. Mom does too. To everyone else though, they're just portraits of happy people grinning for the camera.

But if I can't make anyone else see what I see, then I'll never be anything more than good.

Mom's office doors are closed when I get home, meaning she's with a client. The glass French doors give the illusion of privacy. She'll give me the complete rundown on this client the second they leave so that when it comes time for me to shoot their love-match photos for their matching session, I'll know everything I need to get the best shots. Knowing what they love—those things that make them light up on the inside—makes all the difference.

That's something Mrs. Clemente doesn't understand about my photos. I'm not just taking portraits. I'm capturing the true essence of my subject's heart and putting it out there for all the world to see. The swirls of rose gold emanating from them might not be visible to anyone but me and Mom, but the love causing it is.

I just have to find a way to make her see it.

Mom's laugh cuts through my thoughts. It's her snuggled-into-the-couch-for-a-mother-daughter-*The-Good-Place*-marathon laugh. Not the polite, reserved version of it she uses with clients. Whoever she's with today is sure to find love if they can make Mom drop her professional defenses and bust a gut.

August was like that the day we met. He came to Portree with his mom for one of her matching appointments, and within five minutes, it felt like I'd known him my whole life. He had this easy way about him. Some deep-rooted openness that made me want to tell him all my secrets. It's why I asked to take his picture that day. To capture that moment of feeling seen. Known. August's photo is a reminder of what I'm holding out for by faking a relationship with him in the first place. The kind of relationship my parents had. My dad's been gone for thirteen years, but the love he and my mom had was the real deal—strong enough to keep her heart intact despite losing him so early into their love story.

True love doesn't break hearts.

That's love rule number one.

If your heart gets broken, it wasn't true love, and you have to get back out there until you find it. Or at least that's what Mom tells all her clients. Her list of love rules, handed out to clients during their first appointment, is meant to put them in the right frame of mind to find love. They're a philosophy. A way of life. Not just for her clients but for me too. So I figure why go through the pain of heartbreak when I can literally see if someone loves me?

August didn't love me that day on the dock, but there was a shimmer about him. The promise of something more.

That's what Mom looks for with her clients. What I help capture in their love-match photos. That spark that will set their hearts on fire. Maybe I just have love on the brain, but when Mom's client emerges from her office half an hour later, I swear he's got a rosy glow trailing him out of the house like glitter. He's got an athletic build, all broad shoulders and serious muscles peeking out from his rolled-up shirtsleeves. I can already see how, when I take his photos, the light will play over his sharp cheekbones and long nose that looks like it's been broken at some point. His smile is easy, genuine. Like he's just had the best date of his life.

Mom pauses on the porch then leans into his open arms. And I have to pick my jaw off the floor. Laughing? Hugging? With a client? Who is this woman?

Maybe this mystery client isn't the only one who has a bit of a love glow.

I pin Mom with a questioning look when she waves him off with one final laugh and closes the door. Presumably to keep herself from following him home. Since my dad died when I was four, I've never once seen her like this. Mooning over a man. Her focus has always been on finding love for others so they could find what she and Dad had. But she's been lovestruck by this guy for sure. She's all heart eyes and wistful sighs when she comes back inside from seeing him off.

"He seems nice. Are you sure you want to set him up with someone else?" I ask.

She's careful not to look at me as she walks to her office. As if going right into work mode will stop me from calling her out. "That is what we do here, Imogen."

"But he's cute. And you're clearly into him. You don't hug clients. 'Love can be conveyed in as little as a look or a touch.' Rule number six, remember? But you hugged him."

"Alex is an old friend."

"How old? Did you date him? Because I'm definitely getting some more-than-friend vibes."

"Older than you. And there are no vibes. He is just a friend." She settles into her chair, collecting whatever notes she took during Alex's session so she can transcribe them into an electronic file later. "How did things go with your adviser?"

I drop onto the wingback chair across the desk from her, throwing my legs over one arm and letting my head hang off the other side so my hair drags on the floor, an auburn cascade of waves. "Not as good as I hoped. She wants me to try something other than portraits. Because apparently my portraits aren't 'wow' enough." I explode my hands in the air like fireworks for emphasis.

Used to my over-the-top-ness, Mom shakes her head and sighs. "I'm sure that's not what Mrs. Clemente said."

"Not in those words. But I could see it on her face, Mom. She was bored. And if she's bored, the admission committee will be too, and there goes my shot at getting into Kinsey. Not just for the summer but for good." I have to step it up so that doesn't happen. I just don't know how yet.

"Okay, let's dial the drama back a teensy bit, shall we?" Mom's always been levelheaded, focused. When I overcomplicate things, she's there to cut away the clutter and help me see a path forward. "It sounds to me like she just wants you to show a wider range. Your passion for photography will come through no matter the subject you're shooting. I say you use this as an opportunity to showcase every ounce of talent you've got. Make them remember your name."

"I'm not one of your clients, Mom. This self-esteem pep talk isn't going to work. Kinsey isn't looking to date me."

She smiles, like this isn't the biggest opportunity of my life. "Not with that attitude, they're not."

"Believe me, I'm not lacking in confidence. My problem is that no one sees my portraits the way I do." No one sees *love* the way I do. No one but my mom, who deals in it for a living. "Being able to get my point of view across without words is the whole point of photography. If I'm failing at that, I'm not good enough for Kinsey anyway."

"Rule number four: *Don't self-reject*," Mom says.

I counter with, "Rule number twelve: *When you know, you know*."

And if I can't find a way to elevate my photography game, my summer plans—hell, let's face it, my life plans—will be as hopeless as my love life.

Chapter THREE

Love Rule #2: Welcome love with an open heart, and it will come to you willingly.

I don't remember my dad. The guy I see when I close my eyes and try—really try—to remember him is an amalgamation at best. An idea cobbled together of things I've been told and pictures I've seen. Digital wasn't a thing when my parents were growing up, so the only photos I have of him are faded. But I can tell I have his smile. And, according to mom, his love of breakfast for dinner.

That's why I work at Yeastie Boys. Well, in a roundabout way. When Gemma's dads first opened the place, my dad fell in love. A biscuit-and-egg joint that served breakfast all day? Heaven. He became friends with Lee and Gabe immediately, cementing my best friend status with Gemma at the age of two and my love of all things biscuits by age four. I basically grew up in the booths here. Then, one day, they gave me an eggy-yellow diner dress uniform with my name stitched on the chest and put me to work. Of course, Gemma altered my uniform so now my name reads MO.

I pop a kiss on Lee's cheek as I lean around him to clock in for my shift on Saturday morning.

"A package came for you," he says, pointing toward a padded envelope tucked in next to the register. His hands are caked in sticky dough, and he uses the interruption to sprinkle another dusting of flour on the counter. Then he turns his attention back to folding, turning, and folding the dough again to build half a dozen flaky layers into the biscuits.

"Ooh, what are the odds they fit a new car in here?"

"Sadly, not as high as you need."

"Hey! Shouldn't you be trying to inspire the youth around here, not crushing their dreams?"

Dough sufficiently laminated, he shakes a handful of flour on the silicone mat to roll it out. He flicks his fingers at me, speckling the front of my uniform. "Since when is it your dream to get a free car?"

Since my adviser said I'm not good enough. But I don't want this conversation to take a turn into serious territory, so I counter with, "Who wouldn't want to get a surprise free car? In the mail no less!" I waggle my eyebrows at him, and he barks out a laugh. Quasi-parental crisis averted.

Leaving him to the biscuit dough, I head out front to see what my not-a-car package is. The envelope is so featherlight, it almost flies out of my hand when I pull it from its slot in the plastic mail holder. There's no return address. Only a note written in black marker on the back of the envelope.

Sorry this gift is late. Hope it makes you smile. -August

I double-check my name, written to the care of the café, and peel the flap up. At first glance, the envelope is as empty as it feels. I turn it upside down, shaking out my confusion and a prick of disappointment along with a piece of paper. The page ripped from a book is covered in thick swipes of marker blacking out most of the printed words. The words still visible read:

there's
A
secret
in
my
heart
whispering
To
be

set
free.
Maybe
your
heart
Is
the
key
?

I read it through twice, absorbing the words as if they were meant for me. For five seconds, ten, I forget the poem's not from August. That August's not my boyfriend.

As that realization hits, another follows right on its heels.

August knows.

I don't know how, but he found out, and this poem is his way of calling me out.

Cutting off my panic at the knees before it can consume me, I settle in next to Gemma at the counter and hip check her. "Please tell me you did this."

Gemma looks up from a stack of menus she's wiping down ahead of the breakfast rush. Confusion draws her pencil-thin eyebrows into a sharp V. "Do what?"

"This." I hold the blackout poem up, dancing it back and forth like a paper doll on an acid trip.

"Is that supposed to be a ransom note?"

"No. It's a love poem. I think," I say.

"Someone's got a fucked-up sense of love if this dark shit is what they think is romantic." She waits a beat then unleashes a wicked grin. "I love it."

Which is exactly why I'm hoping she's behind it. "You seriously didn't send this to me?"

"I mean, that would've been super nice of me. But I'm not in the habit of making art or poetry or whatever this is for fake anniversaries. Obviously, it's not from me, so who does it say it's from?" Gemma examines it again, holding the poem up to the light as if there's a hidden message lurking somewhere in all the black marker. When she comes up empty, she moves on to the envelope, as if I haven't already done my best amateur *CSI*-sleuthing already.

"August," I say. There's no other explanation.

"Like *August* August?"

I stare at her, looking for any sign of a lie. A flinch. A twitch. A hitch in her breath. I need it to be from Gemma. The alternative means August really knows what I've done, and I don't know how to deal with that reality. The paper shakes in my hand. "I don't know! It's either him or someone sent it pretending to be him. Do you think someone knows? Are they blackmailing me?"

Holy Shit—capital *S*.

If he knows I've been faking a relationship with him, what's to stop him from telling everyone I'm a liar, a fraud?

"Holy shit," Gemma says, reading my thoughts. "How did he find out?"

"Better question. Why did he send this? And what does he want?" He must have some hidden agenda if he sent me a love poem instead of calling me out directly. But whatever he wants, I'm not stupid enough to take the bait.

"That's two questions. But if it is blackmail, there's got to be a note or demand or something. What else is in there?"

Handing Gemma the poem as if it might self-destruct if left unattended, I grab a pair of scissors and cut down the side seams of the envelope before exposing its bare insides. "Nothing. Just the note on the back saying he's sorry he's a few days late and hopes I like it."

"Yeah, that's not creepy or anything."

"I know, but it's also kind of perfect. Totally something I would swoon over if a boy gave it to me in real life." Just my luck to get trolled with something I actually love.

"It really is." Gemma runs her fingers over the tracks of black marker, tapping each word of the poem as she makes her way down the page. "What are you going to do?"

"The only thing I can. I have to end things now before he decides to rat me out publicly. If anyone else finds out, I'm so screwed."

"But at least you have this last declaration of love to help you through your breakup."

"Not funny, Gemma."

As much as I want to believe the feelings in the poem are real, experience says the joke's on me.

Saturday morning breakfast is in full swing by eight thirty. But I'm so distracted by the poem—and who sent it—that I've messed up three orders and delivered the wrong food to tables twice. Gemma shoots me a death glare every time I get too close to where I stashed the poem back by the register.

"If you don't get your head on straight in the next five minutes, I'm taking that thing and burying it in the compost," she says. It's coming from a place of love, so I can't be mad at her. Plus, she's had to fix my mistakes this morning on top of taking care of her own tables.

"I know. I'm sorry. I'll be better starting now."

"Your newest table says otherwise."

Following her gaze, my heart does acrobatics in my chest. It's not just a somersault or a flip. It's a whole high-flying routine. And it's all because of Ren. He and Lana have a standing breakfast date every week. Only today it's just Ren, looking lost and alone, like he's accidentally slipped into an alternate reality with no idea of how to get back to his real life. Except this is real life.

"Maybe you should take it," I say, giving Gemma a little shove toward his table.

She rubs her hands together like she's washing her hands of me. "Your section. Your crush. Your customer."

"Shh!" I slap a hand over her mouth to keep the word *crush* from traveling to any other ears. I'm supposed to be *so in love* with August. I cannot have a crush on anyone. Especially not Ren, who just broke up with his forever girlfriend. "If you're trying to convince me you didn't send that poem, comments like that are not helping your case."

"Compost," she sings to me as she heads in the opposite direction, leaving me no choice but to wait on Ren.

His head whips up when I approach, a burst of hope shooting out of him like a flashbulb. It dies as soon as he realizes I'm me. But the disappointment that flares to life in my chest burns bright, an eternal flame. I paste on a smile. He does too.

"Hey, Mo." His voice is about as convincing as his smile. Which is not at all. Even without the coppery-teal wisps of aura clinging tight to his body, I can sense his heartbreak. There's a Lana-shaped hole in his heart. In his life.

I'm kidding myself if I think I can fill it. My epic love story is made up. As much as I want to believe I have love all figured out, I don't have any practical experience to back me up. No one wants to date the girl who can magically see love. Too much pressure. The few guys I've kissed didn't stick around for a relationship.

Love rule number five: A good kiss can't make up for what's lacking in your heart.

"Hey, Ren. I wasn't expecting to see you today."

He glances at the empty seat across from him, and then his eyes snap back to mine. They're clear and focused. Like he's determined to keep some semblance of his normal life without Lana by his side. "No? Saturday mornings are kind of our thing."

Our thing? I know I always looked forward to him coming in, even if his mouth was attached to Lana's half the time. But I never allowed myself to hope he came in here because of me. I was the one who did things because of him. Like taking his dad's surfing camp when I was ten because Ren was helping with the lessons even though I can't hold my breath underwater without pinching my nose shut. Or doing a semester-long photography project on wabi-sabi after Ren's grandfather told me on one of his yearly visits from Japan that it meant finding beauty in the nature and impermanence of things.

Maybe getting him to notice me won't be as impossible as I thought. "Yeah, I guess they are. Do you want your usual?"

"I think I'll change it up today. Try something new. What's your Frankenbiscuit today?"

Frankenbiscuits—so named for their resemblance to Frankenstein's monster—are our weekend specials. A chaotic mishmash of ingredients that Gemma and I take turns designing. Her dads have veto power, but they've only used it twice. Once for each of us. We sell out both days every week, so if you don't get here early, you miss out.

"This week's is an Easter explosion. It's your basic buttermilk biscuit with a Cadbury Creme Egg baked inside and then topped with fried chicken. There's also a creme egg sauce on the side, but..." I leave that unwise decision up to him commentary-free.

Gemma, however, has no such qualms. Despite saying Ren was all mine to look after, she's clearly listening in. "The sauce is not optional," she calls from across the room. "You know the rules, Mo. No changes or substitutions to Frankenbiscuits. Customers either eat it as is, or they get something else. Plus, that sauce is the best part."

I exaggerate my full-body cringe for effect. "That sauce is a week's worth of sugar in a single serving."

"What's your point? No one orders Frankenbiscuits because they're the healthy option," Gemma says.

"How much respect will you lose for me if I don't order that?" Ren asks, a grimace bowing his lips.

"Oh, my respect for you would go up," I assure him. If I had veto power, I would've used it on the sauce alone.

"Gemma, on the other hand, may change your order and force you to eat it just to spite you."

"Man, I gotta do it then."

Gemma whoops in victory. Half the customers startle, dropping their silverware or knocking drinks over. "Sorry," she says to the room at large and grabs a handful of towels to do a round-robin of cleanup and refills.

Turning back to Ren, I shake my head, laughing. "You don't have to get it. Really."

"Kinda feels like a challenge now. So same question but reversed."

"Will I lose respect for you? No. Will I tell you I told you so if you puke it up in the parking lot? Absolutely."

"Well, I do seem to be in the market for someone to point out my deficiencies." He gives a sad half laugh, like he's not entirely joking. "And maybe someone who's willing to hold my hair back if needed."

It's not exactly a profession of love, but it's a start. Just the prospect of being able to run my hands through his thick black waves sends a thrill through me. I manage to keep that thought to myself. "Don't worry. I've got you covered."

I leave to put in his order and check on my other tables, which I've been neglecting while talking to Ren. Gemma makes kissy noises at me as I pass her. Thankfully, Ren is too engrossed in his phone to notice. I, on the other hand, silently threaten her with a roll of duct tape from behind the counter. She calls my bluff by planting a kiss right on my cheek.

"I hate you," I whisper to her under my breath.

"You love me and you know it," she says. With her back to the dining room, she adds so only I can hear, "And if you stay glued to Ren's table, everyone will know you love him too."

Staying away as long as I can, I make sure everyone else is taken care of so I can give him my undivided attention for a few minutes at least. He's putting on a good front. Most people would buy that he's dealing with his breakup better than expected. But I can see how he really feels. And right now, Ren needs a friend. To know someone cares about him.

"Are you doing okay? With everything, I mean," I ask when I return with his food.

Ren sizes up the Frankenbiscuit in front of him, a flash of regret pinching his lips. Then he looks up at me, shaking it off. He's not one to dwell on things that are already done. "Yeah. Okay, I guess. That's actually why I came to see you." His heartbreak cloud brightens, the copper morphing into a rosy sheen and the teal dispersing altogether. It's a hopeful kind of love. The kind people don't sense yet or aren't ready to admit they feel.

Hope stages a full-on invasion in my body, spreading through me with every frantic beat of my heart. If Ren is having even the slightest feelings of love toward me, I have to act now. Let him know I feel the same way. "Oh, I'm really glad you did."

"Me too. You are literally the only person who knows what's going on right now. And I thought maybe you'd be able to tell me how Lana is. How she's handling the breakup. I was sitting in the parking lot for like half an hour before I came in, just in case she was here, but she didn't show. So I figured I'd come in, do my normal thing. Hang out with you."

"And ask me about Lana?" The disappointment is like a bag of sand tied to my ankles, pulling me beneath churning ocean waves. Of course, he's not here for me. He's here for my magic. To see if Lana still loves him. His glow grows brighter still at the mention of her name, his love for her on full display.

Stupid, Mo. So fucking stupid. I can't believe I thought he was about to ask me out.

Always the magical love maestro, never the one being maestro-ed for.

"Yeah. You can see if she's still in love with me, right? I mean, if she comes in. Or maybe at school on Monday. And then I'll know if I have a shot at getting her back or if I ruined things for good."

"Why didn't you tell her you still love her when she broke up with you?"

"I don't know. She didn't seem happy, like, with anything I've been doing. If we were going to end, I didn't want to make it harder on her, you know?" Dropping his elbows to the table, he hangs his head in his hands. "I thought it would be easier somehow. Let me tell you, it's not. But I think that's because I don't know if she's this upset too." He looks up at me again like I'm his only hope.

It's the desperation that does it. Snaps the tenuous hold I

have on the anger burning me up from the inside out. I'm all fire and frustration when I say, "You could try asking her."

His head whips toward the door, as if he's manifested her right here, right now. Finding it empty, he deflates. "I've tried. I think she blocked me. Or she's just ignoring my calls and texts."

"I've got to get to my other tables." I turn away, but my feelings for him won't let me leave. He's hurting, and he came to *me* for help. That must mean something, even if he only sees me as a friend for now. And a friend wouldn't leave him hopeless. "But you know what? Maybe it's a sign that there's someone else out there who's a better fit for you. Someone you haven't even thought of in that way before."

"You think?"

"I don't know. But you'll never know what love has in store for you if you don't put yourself out there."

That's rule number thirty-one.

Yet another one of Mom's rules I've never been brave enough to believe. Until now.

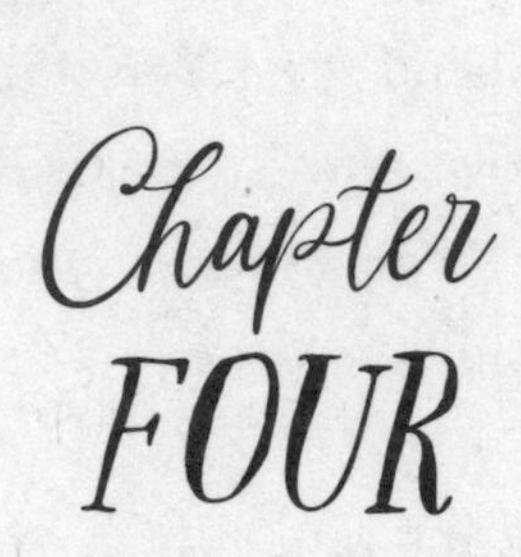

Chapter FOUR

Love Rule #30: True love never lies.

What I said to Ren has played on a loop in my head for days.

I have to end things with August. It's my only option. Between the anonymous poem and talking to Ren about putting yourself out there, I can't keep lying to everyone. Especially my mom.

But how do I convince everyone that my quite literally picture-perfect relationship is suddenly over without admitting the truth?

All I know is it can't be my choice. August has to do the dumping for this to have any chance of working. Figuring out the why and how is easier said than done. But once it's over, I'll have a clean slate.

No more lies.

No stories to keep straight.

Just the lightness of relief that it's all behind me.

And maybe one day soon, I'll be able to put Mom's rules

to real use. But for that to happen, I have to let August go. Ignoring the small pinch in my chest at the thought, I go find Mom as a first step in getting my love life back on track. When I reach her office, I instantly regret my timing as her voice greets me from the open doors, her patience chipping away with every syllable despite the sweet outer coating.

"We'll keep trying until we find the one. See you Thursday, Delaney," she says before hanging up.

It may be past nine on a Tuesday night, but love doesn't have office hours, so neither does a matchmaker. Or at least my mother doesn't. Even if she did, I doubt Delaney would respect it. That woman hasn't met a boundary she wouldn't cross. Lucky for her, my mom's a sucker for helping people find their happy ending.

Which is why I have to stop lying to her. She wholeheartedly believes in true love, and here I am, giving it the middle finger with all my lies.

"Got a minute?" I ask, hesitating in the doorway.

"For you, I have two." She gives me a once-over, her mouth bowing down at whatever she sees. "Though I'm guessing, with the teal glow brewing around you, it may take a bit longer."

Before I can retreat from her unwanted observation, she comes around the desk, takes me by the shoulders, and steers me into the den. I curl into my normal corner of the couch. She follows suit on the other half. It's been just the two of us for so long, we instinctively take up all the space, mirror images of each other. Same choppy auburn hair. Same golden-brown eyes. Same sense of hesitation to broach the subject Mom started back in the office.

I can't ignore it forever. Not what she said or the dark pebble of regret in my heart at having to cut August out of my life. "There's no way you can see that. I haven't—nothing's happened yet."

"That doesn't mean your heart hasn't already made up its mind."

"Maybe my heart's confused?"

"Or maybe it's trying to tell you it's time to move on, but you're not ready to hear it." She reaches out and squeezes my socked foot when I let out an affronted noise. "No, hear me out. You've invested a lot of time and emotional energy on this relationship. And I know you loved him. I saw it every time you talked about him. But long-distance relationships are hard. Even more so when you're young."

"Or when my mom hasn't even met my boyfriend to analyze if he's a good match or not?"

"Nice try. But we're talking about your feelings. When it comes to you, I'm just your mom, not a matchmaker. Your happiness is all that matters. Though as your mom, it would have been nice to know firsthand who's been making you so happy this past year."

"It's not my fault the universe intervened anytime I tried to get you to meet August," I say. Another lie. I pretended to plan a few meetups that fell apart at the last minute due to faked emergencies or bad weather. A couple of times, I waited until I knew she was with a client to stage a call with him and would wave to her through the closed office door as if he were virtually telling her hi.

That level of deception is one thing I won't miss when this fake relationship is over. I've wanted to come clean to Mom countless times this past year, but I'm a coward. The guilt from lying to her is easier to stomach than facing her disappointment that I have not only lied about finding love, I've effectively spit in the face of her love rules.

"Sorry, hon. Delaney has a lock on the universe conspiring against her. You'll have to find another excuse," she says, with a defeated shake of her head.

I won't need an excuse much longer. "She's causing problems again?"

"When isn't she?" Her eyes meet mine, her dark pupils going wide. "Pretend you didn't hear me say that about a client. Besides, we're not talking about Delaney right now. Her heartbreak is all in her head. Yours, however…" She draws a circle in the air, indicating the very real loss I apparently feel from my very fake relationship going up in flames.

Taking the hint, I set the stage for what will hopefully be my last lie where August is concerned. "August is taking the *distance* part of a long-distance relationship literally. I was hoping to get actual face time with him over spring break, but he keeps evading the topic when I bring it up. He said he doesn't have other plans, which means he just doesn't want to see me."

"Let's not jump to conclusions. He wouldn't have sent you that beautiful necklace for your anniversary if he didn't care about you."

Leave it to my mom to be logical in this situation. "He

would if he feels guilty. Maybe he knows I'm more invested in our relationship than he is and that was his way of trying to convince us both I mean more to him than I do. You said it yourself. Long-distance doesn't work."

More to the point, I'm not interested in a boyfriend who's not here. August was a convenient lie. Not seen. Not heard. Just present enough that everyone was assured of his existence. But I want a boyfriend I can go on real dates with. One I can hold hands with and kiss and sit there next to saying nothing if that's what we want. I've been alone long enough.

Mom's look is all pity. "That's not exactly what I said. I think you're disappointed you won't get to see him and are looking for problems because it's easier to be mad at him than sad. But if it's bothering you, try to talk to him again. I'm sure you can find a time that works for you both."

"What if we can't?"

"Then you'll have a harder conversation and decide if being in a relationship is something you both still want. But remember, my rules aren't just for finding love. They're to help you see when something's not true love too."

"I know," I say, hoping she doesn't see right through me.

I give Gemma a heads-up so she's not surprised by the breakup photo I post on Insta. A real post this time, not just a story, to make sure people don't miss it. It takes watching *Brave* to get the tears flowing, because who doesn't sob when Merida's almost too late to save her mom and thinks she'll stay a bear forever? But once they do come, my mascara-streaked face makes a moving selfie. A black-and-white tone sells the sadness. I rarely post photos of myself, which is how I could get away with not posting photos of August either. So this one will definitely get people's attention.

A message notification from someone with the username @TheRealAugust pops up on my phone within minutes. Just long enough for someone to have seen my post and created a fake account.

The spike of panic hits me like a tidal wave, sending my thoughts whirling. I should ignore the message. Block the account and forget it ever existed. But if someone else out there knows I've been lying about August this whole time, I have to know. I can't do any damage control if I don't know what the specific damage is. I click the message before I can talk myself out of it.

TheRealAugust: It was the poem, wasn't it?
TheRealAugust: I knew it might freak you out. But I thought you'd at least like what it said.
TheRealAugust: I didn't think you'd break up with me because of it.

The poem has been banished to the top drawer of my nightstand. I've rescued it a hundred times to reread the words on the off chance that whoever sent it actually believes what the poem says about me.

I *really* want someone to feel that way about me. Just once.

August knowing I faked a relationship with him is the worst-case scenario.

Some rando using a fake name to trick me into coming clean, that I can shut down. But August? The *real* August confronting me and seeming disappointed about the breakup instead of pissed? That's too much to hope for.

MoGlows: I don't know who you are, but it's illegal to impersonate another person, you know.

TheRealAugust: And what would you call pretending to date a guy you've only met once?

TheRealAugust: I won't even get into how messed up it is that you then broke up with said guy without any explanation.

TheRealAugust: Actually, yes, I will. That's just cold, Imogen. Based on your status updates, I've been the perfect boyfriend. I think I deserve an explanation at a minimum.

TheRealAugust: I'll just be over here waiting...

There's no explanation that makes what I did okay. And even if there were, I wouldn't admit it to a total stranger. Especially not one who may be the boy who supposedly just broke my heart. That is a secret I hope to take to the grave.

August or not, they're going to be waiting a very long time.

Chapter FIVE

Love Rule #9: Falling in love is easy.
Staying in love takes work.

When I meet Gemma in the school parking lot the next morning, she holds out her hand, demanding to see my phone before she even says hello. I sent her screenshots of the messages from TheRealAugust last night, but apparently I can't be trusted not to be faking this right along with my relationship. She clicks on his profile and curses when it's set to private. Like I didn't try to cyberstalk him last night. After opening my email app, she scrolls through my August folder, where I've saved fake emails and the ones for the Insta account I did make for him since I couldn't tag the actual August in any of my #mostloved posts.

"Just making sure you don't have a 'Welcome to Instagram' email for this new account hiding in here," she says.

I steal my phone back before she can message this impostor and make things worse. "I swear to you, this is not me. Whoever it is knows our relationship wasn't real though. So, if it's not you, and it's not me, who the hell is it?"

"Maybe it's him. Just like the handle says. The *real* August."

"How would he even know?"

Gemma rolls her black-lined eyes like it's the most obvious answer. "You do know him. It was only one day, but what if he decided to look you up at any time in the past two years? Out of curiosity or because he's had a mad crush on you and is finally ready to come clean."

That does sort of make sense. The curiosity part anyway. Tightening my grip on the phone, I admit, "I doubt he's even thought of me since that day."

"And how would you know that?"

"I may have kept tabs on him. Just a little. To make sure there wasn't anything that would come back to bite me in the ass."

"I'm sure it had nothing to do with how hot he is. He is still hot, isn't he?" she asks.

I scan the parking lot to make sure no one's eavesdropping and keep my voice whisper soft to be safe. "He's only on a few socials, and those he keeps locked down. He was in the paper in Winston-Salem for some teen art curators program. There *may* have been a photo. And he *may* be even hotter now."

"Oh, well, now we're doing a full-on deep dive into his online life at lunch to see if we can figure out if this is him or not. Full disclosure, I'm really, *really* hoping it's him."

"Why would you want that? That is the worst possible scenario."

"You'd rather pine after Ren for the rest of your life?"

"I'm not pining," I say. After breakfast on Saturday, it's

clear he's not interested in me. Not in a romantic way. But I'm still stubbornly holding out hope he'll miraculously change his mind. "And if this *is* August, do you really think he'd want to date me after what I've done? He'll probably slap a restraining order on me."

"Those messages don't seem mad. Not about the fake relationship anyway. He does, however, seem a bit miffed about the breakup. Kind of like he's known about the relationship for a while." Gemma jumps up and down, slapping my shoulder, as if she didn't already have my attention. "Oh, oh. That poem. I bet it really is from him. The *real* August, just like his username says. You said he was artsy, right? What if he likes you, Mo?"

Not only did she get my attention, but a dozen other people are staring now too. I manage to hold her in place with both hands shoving down on her shoulders. She's four inches shorter than me, but she has the energy of a cheetah on speed when she's excited. And apparently the prospect of my worst nightmare coming true excites her. I may need a new best friend along with a new boyfriend.

"He does not," I say. He can't. There's no good way to spin what I've done. No way I come out of this on top, whether it's August or someone else who knows the truth.

"We'll never know until we ask him."

She wrangles my phone away from me and dances a few yards ahead. Then she types out a message too fast for me to read and sends it before I can snatch my phone back out of her hand. Checking the screen, my heart rate settles back into a normal rhythm when I read what she wrote.

MoGlows: This is Gemma. Not to get all middle school on you, but do you like Mo?

"Was that really necessary?"

"Damn right it was. We have to know what we're working with here."

"No, what matters is *who* it is." I wait for a crowd of seniors to go through the doors ahead of us, my hand half raised to muzzle Gemma if needed. When we're alone again, I say, "As I've proven over the past year, you can say anything online, and unless someone else has irrefutable proof against you, people will believe you."

Gemma pulls the door open, waving me through. "Good point. But why would the real August lie about it?"

"Because it's not him."

My life must be one big cosmic joke because my phone chooses that moment to buzz with a new notification. I pull up short, and Gemma crashes into my back. She grabs my wrist so I can't move the phone out of her view. I guess it's only fair that she witnesses the destruction of my life firsthand since she helped me keep the lie going this whole time.

TheRealAugust: Nice to meet you, Gemma. I'll answer your question, if Imogen answers mine.

TheRealAugust: Also, I'm trusting that this really is Gemma and not Imogen pretending to be you so she doesn't have to talk to me. Though I bet she's reading this too. So, hello, Imogen. I'm still waiting for an answer.

Well, he can keep on waiting. Until I know who he is, I'm not engaging. No matter how charming he pretends to be.

"Oh, I like him," Gemma says. Tugging on my arm, she leads me out of the mass of foot traffic to some rooms off the main hallway that rarely get used this time of day. "If this were somebody just messing with you, they would have made some sort of demand by now. And he definitely wouldn't be flirting with you."

I hold the phone up as irrefutable evidence. "This is not flirting. This is him baiting me to incriminate myself."

"I never thought I'd see the day Imogen Finch turned into a cynic."

"Forgive me for being cautious. I'm just trying to keep this all from blowing up in my face." My lies about August haven't hurt anyone, but that doesn't mean there won't be some backlash if the truth gets out. Hopefully, ending my fake relationship will stop any consequences in their tracks.

"Do you trust me?" She holds out her hand for my phone again.

I pull it back out of reach. Trusting Gemma isn't the issue. What I'm struggling with is believing in the good intentions of whoever is on the other end of these messages. "Using our friendship against me is cheating, you know."

"As your accomplice in this whole thing, I'm well within the blast radius. So I'm doing this as much for me as for you. Or at least partially for me anyway." She takes my phone again, this time with no struggle from me, and responds.

I read over her shoulder. Even though it's my account—not to mention my *life*—I don't get a say in what she writes. I just get to watch as the back-and-forth unfolds.

MoGlows: Definitely Gemma. Mo would say hi back, but she's being "cautious." Cool if I answer your question on her behalf?

TheRealAugust: If anyone has cause to be cautious here, it's the guy whose identity was stolen.

TheRealAugust: But sure, as long as it's the truth, I don't care who tells me.

TheRealAugust: I just want to know why the sudden breakup.

MoGlows: Mo's longtime crush just got dumped and she had to ditch you to have a shot with him. It's not personal. This guy is here and you're, well, you know the situation.

TheRealAugust: Did you just "It's not you, it's Mo" me?

MoGlows: Technically yes. But I am #TeamAugust,

so if you're legit and not some asshat who's just messing with Mo, I'll work on her for you.

I throw myself on her, batting my phone from her grasp. It flies to the floor, but I don't release my grip on her. "Nope. That's it. Trust revoked. Best friend status is now in question too."

Gemma's body shakes against mine as laughter rocks through her. After a minute, she regains control and shoves me away. "You can't tell me this guy isn't crush worthy. Or date worthy for that matter. I'm fully on board with you dating him for real. Forget about Ren. August is the boy for you, and I won't hear any objections."

"He is not—"

"Lalalalalalala," she sings, her fingers in her ears for the full ignoring-me effect. The sound flies out of the room like a siren.

Slapping a hand over her mouth, I relent. "Okay, I get it. August is perfect, and my life will be meaningless without him."

"'Meaningless' might be a bit much, but he'd definitely make you happy," Gemma says after yanking my hand away.

"Oh, please," a voice says, breaking our privacy. Lana leans into the room, the hallway dark behind her. "Your mom's a freakin' matchmaker, Mo. It's not like you'll be single for long. I bet you could pick any name from her list, and she'd have you set up before the end of the day."

My heart stutters, waiting for Lana to call me out on everything else she overheard. When she just stares at me, I let out a ragged breath. Then I fill the silence before she realizes anything is off. "Considering she has a minimum age of twenty-five, that would be gross."

Lana rests her head against the doorframe. The circles under her eyes are a few shades darker than her skin. She didn't try to cover them with makeup. Her eyelashes are free from mascara too, as if she expects to shed a few tears at some point in the day. I wish I'd thought of that to help sell my breakup too. "You know what I mean. Unlike the rest of us, you have an advantage. You literally live with someone who deals in love for a living. I'm sure you know every trick she has for attracting guys."

Is that what she thinks? What everyone thinks? That I can have any guy I want just by batting my eyelashes? Sure, Mom has her rules, but they haven't done me any favors yet.

My jaw aches from clenching it so I don't spill the truth of my lackluster love life right here and now. Releasing the tension, I let a little of my truth escape. "There aren't any tricks. You can't make someone like you just because you want them to."

Gemma squeezes my hand that's still grasping my phone. "Don't forget about Claire's Fifty Rules for Finding Your Soul Match."

"Not helping," I sing to her under my breath. Lana latches on to the idea and stares me down until I cave. "The rules are supposed to put a person into the right mindset to find love. It's not a step-by-step instruction guide."

"The point is," Lana says with enough authority that I don't dare interrupt her, "that you still have an advantage over the rest of us. You don't need to be over here pining for August when you can go out and find someone new in no time. I, on the other hand, have been with Ren so long, no one will even look at me, let alone date me."

"And you think I had a long-distance boyfriend for fun? The whole reason it all went south with August is because we never saw each other. But no one in Portree has *ever* wanted to date me. The only thing anyone here wants from me is to know if the person they like likes them back. Not exactly a prime dating pool."

The five-minute warning bell rings, but none of us makes a move to get to class.

"What are you talking about? Everyone loves you," Lana says.

I meet her disbelieving stare with one of my own. "As a friend, yeah. But I can literally see how people feel. No one has ever felt anything remotely close to love where I'm concerned."

Gemma jabs her finger into my chest. When I look at her, she pouts for full effect. "That's just hurtful."

"Romantically," I say to appease her imagined hurt feelings.

Lana's heartbreak builds around her, all teal flecked with copper. She glows as it consumes her. "So August was your first big love too?"

I'm so far into this lie, I can't even see the light of truth far above me. The only thing I can do is dig in deeper. "I know it's not like what you and Ren had, but aside from Gemma here, it's the longest relationship I've had."

And it's not even real.

God, I'm so pathetic. No wonder no one wants to date me.

"Well, I don't need your matchmaker powers to see he broke your heart," Lana says. She waves her hand in a circle to indicate all of me like she's the one with the power to see heartbreak clinging to people. "We should start a club. Like matchmaking for the brokenhearted."

"You could call it *Rebounds 'R' Us*," Gemma says.

She laughs. Lana and I don't.

Instead, Lana says, "I'm not talking about a rebound. I'm talking about Mo helping us all find real love again."

Love rule number sixteen: You can fall in love in an instant, but heartbreak will linger until you're ready to let it go.

So until Lana is ready to leave Ren behind, she won't be able to move on. But the deep rusty teal enveloping her like a cocoon says I'll be smart to keep that to myself if I don't want to send Lana bad-mouthing me all over school.

I say, "My mom's the matchmaker, not me. And besides, isn't it a little too soon to be thinking about dating again? Are you really ready to move on?"

Gemma digs her elbow into my side. As if I need the reminder that I did all this to have a shot with Ren in the first place. I should be finding every eligible guy to set Lana up with.

"I just think getting Ren out of my system is the only way to be okay again," Lana says. Her face is set, like that's the mantra she repeats in the mirror a hundred times each morning before leaving the house. "And he's been this major part of my life for so long, it's going to take drastic measures to put my heart back together without little pieces of him getting put back too. Falling in love with someone new is about as drastic as it gets."

"You really want to get over him?" It's selfish to want her to say yes. Especially knowing that just two days ago, Ren was asking me how she was handling their breakup. But if she's ready to move on, that's her decision. Who am I to stand in the way of that?

Lana nods so fast, she looks like a bobblehead. "Yes, I do." The resolve in her voice is razor-sharp, but the cloud of heartbreak around her intensifies, deepening to a teal so dark, it's almost black.

And I can't help but stare at her. She's gorgeous on a normal day, with her smooth dark skin, defined cheekbones, and perfectly pouty lips. But this level of heartache is mesmerizing. I might not be up for being the leader of the broken hearts, but capturing this raw emotion may be the thing my portfolio needs to show Mrs. Clemente and the submission panel at Kinsey that I have what it takes to be part of their summer arts program.

Chapter SIX

Love Rule #25: Don't confuse attraction for love. Attraction is surface level and wanes over time, whereas true love becomes a part of you forever.

Tomorrow's the first full day of spring break, so a lot of people will be headed out of town. But Ren is sticking around this week. His usual camping trip with Lana's family is off the table this year, which means this is my chance to get him to see me as more than a friend. Plus, I'll be able to make progress on my portfolio too.

Two birds, one stone, and all that.

It takes me thirty minutes to stage a photo I'm happy with. Black-and-white prints of all the portraits I've taken are spread across the table in the studio. Each one is ripped down the middle and the pieces are layered over each other at dozens of different angles. Even in grayscale, the rosy glow of love emanates from the photo halves. But I think the destruction gets the point across.

MoGlows: OPEN CALL: Photographer seeks subjects with broken hearts for photography project. Learn more in person at Yeastie Boys in Portree, 9 a.m. Saturday, March 30. #brokenheartsclub #photography #freeportraits #modelswanted #springbreak

My eyes drift to the message string with TheRealAugust. He's gone silent since he and Gemma chatted a few days ago. I can only hope he took the news of me having a crush on another guy as a sign that I'm moving on and he should too.

It's not hard to pick up on someone's routine. Not in a small town like Portree where choices are school, work, their house, or the beach. Not when you've been half in love with someone for most of your life.

I could set my watch to Ren's surf schedule. As soon as the weather's not winter miserable, he's out on the water after school most days and up with the sunrise on the weekends. I spot his truck and pull into the parking lot. The note I plan to leave on his windshield personally inviting him to be a part of my broken-hearts project waits folded in my jacket pocket.

Out at the north end of the beach, a cluster of restaurants lets locals park for free in their lots once the on-street parking goes into effect during the tourist season. Most people take the free parking and run. But I work for a local business and know how every dollar counts. I support at least one of the businesses here every time I take them up on their offer. Tonight it's Coastal Creamery.

I love ice cream for dinner almost as much as breakfast for dinner. It's a tradition Mom started after dad died. A reminder to live life to the fullest by indulging in the things you love. On an occasional basis, that is.

Before my mouth can even start watering at the thought of my usual salted caramel ice cream in a chocolate-dipped waffle cone, I notice Ren across the parking lot, cowering from the all-of-five-foot-two presence of Astrid Knight as she blocks his path from the beach. She's in a black minidress and a face full of makeup that probably took her an hour to make look natural. Wedge heels hang from her fingers by the straps. A stark contrast to Ren. His hair is slicked back with ocean water, and his wet suit hangs low on his hips, the top half stripped from his chest and arms despite the chill in the air. My eyes drag over him, taking in every curve and cut of muscle. I've spent years noticing Ren. I know all his tells. And the constant readjusting of the board tucked under his arm has less to do with its weight than the girl holding him hostage with her constant chatter.

He's too nice to cut her off.

Or maybe he just can't get a word in to try.

I wave and pivot toward him instead. With as vibrant as

his heartbreak has been the last few times I've seen him, he could probably use some ice cream tonight too. And a rescue from Astrid's advances. "You forgot, didn't you?" I improvise as I reach them.

"Forgot?" Ren asks with another jiggle of his board.

"That we had plans? You're not trying to use Astrid as an excuse to bail on me, are you?" I cut my eyes to Astrid and back to him, the implication clear. I'm here to save him from *her*.

"Yeah, no. Not bailing." Turning to Astrid, he says, "Maybe some other time."

Her smile pulls tight, like she's not used to being turned down. With an outstretched finger, she taps his bare chest. "You can count on it. Be good tonight, you two." Astrid glances down the beach toward Tower Seven, the lifeguard tower that gets used as a make-out spot as soon as the sun goes down.

I give a small laugh as if that's the last thing on my mind. Even if I were as straightforward as Astrid about what I want, Ren's heartbreak over Lana is going to take time to heal. He has to live in the sadness for a while, let it work its way through his system before he's ready to move on. But I can be a friend if that's what he needs now. Someone who understands what he's going through.

"Do you have to go home immediately?" I ask when we're alone. There's a quiver to my voice. I pray he mistakes it for a reaction to the cool night air rather than his presence.

Ren's smile comes slow, easy. His heartbreak stays contained for the moment. "I can hang out for a bit. I owe you for getting me out of that."

"I think that deserves ice cream at least."

"Just lemme change so I'm not in this wet suit longer than I have to be. I think I've got something in my car." He stows his surfboard in the bed of his truck before climbing into the cab to throw on a dark gray Henley and wrap a towel around his waist. Then he twirls a finger at me to turn around so he can strip in relative privacy with only the towel and truck door as cover. Once he's dressed, he walks back to me and tugs on a lock of my hair. "Shouldn't we get dinner first?"

I grab his hand, ready to drag him along if I have to. "Look at you, following the rules. You probably never eat breakfast for dinner either."

"Is that a real thing or just a Yeastie Boys influence?" He shifts his grip so our fingers interlock, our hands swinging between us like we're out for a romantic stroll.

My hand feels so nice in his, I don't let go. "I'm going to pretend like you didn't just ask me that. But if you keep talking like that, I'm going to be forced to tell Astrid you only made plans with me *after* she cornered you into a date."

He lifts our joined hands to his heart, wounded. "That's cold, Mo. I can be a breakfast-for-dinner convert. Or an ice-cream-for-dinner convert. Whatever you want, that's what I'll be."

There's not a single thing I would change about him. "Such a gentleman."

Living up to that moniker, Ren buys my ice cream. We take our cones—mine a single salted caramel scoop, his a double scoop of espresso chocolate chunk and Mayan hot chocolate—out to the beach.

"Good call on the ice cream," he says around a mouthful. "First you save me from what would have been an absolute disaster of a date. And then you take it to the next level by going dessert first. You're just full of surprises, aren't you?"

I dip into a quick half curtsy, half bow, basking in his newfound admiration for me. "I do what I can." After breaking off a piece of my waffle cone, I use it like a spoon to scoop up a bite of ice cream and pop the whole thing in my mouth. The salty and sweet mixed with the buttery cone is everything good in the world in a single bite.

Then Ren ruins it by asking, "So what happened with you and August? I thought y'all were solid."

So far, I've gotten away with pretending to be too upset to talk about it so I could buy myself some time to come up with a plausible excuse. But now that it's Ren asking, I blurt out the first thing that comes to mind. "He cheated on me." The lie makes me flinch. All my other lies about August put him in a positive light. This one, though, is dragging his name through the mud. All to make *me* look better. Garner sympathy.

It was one thing to use his name for my benefit, but this is crossing a line. One I can't come back from.

But Ren must think my reaction is from the pain of what August supposedly did to me. He smiles at me, a puff of teal clouding around him, like my heartache is his. "Damn. What an asshole. You don't want to be in love with a guy like that."

"Who should I be in love with then?" I ask. *Hint, hint.*

"I'm the last person you should be asking about love. I had my shot at it already. Maybe that's all I get." He takes a bite of his ice cream, right where the two flavors meet. A better compromise than the one he's settling for relationship-wise. "You and your mom know a lot about love. I mean, I know you can see it and everything, but also just, like, with your mom's job. She's pretty successful at matching people who belong together. At least that's what I read anyway."

"You read up on us?"

"Yeah, kinda. Not to, like, hire you or anything. Just everyone around here talks about you and your mom like you really get this stuff, so I wanted to see what all the fuss was about."

Maybe I haven't been as invisible to Ren as I'd thought. "And did you?"

"Not really. At least not from anything I read. But you're really cool, Mo. Why haven't we hung out before?" he asks.

"You never needed to," I say, my voice light and blame-free.

"Right, but we've had parties and group things. You've never come to any of those. Please tell me that's not because I almost let you drown when we were kids. Because I was not prepared for your serious lack of swimming skills." He wipes his mouth on his shoulder, leaving a wet trace of ice cream on the fabric. A stubborn cone crumb clings to the corner of his mouth for a second before he licks it away.

I smile at him because even if he's a sticky mess with questionable manners, Ren is a catch. Digging in my pocket for one of the napkins I stuffed in there, I hand it to him. "I tried to tell you."

"Yeah, I thought you were just saying that to keep me close."

"If I'd known that would work, I might have tried it."

Ren feathers the unused napkin over my face to get me to look at him. When I do, the playfulness fades from his expression. "Nah. You're way cooler for being real and not faking things to get a guy's attention."

Except that's exactly what I've done. He just doesn't know it.

And he never can.

"I'm not that cool," I say. Because I can't admit to my lies. Because it's true.

"You totally are. Whatever kept you from coming around, I like that we're hanging out with each other now. Being around you makes me forget I'm supposed to be sad."

That might be the best compliment anyone's ever given me. My whole body warms at his words, melting me from the inside out, despite the guilt threatening to taint this moment. "Who says you're forgetting to be sad? Maybe you're just *not* sad anymore. Or working on it anyway."

Ren cocks his head to study me. "Do you think people can have more than one soulmate?"

"My mom has these rules about love. She says if you follow them, you'll find your happily ever after. I'd guess a good seventy-five percent of her clients laugh at her when she introduces the rules and insists they follow them. But by the end, they all swear by them like they're commandments straight from God." I raise my free hand toward the heavens like a religious zealot praising Him for a miracle. When I turn to look at Ren, my smile falters. I'm about to break his heart all over again. And it's like seeing an animal dash in front of your car and knowing you can't stop in time. "One of them is that true love doesn't break hearts. Meaning you can absolutely love multiple people throughout your life and probably be relatively happy with them, but everyone only has one soul mate, so all the others are just regular love. Lowercase *l*. If you're lucky, you find your one."

"Wait. So does that mean Lana wasn't my soulmate because she broke my heart?"

"That's what my mom would say. It doesn't mean you didn't love Lana because you obviously did—do. But statistically, how many people find their soulmate as a teenager? Don't actually ask me for the stats because I don't have them. I just know it's rare. Not impossible, but my mom wouldn't have such a booming business if everyone stayed with their first love."

"You know what? That's enough of this depressing talk. I've got ice cream and a whole night to hang out with a smart, pretty girl who doesn't see all my faults yet. On the whole, my life's pretty sweet." He shrugs, taking his bleak romantic outlook in stride.

I bump my cone against his, careful not to contaminate his ice cream with mine. "I've always admired that about you."

"What?"

"Your optimism. You can find the silver lining in any situation."

Ren looks down at me, a tinge of rose-gold aura softening his features in the dying sunlight. "Well, I've always thought you were magnetic. The way you make everyone your friend, like, instantly. Even when they're just one of your customers. That's why I like Yeastie Boys so much. Well, you and the fact the food is banging. But you always make me feel like me showing up is the best part of your day. I know that's just your personality and has nothing to do with me—"

"It was definitely you," I say. I don't know if it's the soft lull of the waves lapping at the shore, the beauty of the sunset spilling pink and gold across the horizon, or the way he's looking at me that brings the admission out, but in the end, it doesn't matter why. The truth is out there now.

"Nah. I've watched you with customers. You're that way with all of them," he says. But he grins like my admission is having more effect than he's willing to cop to. "And that's my point. You treat us all the same, and somehow it still feels like you're seeing right into our individual souls and filling the cracks with a little bit of your Mo glow so we all go around shining for the rest of the day."

"If people are glowing, it's not because of me. I can guarantee that."

"What makes you so sure, huh?" he presses.

"Just trust me. I'm good at reading people."

"If you're so good, then what am I thinking right now?" His eyes close as if that will somehow protect his mind from me.

I pause to think, taking a long lick of my salted caramel ice cream. The outer layer is melted, but it's cool enough outside that it's not dripping onto the cone. "You're thinking it's too cold to be eating ice cream now that the sun's going down, but you feel like you owe me, so you're keeping that particular opinion to yourself since you already said it was a good idea."

He tilts his head to study me, a smile tugging at his lips. Pointing at me with what's left of his ice cream, he says, "That is not…inaccurate."

"Believe me now?"

"I do not. You wanna know why?" Having polished off his first scoop, he takes a bite out of his Mayan hot chocolate, breathing through his open mouth to expel some of the cold before it gives him brain freeze. "Despite the temperature and the ice cream, I'm all warm inside just from being around you. You might not be able to see my glow, but I know it's there. And it's all because of you."

When I look at him, there's a faint rose-gold light flickering around him. It's not love. Not yet. But it could be if someone took the time to fan the flames.

"I have to say, you are living up to all my expectations," I say.

"Sounds like you need to raise your expectations. Based on recent feedback, I can do better."

"Oh, please. You're already perfect. I don't think you *can* do better."

"No harm in trying." His glow intensifies, flaring bright for a few seconds before dimming to a subtle rosy shine in the evening air. Only a few flecks of teal mar the air.

And I can't help but wonder if he's just talking about doing better or if his glow means there's something else he thinks would be worth trying. If after all my pining, I might finally have a chance with Ren Kano.

I just need to convince him that's something he wants too.

Chapter SEVEN

Love Rule #29: True love will never ask you to be someone you're not.

There's a line wrapping around the building. Yeastie Boys always has a line on Saturday mornings, even without the added spring break crowd, but this is something else. Locals who avoid the café when tourists descend on Portree are standing outside, squinting against the sun to see through the windows.

"Are we suddenly doing stripteases at every table turnover?" Gemma asks, shimmying her hips as she passes me.

"How are we supposed to tear away these dresses?" I pluck at the fabric. It snaps right back into place, keeping me modestly covered. "That would be easier to do if the uniforms had buttons up the front."

Gemma mimes undoing a few imaginary buttons then shakes her head. "It would need to be Velcro. Buttons would make it more like a slow-motion striptease rather than a *Magic Mike* reveal. And with this line, we don't have time for that."

"There go our tips."

"Guess we'll have to earn them the old-fashioned way. With the line outside, I think we'll be just fine." Her gaze lingers on Greer Latimore three-people deep in the line outside.

Greer's been here a handful of times, always with a group of friends. And always when Gemma is working. It may be a coincidence, but the amount of looking away and blushing when eye contact is made between the two of them is enough to get my matchmaking senses tingling. Not that Gemma has admitted to having a crush. There's no love-glow between them yet, but given more time, there could be if this crush tips into something more.

After we drop off plates and refill drinks, we reconvene behind the counter. "Do you think they're all here because of my project?" My casting call post got hundreds of likes within hours. And word spreads like wildfire in Portree, so it's possible some of them are here for me.

"Do you really think there are that many people willing to relive their heartbreak just so you can take their picture?" Gemma asks, cocking one eyebrow in skepticism.

"Hey, I take damn good pictures, thank you very much."

She scoops coffee grounds into the filter basket and starts a new pot. When she turns back to me, her expression softens. "That wasn't a knock on your talent. Just that heartbroken people are desperate for someone to care. Not to mention the daughter of the local matchmaker invited them here. There are definitely some unrealistic expectations waiting out there."

"Shit. I didn't think of that." Scanning the amassing crowd, I spot Ren with two of his friends. He's back, and I can't help but hope he's here to take me up on my offer to include him in my portfolio. A little one-on-one time to show him moving on is what's best for us both.

Oddly, it feels like I'm moving on too. My relationship with August took up so much of my life, it's as if a part of me is missing now that I'm done with it. Which makes no sense. I was both sides of that relationship. If anything, I should be fuller somehow, having been on the giving and receiving end of things. But, while my brain understands the intricacies of this situation, my heart is throwing a temper tantrum at losing someone whose sole mission was to make me feel loved. Even if that person wasn't real.

So maybe I do have some idea—albeit small—what these people have come here for me to help them with.

Tapping a customer at the counter on the shoulder, I ask to borrow his stool. When he vacates it, I climb onto the seat and sway as the stool twists under my weight. The customer offers his hand to steady me before I fall. "Hey, everyone, can I have your attention?" My voice cuts through the chatter and skillet sizzling. All eyes in the front and back of the house zero in on me. "Thanks. I'm just trying to see who's here for breakfast and who's here to learn about my photography project. So hands up if you're here for me."

"What if we're here for both?" someone asks.

"Even better! But put your hand up now, and I'll take your

order as soon as I've explained the project and passed out the sign-up sheet." Two-thirds of the hands in the room go up. Someone must've opened the door and passed the word to the crowd forming out there because a smattering of hands rise outside as well. I'll probably lose most of them when they realize there's no monetary compensation for their time, but this turnout is way bigger than I hoped. As long as a handful of them agree to help, I'll have what I need to round out my portfolio before the end of spring break. Ren waves to get my attention. Which thankfully means he hasn't caught on to the fact I've purposely kept him in my periphery, stealing quick glances at him for any sign that he's going to bail. I make note of the just-here-to-eat tables and hop off the stool. "Gemma, can you manage the other tables until I'm done? Five minutes. Ten, tops."

"If you're done in an hour, I'll be surprised." She grabs a pot of coffee in one hand and a stack of menus in the other. Using the menus like a sword, she jabs me in the side. "But I'm holding you to ten minutes. And you're splitting your tips with me. So flip the non-eaters quickly, okay?"

"Don't worry. They'll be gone before the spring breakers descend on us." Most of the tourists won't get into town until early afternoon anyway when they can check into their rental houses. Tomorrow morning's the one we have to worry about. And every day for the next few weeks as various parts of the country roll through their spring breaks. It's a small taste of what summer brings.

If I can't up my portfolio's game enough to get accepted into Kinsey's summer arts program, I'll be stuck here waiting tables. Possibly for the rest of my life.

I take the clipboard I borrowed from Soul Match—my sign-up sheet already in place under the clip—and get started. I make it through three tables, with two senior girls from my school taking time slots for midweek, before I get to Ren. His aura is more teal than rose gold today, his heartbreak having intensified in the week since his breakup. The color is thick like storm clouds. It's a riot of emotion clinging to him, and I half expect for little lightning bolts to streak through, lighting the darkness.

"I'm glad you showed up," I say.

He smiles at me, and the teal recedes a fraction. "Looks like I have some competition for you this morning."

Maybe for my time, but not for my heart. That is still up for grabs if he wants it. "It's really not that much." I hold the sign-up sheet out to him as proof. "But I'd love it if you wanted to be a part of my project. I'm doing portraits of people who've had their hearts broken to juxtapose with some of the others I have of people who are in love. To show how love and heartbreak can change a person."

"So you just want to take our pictures?" Evans asks in his slow, half-confused way, dragging my attention to the two other people at Ren's table. Evans looks every bit a stereotypical surfer. Shaggy blond hair. Button-up tee with only one button in the middle done so he can claim his shirt is closed while in the café. Sand from his early morning session clinging to his feet and flip-flops.

"It's a little more detailed than that. As part of the shoot, I'll be asking some personal questions about your relationship to really bring out the raw emotion in the photos." Not everyone's going to want to rehash their breakups or tell me personal details about their relationships, but that's what I need to make sure I'm getting something unique. Something that'll stand out.

"And if we're not into that?"

"Then you say, 'No thanks,' and go," I say. I bump up the wattage of my smile to show there will be no hurt feelings if someone chooses not to participate.

Ren rubs the back of his neck, like he's thinking it all over. "Is there some sort of confidentiality for what we tell you?" he asks.

"Yes, absolutely. My mom uses confidentiality agreements at Soul Match that people can sign if they're worried about that kind of thing. But I'm just interested in the photos. Anything you say to me will stay with only me. The stories are not a part of the project, just the physical manifestations of the heartbreak the story evokes."

"And what are you doing with the photos exactly? Who will see them?" someone else at another table asks.

I turn toward the voice, unsure who asked the question. After locking eyes with a few people seated at the surrounding tables, I swing my gaze back toward Ren. I need a handful of people to agree to help, but if I can get Ren on board, the rest will line up. "I'm applying to a summer arts program and will use the portraits in my portfolio. So my adviser, Mrs. Clemente, will see them, along with the admissions committee at Kinsey. Probably my mom and Gemma since they see everything I do. But that's it. And if you want a copy of the photo, I'm happy to get you a print. They won't be available to anyone else though. I'm not looking to sell them or anything like that."

"What kind of compensation are we talking about here?" Evans asks.

Ren smacks his arm. "It's a volunteer thing. You know, something we do because Mo's seriously cool and is asking for our help."

"Dude, you really have to get out more. No offense, Mo."

Too late. Offense taken. Any thrill I may have gotten from Ren calling me "seriously cool" is tempered by Evans's reminder that I'm just the waitress. Someone they share a few classes with. Not worth his time if there's nothing in it for him. I tap, tap, tap my pen on the table to keep from snapping at him. "There's no pressure to sign up now," I say to Ren, struggling to keep a smile on my face. "Or at all. That's totally okay."

Taking the sign-up sheet, Ren signs his name next to a time slot early next week. "No, I want to help. Just because Evans is too scared to admit he has emotions, let alone let anyone see them, doesn't mean the rest of us are too."

"Look, I'll sign up if you need me to," Evans says. He reaches for the sheet, but I take it from Ren before he can get it and stuff it between pages of my order pad.

"I appreciate it, but you don't look very heartbroken to me. Though you do look hungry. Let me grab your orders and finish things up before Gemma kills me."

He spouts off his order, unfazed by my disinterest in him. Holding up his menu to hide his face, Ren gives me a look that says he's sorry for his friend's lack of manners. We exchange smiles, and hope worms its way back in. Ren may not be ready to move on from his feelings for Lana yet, but I can wait.

I finish up with them and hit the last few tables, collecting two more willing participants. Then I jump back into full-time waitressing mode. I'm so caught up in the nonstop trips from kitchen to table to kitchen that I don't hear the first time he says my name.

"Imogen."

When it registers, the world comes to a screeching halt.

The boy standing there can't be real. Not here. Not now. I close my eyes, trying to blink the hallucination away.

He says my name again. My full name. Because he doesn't know to call me *Mo*. Because he doesn't know me at all.

August Tate. My fake boyfriend—no, former fake boyfriend—is standing two feet away from me, only a diner counter separating us instead of the two hundred and fifty plus miles that should be between us.

"You can't be here," I say. No one knows what he looks

like other than Gemma, but it won't take anyone long to guess with as freaked out as I am at his presence. He has to go before anyone figures out who he is. And, more importantly, that he's *never* been my boyfriend.

"Why not? You said it was open to all." He stuffs his hands in his pockets, casual, confident. Not at all concerned that he's about to ruin my life.

The diners closest to us stare, their breakfasts temporarily forgotten at the prospect of drama about to unfold. I grip his arm, silently begging him to understand. To walk away before this goes any further.

Gemma catches my eye from across the room and nods to her dad. "Mo?"

My brain is full of static. I can't tell if she's telling me not to make a scene in front of her dad or if she's offering to bring him in to act as bouncer and boot August. I shake my head, not sure what my response means either.

"August." My voice catches on his name. I've said it countless times over the past year. It's as familiar to me as Gemma's. But saying it to him feels wrong. Like the lie I've spun is altering reality. "Exes aren't allowed. I thought that was implied by the name of it."

"No, the name implies that anyone with a broken heart is welcome. Seeing as how I fit that description, you can't kick me out." He shoots me a smug smile. He's even better looking than I remember. All sharp-jawed and full-lipped. "But I'll make you a deal. Tell me why you broke up with me, and I'll go."

If he's asking, then he's clearly not TheRealAugust or he would have that answer from Gemma already. But I don't have time to worry about that now. August being here in person takes precedence over being catfished online. "You broke up with me. Remember?" I say.

"Clearly I don't remember that. So maybe this is all some big misunderstanding and we're actually still together."

"We're not." I finally come to my senses and drag him out of the dining area. The hall leading to the bathrooms isn't exactly private, but it's better than being right out in the open where everyone can gawk without even trying. "If this is some kind of April Fools' joke, you're a day early. And it is not funny."

"It's not a joke. And don't change the subject." His voice is calm, verging on teasing. The same as it was two years ago when we met.

The smile he slips me now that we're alone is like putting on my favorite sweater. And I'm smiling back at him before I remember he supposedly just broke my heart. I dip my head until I get my mouth under control. "I know you drove a long way for this, but I really need you to leave. Please."

"Okay, I'll go. But I need you to answer a question for me first."

"What's that?"

August drags a hand through his hair. The first sign of nerves he's shown. "Did you not like the poem? I know it's weird that I sent it, when you know, we're not really—"

The words of the poem burn bright in my mind. I bite the inside of my cheek to keep from reciting it back to him from memory now. Then my brain catches up, sending my warm and fuzzy feelings scattering like mice. If he knows about the poem, then he's the one who sent it. He *is* TheRealAugust. So why is he here when he already knows why I ended our fake relationship? What does he want from me if not to expose my lies?

"The poem was perfect. But how did you even know to send it? Scratch that. You obviously follow me on Insta." I guess I should be lucky he didn't confront me until after I ended things, but that doesn't make this moment any less panic inducing. My heart went into warp speed the moment I heard him say my name and hasn't slowed down since.

"Not until recently. Then I saw your stories and put two and two together. Gotta say, that was not what I was expecting to find when I looked you up. Though I'm a little flattered you picked me. Is that weird?"

"Of the two of us, you are not the weird one."

"So what happened? Why did you end things? Was it really so you could date some other guy like Gemma said?"

My gaze gives me away as it shifts across the room to where Ren sits.

August turns, assesses the competition, and continues speaking though I haven't verbally responded. "That guy? You broke up with me for him?"

"Keep your voice down," I say. I clap my hand over his mouth to keep any more of my secrets from spilling out. Not that he knows any. He barely even knows me despite what my online persona suggests. "Do you promise to leave if I answer you?"

Drawing a cross over his heart, he says, "And hope to die."

Ren and Evans are watching us now, eyes narrowing as August's identity dawns on them. Tugging on his arm, I try to pull August away from their prying eyes. "I wanted a chance at real love, okay? And I think I could have it with Ren. You being here *in person* kinda puts that all in jeopardy." It's not fair of me to put that on August when I'm the one who's been using him, but he was *not* supposed to show up here. He wasn't supposed to even know I'd used him. How the hell do I make this right so he'll leave without making a scene?

My deer-in-headlights look must jolt some latent white knight instinct in Ren because he calls from across the room, "You okay, Mo?"

Ren's question reaches me in slow motion, as if my ears are waterlogged. I nod, my muscles regaining control before my brain. After an awkward moment, I manage, "Oh, yeah. I'm great. August and I were just—"

"Talking about how you're better off without him?" Ren fills in. His breakup with Lana is still fresh enough for the bruises to show. Apparently, any breakup is enough to trigger him. Though my heart tries to rip out of my chest and throw itself at his feet over his worry at how August suddenly showing up here is affecting me.

August holds up both hands to show he means no harm.

"Hey, man. I appreciate that you're looking out for Imogen, but this doesn't concern you. I'm just here to get some answers. If she wants me to go, I'll go. I'm not here to make things harder on her." He looks at me, the same kindness that pulled at my heart two years ago slamming into my chest like a direct sunbeam.

I lay my hand on his arm, a silent plea for him to understand. "I can't do this right now. I need some time to figure out where we stand, okay?"

"Yeah, sure." He pulls his arm away, and I can't blame him for wanting nothing to do with me. "You know how to get in touch."

"I do." Though I don't know how I'll ever be able to talk to him again now that he knows I made up a whole relationship with him.

Chapter EIGHT

Love Rule #15: Be vulnerable. Love requires you to reveal your truest, most genuine self.

By the time my shift's over, I'm equal parts shock and guilt. I've managed to avoid talking to Gemma about August's very sudden and very inconvenient arrival, pretending to be fully dedicated to my tables—when I had them—and to cleaning when I didn't.

But Gemma's on to me. She corners me by the supply closet when I return the package of napkins I was using to roll more silverware sets. "So August's even hotter than I expected."

I stare at her open-mouthed and feign stupidity. "I think you need a calendar. It's only March, not the dead of summer. And I wouldn't call seventy a heat wave."

"Har har." She needles her finger into my ribs, backing me into a literal corner. "I've left you alone all morning so you could process what happened. You don't get to shut me out now."

"August showing up here is going to take more than a

few hours to process," I say. Panic is a constant hum beneath my skin. I never expected to see him again after that first day, much less thought that he'd find out about Fake August.

"At least now we know he's TheRealAugust. So as long as you stay on his good side, I think your secret's safe."

I wedge my arm between us and pry her away so I can escape. She moves back a step but continues to block the hallway leading back out front. Her message is clear: the only way to get away is to have this conversation.

Relaxing my stance, I say, "How do you figure that? Because from where I'm standing, him just being here threatens to implode my whole life. It'll take five seconds for word to get out that he's here, and then everyone's going to start asking why since they all think he broke up with me last week. What was he thinking showing up like that?"

"What was *he* thinking?" Gemma's accusatory tone leaves no question where she places the blame. Pinching the bridge of her nose, she lets loose an exaggerated sigh. "I love you, Mo, but this isn't his fault."

"I know. I know. I'll add it to the list of things I have to apologize for if he's still even talking to me." And if he accepts my apology, there's a chance he'll also agree to keep my secret.

After pulling my phone from my uniform pocket, I shoot off a message.

MoGlows: Are you still in town? And speaking to me after I was a complete witch this morning?

TheRealAugust: My family's renting a house at the beach for the week, so definitely still here.

TheRealAugust: And I could be persuaded to talk if you bring me a biscuit as recompense.

Not a day-trip then. He's here for a week. I don't even want to think about how many chances he'll have to tell everyone the truth. I have to convince him not to do exactly that the first chance he gets.

MoGlows: Send me your address and I'll be there in a few.

A biscuit is the least I can do. Especially since I have to ask him to play along with my lie until he's out of town—and my life—for good.

To-go bag of biscuits in hand, I walk up the front steps of the beach rental twenty minutes later. The pale aqua house is oceanfront, with one of those cutesy name placards that reads SEAS THE DAY.

Taking the sentiment to heart, I ring the bell. A young boy answers the door, damp hair rioting in a mass of curls around his face. Sand and bits of shell cling to his feet as water drips onto the floor from his bathing suit. He's a mini version of August, with the same megawatt smile and crystal-blue eyes.

"Who are you?" he asks, eyes narrowing with suspicion. Stranger danger is alive and well with this kid.

"I'm Mo. A friend of August's."

"So we're friends now, huh?" a voice says from farther in the house. August appears over his brother's shoulder a moment later, giving me a sly smile.

Holding up my peace offering, I say, "I brought biscuits. And our homemade honeysuckle butter, which is quite possibly the best thing you'll ever eat in your life."

He takes the bag from me, opens it, and inhales like the scent alone will sustain him. "All right, *friend*, do you want to come in?"

"Can we maybe go for a walk?" I'd rather not have any witnesses for this conversation.

"Can I come?" his brother asks before August can answer.

"Imogen and I need to talk. But we'll hang out with you while we eat our biscuits first, okay?"

Crossing his arms over his chest, the little boy glares at us both in turn. "She said her name was Mo."

I offer an explanation, hoping August will pick up on it too so he doesn't accidentally reveal my lie if he runs into anyone this week by calling me the wrong name. "*Mo* is short for *Imogen*. It's what most everyone calls me. And you're Owen, right?" I remember August talking about him the day we met. I didn't, however, remember to factor him into my fake relationship story. Not that I thought I'd ever meet him face-to-face.

"Yep. I don't have a short name though. Neither does August."

"Well, it's nice to meet you, Owen." I follow them into the heart of the house. The back wall is floor-to-ceiling windows, the sliding kind that stack up on one end to literally bring the outside in. A few panels are open, letting in a warm ocean breeze. The water beyond the low dunes is the perfect artist's palette of aqua, teal, and a blue so deep, it's almost black where the ocean meets the horizon. My fingers itch for my camera on days like this. When there's beauty so perfect and fleeting, it'll be gone the second you look away. "Wow. This view. Do y'all vacation here a lot?"

"We normally go to the mountains. Jason—our stepdad, thanks to your mom—is a hiker. He got our mom hooked, so family trips are more trees and dirt than sun and sand," August says.

"Yeah, but the beach is way more fun." Owen hops onto one of the stools at the counter separating the kitchen from the living room. "Jason signed me up for surfing lessons this week. And August is taking me out to look for shark teeth at low tide. I'm so happy August picked here instead of hiking when Mom and Jason let us choose."

August shakes his head at his brother, presumably to get him to shut up before he gives away any more of August's secrets. "She doesn't need our whole life story."

A shot of fear spikes through me, buzzing in my veins. Did he come here to confront me? Or is there something else that brought him back to town—and to me? Instead of letting it show, I beam at him. His life story is exactly what I need if I'm going to find something to hold over him if he doesn't agree to keep my secret out of the goodness of his heart. "As a matter of fact, I absolutely do."

"Trying to get your story straight?" he asks. But he grins back at me, so I have no clue if he's messing with me or if he's on to my digging-up-dirt scheme so soon.

"Just curious." And then it hits me. Not only have I roped August into my lie, I've managed to entangle his entire family. His friends. Everyone he's connected to is a part of this, and they don't even know. I can't blame him for coming to confront me in person when I've tainted every aspect of his life. August doesn't seem mad at me though. If anything, he's intrigued about our fake relationship. Why I picked him. Possibly even a bit confused. But not angry. Maybe he's just being nice to lull me into incriminating myself, but something tells me he's not. That my first instinct about him two years ago was spot on and he's one of the good ones.

Turning his attention to the biscuits, August flips the bag upside down and dumps them on the counter. The plastic cups of honeysuckle butter tumble out, spinning straight off the edge. My waitress instincts kick in, and I lunge to catch them before they splatter on the tile floor, which means I end up plastered to August's chest when he turns to catch them as well. My free hand flies up to grip his shoulder to steady me. He's solid muscle under his shirt. My heart jackhammers at the closeness, putting all my G-rated fantasies about him this past year to shame.

I came here to apologize, not throw myself at him. Literally.

"Nice catch," he says. We're still close enough that his breath is warm on my neck.

I don't register that I've managed to rescue one butter cup and August snagged the other until we finally break apart. "You too."

We set the butter on the counter, careful not to touch again. Owen's on them within seconds.

"What kind of butter did you say this was?"

"Honeysuckle. Sounds weird, I know. But I promise it's good. It's a family recipe from one of Gemma's dads' great-grandmothers or something. They make it from scratch and everything." I'm rambling, but it's better than letting my thoughts drift to the wisps of rose gold shot through with flashes of teal coming off August after our close encounter. Whoever he's thinking about right now, she's done a number on his heart.

"Who's Gemma?" Owen asks.

August answers for me. Like he wants to remind me he knows enough about me to cause trouble. "She's Imogen's best friend. Her dads own the biscuit place where Imogen works." After setting out three plates, he drops a biscuit on each one and slathers a heaping dollop of butter right on top. It's going to melt right off in seconds, leaving most of the butter in a puddle on the plate.

I want to tell him they're biscuits, not pancakes, and the butter belongs on the inside. But no sense in ruffling feathers with how he likes to eat his food when I need to keep him in a good mood. "Been doing your homework, I see." I tip my head toward him. *Touché.*

"I looked you up a few months ago after Mom booked this place. Seeing your stories about your *boyfriend* was a bit of a surprise." He raises an eyebrow at me, a smile tugging his lips to one side.

He's known for months? That bombshell only has about three seconds to wreak havoc on everything I thought I knew before my sense returns. I have so many questions for him, I don't know which to ask first.

Why did he look me up in the first place?

Why didn't he say anything before now?

Does he know how embarrassed I am that he knows?

Owen interrupts my silent question tornado with a full-mouthed exclamation. "I feel like I died and ate heaven!"

August and I lock eyes and burst out laughing at the same time. The awkwardness of the situation pauses in the name of mutual amusement.

"Don't talk with your mouth full," August says. He has trouble saying it with a straight face.

"Oh my God. I want to get that printed on a shirt," I say. It would also make a gram-worthy caption to my next biscuit-themed post.

"What's so funny?" Owen asks.

I love his phrasing too much to correct him.

August shakes his head, like he's having the same crisis of conscience. Then he says, "It's that good, huh?"

Picking up his biscuit to take another bite, Owen looks at August and says, "If you're not going to eat yours, can I have it?"

"He's going to eat it," I say. One biscuit doesn't begin to make up for apparently not-so-secretly using his name throughout the past year, but it's a start. I barely know the real August, but if the past few minutes are any indicator, he seems like the kind of guy who would give in to his brother's request. I nudge my plate closer to Owen. "I eat them all the time, so this one's all yours."

"I love you," he says. And in that moment, he does. A wispy puff of rose gold hangs in the air before dissipating as his attention turns back to his meal.

"She does have that effect on people." August smiles at me like he means it. Then he breaks off a hunk of his own, melted butter dribbling down his fingers as he pops the bite in his mouth. "Yeah, okay. I think I've died and eaten heaven too."

"Oh, that's definitely going on a shirt." As soon as I have the August situation under control.

They polish off their biscuits in record time. August uses the last few bites of his to mop up extra butter pooled on Owen's plate. Not willing to be cheated out of a final taste, Owen goes to lick the butter ramekin clean, but August stops him with a don't-even-think-about-it look. Then he motions to the dirty dishes, which Owen obediently rinses in the sink before loading into the dishwasher.

"All right, Mom and Jason are out, so we're sticking close to the house for a bit. You can either go out back and practice your soccer sprints or go in our room and play *Minecraft*. Imogen and I are going out on the back porch to talk."

"You'll take me to the beach when you're done?" Owen asks.

August holds one hand up, fingers splayed, like it's part of an unbreakable brotherly pact. "Yep. And we can stay out there until dinner as long as you're wearing sunscreen."

"Deal!" Owen high-fives him and runs off down the hall. A few seconds later, he sticks his head back out and shouts, "Bye, Mo!"

I call "bye" back, laughing at Owen's enthusiasm, and follow August through the sliding glass doors to the deck. There's a strong breeze rolling off the ocean, keeping the temperature a good five degrees cooler than inland. It's technically spring, but Mother Nature likes to give us multiple seasons within a week in North Carolina this time of year. Thankfully, today is a good day. The ocean stretches out on the other side of the dunes, the constant crash of waves dulled by the distance.

We sit in rocking chairs side by side. Maybe this will be less awkward if we don't have to look directly at each other.

I go first. "Let me start by saying I am so, so sorry. I know what I did was weird and inexcusable."

"'Weird' is a good way of putting it," he says, not unkindly.

"And I'm also sorry for basically kicking you out of the café earlier. I wasn't expecting you, and with so many other people there who know about you—well, not *you* you but the fake you—I freaked. And I totally get if you want me to come clean to everyone and tell them I made it all up."

August turns his chair before hopping it along the wood until he's perpendicular to me. "Why did you make up a relationship?"

My fingers itch to pull down my sunglasses from their perch on top of my head, but then he'd know I'm trying to hide from him in plain sight. Can't have him thinking he has the upper hand here even if it means opening up about my most embarrassing decisions. "Do you remember the day we met? And the stuff I told you about me and love?"

"Of course I do. You're not an easy girl to forget." He looks away like he didn't mean to say that out loud. "And yes, I remember that you can see when people are in love too. That's actually part of why I wanted to see you again."

"Well, you're not the only one who likes that about me. Turns out nobody wants to *date* a girl who's basically a living love detector. The few times someone did ask me out, they were either not actually that into me—I could tell—or, more often, hoping I'd give them the scoop on the person they actually liked. I was just so over it. I mean, just once it would have been nice to find someone with actual feelings for me. And believe me, I know how pathetic and whiny I sound. My life is great; so what if I don't have a boyfriend? It's not like being the daughter of a matchmaker has given me unrealistic expectations of love or anything." I laugh, like it's not the truest thing I've said all day.

"Okay, I can see why you might prefer to lie about having a boyfriend under those circumstances. Since you seem to be in a sharing mood: Why me? Why not make up a guy who didn't actually exist? You never shared pictures of me. Thanks for that, by the way. And you made up fake accounts for me—him. So why risk using a real person?"

I rock back and forth, trying to find the right way to explain. If there even is a way that doesn't make me sound sketchy as hell. "I mean, the obvious one is that you didn't live here. There was supposed to be zero chance of this"—I motion to the less than a foot of space between us—"happening. But you were out there, searchable online should anyone try to verify your existence. Made it seem more plausible, I guess."

"Ah, so I was simply a logical choice."

As if there's anything logical about faking a relationship. It's desperation, pure and simple.

"Not entirely, no," I admit. The fact he's talking to me instead of revealing my lies all over town is another point in his favor. He deserves to know there were other factors at play in choosing him specifically. "You were also incredibly cute and easy to talk to. If I couldn't be with Ren, at least I could make everyone think I had the next best thing."

Sinking back into his chair, August exhales a small laugh. "That may have sounded like a compliment in your head, but nobody wants to hear they're second best. That who they are isn't enough. You and Shay should compare notes." The lightness in his voice is undercut by the aura of heartache blooming around him: a hazy teal so pale, I have to squint to see it. It's barely there. Like he's doing all he can to lock the emotions inside.

"That's not what I was saying. At all. But I'm sorry Shay, whom I'm assuming is your ex by the heartache coming off you right now, messed you up so badly that you think that of yourself."

"She's not... I don't know what to think. About me. Or Shay. I was never good enough for her. I didn't say or do the right things in our relationship. She constantly wanted me to be someone I wasn't. We weren't good together and neither of us was really happy *being* together. And now I don't know *what* I want. But maybe you can tell me."

There it is. The reason he's being so civil about all this. He wants my help.

And I can't tell him no. Not after all I've done in his name.

That doesn't mean I have to cave at the slightest pressure. "Knowing what you want isn't all it's cracked up to be. You can do everything right—be everything you're supposed to be—and still not have it."

August taps his fingers on the arm of the chair, lost in thought for a moment. "But that's what you're hoping for with the guy from the café earlier. Ren? You ended what everyone else thinks was a real relationship to be with him, so you must think it's a possibility."

I don't know how to answer him. It's different with Ren. I've had a crush on him for so long, I don't know how to separate myself from my feelings for him. They're too entangled. Too deep-rooted to rip free. Evans was right earlier though. I'm just a side character in Ren's life. Why would he have ever looked at me twice? Unless I give him a reason to see me as something more. With August's help, I might have a shot.

"It wasn't *for* him, and no one besides Gemma thinks that because for all they know, you cheated on me. But back to the point. I know Gemma said I broke up with fake you for Ren, but it was because of you too. The real you. When I got the poem in the mail, I thought it was a prank. Like someone found out it was all a lie and was baiting me or about to blackmail me or something. I knew if I kept lying about it that eventually the truth would get out, and I couldn't let that happen. Staging a breakup was the only way I could think to make it all go away. And then you showed up today and blew that plan all to hell. What I don't get is why you didn't say anything before now. If you've known for a few months, why let it go on?"

"I wanted to message you when I realized the *boyfriend* you were talking about was me. But I don't know, like I said earlier, after the initial shock wore off, I kinda liked that you picked me. It didn't make any sense, but it wasn't hurting me either. So I left the message to you as a draft. Since we were coming to Portree, I figured I could use it as leverage to get you to help me with Shay. But then I saw the version of me you made up, and that was closer to the real me than who Shay wants, and here we are." He shakes his head, his dark hair falling into his eyes. He drags it back with both hands and holds his head like he can't believe he just admitted that to me.

I kind of can't believe he said it either.

"Here we are," I say.

"Right. And now the guy you like knows your supposed ex is in town to see you," he says. Not a hint of regret in his voice.

"Exactly. So what if we help each other out? I know I'm not really in a position to ask you for anything, but here goes: Will you pretend to be my ex for the week? I think I can get Ren to help me if I tell him you're on a mission to win me back and I need him to run interference. You know, make you—and Lana, in his case—think we're moving on from our respective breakups."

"And what's in it for me?"

"I'll help you figure out what you're feeling about Shay post-breakup. If you still love her despite how she made you feel, or if deep down, you're relieved it's over. That's what you wanted to ask me about right? Your leverage?"

He rocks back, a small laugh escaping him. "It's not exactly leverage if you're getting what you want too. But I'm willing to agree to your terms, being a nice guy and all."

"If it makes you feel any better, your ex wasn't the one."

"And you know that how?"

"True love doesn't break hearts. It'll sustain you even if the person you love is gone. My mom is living proof of that."

"You see heartbreak around me then?" A watery-teal mist forms in the air around him as he speaks.

"Well, I do now. But you've been all over the place today. I won't really know what you're feeling until that's all you're focused on. If you were serious earlier about wanting to be a part of my project, I can get to the heart of things with you and Shay. I know you and Owen have brother beach day this afternoon, but let me know when you're free, and we can work something out."

He looks over my shoulder into the house, a hint of guilt pinching the corners of his eyes. "You're not worried about anyone finding out?"

I've been able to keep him a secret this long—what's another week? "If they do, it'll support our story that you're trying to win me back."

"That sounds like something I would do if I were stupid enough to let you go in the first place."

Turns out I made a mistake. I thought using August as my fake boyfriend was harmless. A lie that would never come out. Yet here he is. Helping me when he has every right to hate me. But I can't take it back now. So I'm going to have to find a way to give him what he wants. Once I figure out what exactly that is.

Chapter NINE

Love Rule #8: Secrets are the enemy of love.

I'm not the only Finch with romance on the brain. When I get back to the house on Sunday after working a double, Mom's stepping into a pair of black heels as she shuffles to the front door. Her hair falls in loose waves around her shoulders, and the classic little black dress twirling around her knees screams fun and flirty. As far as I know, she hasn't been on a single date since Dad died. She was only ever interested in finding love for others. But there's no mistaking this look.

Blocking her path, I fan myself. "Damn, Mom. Hot date?" I ask.

Mom startles, dropping her earring. She avoids looking at me as she follows the diamond stud to its final resting place a few feet away. "Meeting a client for dinner. I shouldn't be out too late."

"Does this client happen to be your old—your word, not mine—and very good-looking friend Alex?"

"No, it's not Alex. And even if it were, it would be a business dinner, not whatever it is you're implying." Though Mom's aura betrays her by going the tiniest shade of rose gold.

"I'm implying you should stop trying to set him up with someone else and go on a date with him yourself. There's a connection there. I can see it, whether you're ready to admit it or not."

"Whatever you think you see, you're wrong. Let it go."

"Why won't you just admit you like him?" I ask.

"I said let. It. Go." She punctuates each word with a pause, grinding her teeth to keep from yelling at me. It's a losing battle, and she knows it. I can practically hear the enamel chipping off with each passing second, which is a shame because my mom has perfect teeth. All straight and even and whiter than a toothpaste commercial. Not even a cavity would dare blemish them. But she'll grind them to nubs if she doesn't stop trying to convince me her feelings for Alex mean nothing.

Doing as she asks, I change the subject so she doesn't leave the house angry. "So who are you going out with tonight?"

She pulls me into a hug, pressing a kiss to the top of my head. All her anger from a moment before is washed away in a wave of what feels like sympathy. "I really wish you'd come home five minutes later so we could have avoided this. You weren't supposed to know."

"Know what?"

"August's family is here for spring break. I'm having dinner with his mom and Jason."

The words spin like a hurricane in my head, threatening to destroy every relationship I care about. If she talks to August's parents, she'll know I lied. Not just lied but lied about love. To my mom, there is no greater sin.

"What? No. Mom, you can't go."

"I know the breakup's been hard on you, but that's why it's just the parents tonight. You don't have to see August while he's here. I'll make sure he stays away."

"You knew he was coming to town, and you didn't tell me?"

"I only found out this morning when Madeline called and invited me to dinner. But no, I wasn't planning to tell you. You've been through enough with him already. I didn't want to add anymore heartache to an already hard situation."

Why dinner though? If his parents knew what I'd done—that I faked a relationship with August—they wouldn't make it a social event. August's mom would have come straight here to demand answers. And potentially a restraining order.

Gripping her arm, I tug her away from the door. "I'm serious about you not going to dinner with them. Please, Mom. You don't know everything."

"Then tell me," she says. The edge is back to her voice, warning me not to mess with her.

I don't want to keep lying to her, but I can't tell her the truth either. Rock meet hard place.

"August came to the café yesterday." I send a silent apology to the universe, to August, to Mom, and add another lie to the fire. "He said his parents didn't know about us. So if I ran into them not to be surprised if they didn't even remember me. If you go to dinner and talk to them about me and August, you're going to make everything so much worse."

"That doesn't make any sense, Imogen. Why would he do that? Lie to them for an entire year about you?"

"I don't know. People lie for all sorts of reasons. He must've had his."

Just like I had mine. But now I can't remember why it seemed like the right choice. Or how I let it get so out of hand. All I can think about is making sure my lies don't ever come out.

Since Mom didn't listen to me, maybe August will have better luck with his parents. My hands shake as I grab for my phone and type out a message that's sure to get his attention.

MoGlows: shitshitshitshitshitshitshitshitshit!!!

TheRealAugust: Hello to you too.

TheRealAugust: How can I help you today, Imogen?

TheRealAugust: Because that many shits in a row is clearly a cry for help.

MoGlows: This is not a time to be cute. Our parents are on their way to dinner. TOGETHER. My mom thinks we dated for a year. And that you just broke my heart. And when I tried to convince her not to go, I suggested that you maybe hadn't told your parents about dating me so she shouldn't talk about me or us at all. But that backfired and now she's even more pissed at you. So unless you want her unleashing her wrath on your parents and convincing them you've been lying to them, we need to stop them. NOW!

TheRealAugust: Shit.

TheRealAugust: You could've led with that.

TheRealAugust: My mom and Jason just left.

MoGlows: I know where they're going. Meet me there. And try to come up with a plan on the way. I will too.

I send him the restaurant's address, grab my keys, and send a prayer to the universe that we're not too late.

I run into August on the way to the restaurant. He's sitting on the curb with his arms propped on his knees. A bike lies discarded nearby, the front tire deflated. A second smaller bike stands beside it as stoic as Owen sitting rigidly next to him. I swerve into the parking lot. There's no open spot, so I park half in the lane a car length from them to block the two from the street view.

Up close, the mangled state of the bike wheel makes sense. August's got a gash at his temple and a bruise already purpling the skin on his cheek where his face must have smacked the ground. Squatting in front of him, I rest my hands on his knees to get my balance. "Oh my God, August. What happened?"

A smile curves his lips. "I may have gotten a bit overzealous in my *dinner-ruining* ice cream expedition." He tips his head toward Owen, who tracks the flow of blood from August's head wound as it trickles down his jaw.

"A bit? You might need stitches! Let me see."

I feather my fingers across his bruising skin and into his hair to check how large the cut is. He shivers at my touch. Leaning closer, I hold my breath, tensing as I continue my examination. I lay my palm against his temple and press my fingertips as gently as I can along one centimeter, two. The blood is already slowing. At least I think it is. There's so much already soaking his hair, I can't be sure.

My throat tightens when he hisses in a sharp breath. And I hate myself for doing this to him. For hurting him. For pulling him into this whole scheme in the first place.

It was never supposed to go this far.

But I don't know how to stop it without losing everything.

I drop my forehead to his and whisper, "I'm so sorry."

"I'm okay. Really." Reaching up, August tugs my hand away from his temple. He squeezes my fingers but doesn't let go. "But if my parents ask, I'm possibly dying. Just until we're sure dinner is a no-go," he whispers so Owen doesn't hear.

"While I appreciate the commitment to the cause, I—"

"Hey." Ren's smooth voice cuts across the air, dragging my attention from August. He jogs the last few feet of the beach-access path to where we're huddled at the edge of the parking lot. He lays his surfboard on the patch of grass and sand by the abandoned bikes, eyes darting between August and me. "Are you okay, Mo?"

"Yeah, I'm okay," I say, slipping my hand free from August's. I stand and put a foot of space between us.

August's gaze drifts to me, guarded, before landing on Ren. "I'm the one bleeding here."

Ren jerks a shoulder at him, his smile smug. The wet suit pulls tight against his chest with the motion. "Karma's a bitch, huh? Should've treated Mo a hell of a lot better."

"Not in front of my brother, man," August says.

I dig some cash from my purse and hold it out to Owen. "Hey, why don't you go get your ice cream and ask if they'll give you a cup of ice so we can get August cleaned up before your parents get here?"

Owen looks to his brother, worry gluing him to August's side as if his injuries are life-threatening. He only moves away when August takes the money from me, his fingers brushing mine, and waves it in front of his brother, saying, "This might be your only chance. I wouldn't risk Mom making us leave before you get a scoop if I were you."

"Can I get two?" Owen asks.

"I won't be there to stop you," August says. His wince lasts the span of a heartbeat when he smiles at his brother.

Then he regains control of the pain so Owen doesn't see how hurt his big brother is.

"I'll take care of him until you get back," I say to Owen. It's the least I can do after August literally bled to help me keep my secret.

"You better."

Once Owen is out of earshot, August says, "You don't have to stay. I already called my mom, and they should be on their way. Dinner plans officially canceled."

He has no reason to help me. To *keep* helping me. But he is.

I don't want to think about what it says about me that I'm letting him.

Or that part of me is charmed by it. By him.

"I can stay for a minute. At least until he comes back," I say.

"You don't owe him anything, Mo. If you walked away right now, no one would blame you," Ren says, reminding me how this must look to him. To everyone who sees me fawning over my ex.

I shake my head to reset my thoughts. We're so far into this lie, I can't turn back now. "I'm not doing it for him. I just don't want to scare his brother more than he already is." Turning to smile at Ren, I continue, "But I'm really glad you're here with me. Thanks for stopping."

"Anytime," he says. To me, his smile is pure sunlight.

August lurches to his feet. He sways once but holds out a hand to steady himself while the other touches his wounded head. "I know what you're doing, Imogen."

"And that would be?"

"You're pretending to be interested in this guy to prove a point. Make me think you're over me. But I promise, he's not the one for you."

I know he's the one pretending, but he sounds so sincere—so much the ex-boyfriend trying to win me back—I almost believe him.

Ren steps between us, using his height and broad shoulders to his advantage. "Dude, you are the last person who gets to tell her who's good for her or not."

Shooting August an apologetic look from behind Ren, I say, "Ren's right. I'm not doing this with you again, August."

"Just let me come over tomorrow. We'll talk. I know I can fix this if you just give me a chance," he says.

"You must've hit your head harder than I thought if you think that's what I want."

"No, August knows exactly what he's doing. He knows he had a good thing and that he's the one who ruined it." Ren looks back at me, his damp hair falling across his forehead adorably. Then he says to August, "Too bad though. Mo and I already have plans tomorrow. We're working on her project together. She's the only one I trust with my heart right now."

His words light me up until I'm glowing like an entire galaxy of stars.

Ren trusts me.

With his *heart*.

"Me too," August says. "Guess I'll just have to be patient.

On the other hand, Imogen, you should probably get a move on. Unless you want my mom to see you."

I blink the stardust out of my eyes and nod. "Right, I should go. Come by around nine tomorrow morning, Ren."

"It's a date," he says.

Chapter TEN

Love Rule #4: Don't self-reject.

Ren is late. I started watching for him ten minutes before our agreed-on time. That was over an hour ago. Despite our recent run-ins, we haven't managed to exchange numbers, so I have no way to contact him to see if he's okay. Or if he's still coming.

Or *why* he didn't come in the first place.

He seemed so eager to help me last night. So *into* me. I know I didn't imagine it.

If he were here right now like he was supposed to be, I could put that theory to the test.

I dial the café's landline so Gemma doesn't get in trouble for answering her cell, which she undoubtedly has in her apron pocket despite her dads' no-phone-during-shift policy.

"Any chance you secretly have Ren's number? Or access to someone who does and would be willing to hand it over? I sent him a snap half an hour ago since that's the only way I know how to get a hold of him. But he's not responding. Now

I need to get ready for work and don't want him to show up when I'm not here if he got the time wrong, and think I'm the one who stood him up."

"Wow, that was a lot of words for a simple question. Don't shoot the messenger here, but I doubt he's heading your way any time soon."

"Is he there?" *Is he with Lana?* As much as I want to know the reason he didn't show this morning, I can't bring myself to ask that question. I'm not ready to give up on us yet. "Why didn't you remind him he was supposed to be *here*?" My panic over Lana's possible reentry into Ren's life makes it come out harsher than I mean for it to.

Gemma sighs dramatically into the phone. "What did I say not to do to the messenger?"

"Sorry. I've just been sitting here watching the street all morning like an idiot. I thought after ice cream and him wanting to help with my project that I'd finally gotten his attention. How am I supposed to get him to date me when I can't even get him to remember we have plans?"

"Again, lots of words. Take a breath, Mo." She waits for me to comply then says, "He's not here. But I see his truck parked across the street. It's like a surfer convention out on the water today. If he comes in before you get here, I'll tell him off for you."

If I didn't know her so well, I might think she was joking. But I do know her, and she doesn't let anyone mess with the people she loves. "No! We want him to like me, remember?"

"Suit yourself. I'm going back to my tables now. And if

lover boy comes in, I'll do nothing but get his number for you." Gemma's cackle reverberates through the receiver for a few seconds after she hangs up.

My strategy with Ren is to nudge him in my direction until he's over Lana and ready to start something new. Gemma's lack of subtlety could take him from skittish to straight-up blacklisting me. I still have a chance to bring him back from whatever kept him from showing up today. I just have to get to him first.

"It's still there," Gemma says for at least the dozenth time since my shift started.

Dragging my gaze away from the window and the beach beyond, I say, "He could be done any minute. I need to be ready."

"Any minute" turns into forty-two. But thanks to my vigilance, I see him the moment he crests the dunes on the beach-access path.

"I'm taking my break," I call to Gemma, my fingers fumbling on my apron knot. After getting it free, I toss the apron on the ice machine as I leave.

It's the perfect spring beach day—the sun casting the world in a warm glow, the hint of a breeze tickling the fronds of seagrass, a trail of wispy clouds dotting the sky like spun sugar. A line of cars clogs the street, looking for a place to park. I cut between two just as one surges forward, and the car behind it honks at me as if I'm the reason for all the traffic. I give the driver my best smile. Then I jog the rest of the way to the beach entrance.

"Mo!" Evans shouts when he spots me. He stabs the end of his surfboard into the sand and throws his arms above his head as if my presence is something to be celebrated.

Ren grins at me. For a few seconds, I forget why I'm here. That smile directed at me—*because* of me—short-circuits my brain, mainlining a shot of hope right to my heart.

He stops a few feet from me, the smile slipping. "Oh, shit. I legitimately forgot."

"I noticed," I say. When my hands tremble, I wish I'd left my apron on so I could have somewhere to hide them.

"Are y'all, like, hanging out now?" Evans asks. Thick ropes of blond hair whirl around his head and send seawater pinging like missiles as he attempts to dry off.

My heart spasms at the idea that this is more than a one-off encounter. That Ren's friends think it's a possibility there's something more between us. But the fact Evans has to ask means Ren has not been talking me up to his friends. Did I even rate a mention for our ice-cream-for-dinner walk on the beach last week? Or is me showing up here now seen as an act of desperation on scale with Astrid?

Ren shoves Evans's shoulder. "Dude, we both just broke up with someone we *loved*. We're like our own two-person broken hearts club over here. She helped me with the Astrid situation the other night, and I swooped in to rescue her from her jerk of an ex." He slings a well-toned arm around my shoulders, crushing me in a half hug like I'm a cute sidekick.

Or worse, a little sister.

After our ice cream date, I thought he'd see me differently. If not girlfriend material, then at least as a friend. Being relegated to an IOU is demeaning on so many levels. "You maybe could've told me you weren't interested in being a part of my project before I spent all morning waiting for you."

"No, I totally meant to be there. The waves were just so good today. You lose all track of time out there. Back me up here, Evans. I can't have Mo thinking I'm a flake."

"Good waves wait for no man." Evans says it like it's a phrase cross-stitched on pillows for aging surfers everywhere. "Don't feel bad. Lana didn't get it either."

At the mention of his ex-girlfriend, a tendril of teal aura curls around Ren's collarbone.

"I do get it, actually. Not with waves but with my photography. Waiting for the exact right moment to snap. The right light. The right angle. It's probably a lot like waiting for a good wave. If I had a day when everything aligned for one killer photo after another, I'd forget everything else existed too."

"So you're not mad?" Ren asks. His shoulders are curved forward. The slick wet suit pulls tight against his muscles.

"How could I get mad at you for doing something you love?" I'd bet my tuition for Kinsey that Lana was never mad either. But when you're drowning in disappointment, you reach for any lifeline that could save you. Even anger.

"Oh, dude." Evans paws at my shoulder, his fingers tapping against my skin like I'm a typewriter translating thought to text. "You should totally come out with us one day. The pictures you could get of us in action would be sick."

"No way," Ren says.

Not just a no, but a *hell no* packaged in a polite brush-off.

I shrink back at the vehemence in his voice. "No?"

"I already have one near-drowning experience with you on my hands. I'm not chancing a second one. Besides, I didn't even bring Lana out with me more than a couple times. How would it look if Mo were out there sharing one of our boards this soon after...everything?"

"I'm good with my feet planted firmly on the sand; don't worry," I say.

The relief that pours off Ren prickles against my skin like a sunburn.

"I'm sorry about this morning. Really. You're the only reason I'm handling everything with Lana the way I am. Which admittedly isn't great, but I'm working on it." His heartbreak flares to life, dousing him in a teal storm. As dark and violent as ever.

The force of it batters my heart.

I can work around Ren forgetting about our plans because the surf was good. But his feelings for Lana? If he's still this broken up over her, I don't know if he'll ever be ready to move on. Not with me. Not with anyone.

For the rest of my shift, whenever my mood gets too dark, Gemma sideswipes me with a whispered "August" to remind me I'm supposed to be more torn up over him than being blown off by Ren. All it does is make me pull out my phone once I clock out to let August know about my failure.

MoGlows: It's never going to work.

TheRealAugust: What? Our fake-up?

TheRealAugust: Or keeping our parents from finding out we're lying to them?

MoGlows: Ren. He was Mr. To The Rescue yesterday in front of you, but today he bailed on me to go surfing and then basically friendzoned me when his best friend asked if we were hanging out. I thought he liked me. But he just wanted to make you feel like shit and prove that I was better off without you. Plus, he's nowhere near being over his ex. So you pretending to try and win me back is pointless.

TheRealAugust: Give the guy some time to come around.

TheRealAugust: Not everyone is an expert in love like you are.

TheRealAugust: Plus, if we give up now, what am I gonna do for the rest of the week?

I want him to be right. That I just need to be patient and things will work out with Ren. But he didn't see Ren's heartbreak. Or how easily he brushed aside the notion that there was anything going on between us.

MoGlows: Do you really want to spend your whole break chasing after a girl you're never going to get?

TheRealAugust: Who says I won't get her?

TheRealAugust: You did pick me to be your fake boyfriend, so there must be something about me you like. 😉

MoGlows: Under different circumstances, I think we'd be friends.

MoGlows: Speaking of which...I'm free tonight if you want to come over. I owe you a romance evaluation. And since Ren skipped out on his photo session today, I'm down one model for my project. You did say you wanted to be part of it, right?

TheRealAugust: I did say that.

TheRealAugust: And you do owe me.

TheRealAugust: So I guess I'm all yours.

I know I should be thinking of how to get Ren to be more than my friend, but something about August—the real August—saying he's all mine, even as a joke, does something funny to my heart. And I don't have a clue what to do about that.

Chapter ELEVEN

Love Rule #22: You can lie to yourself, but your heart will know the truth.

I've almost convinced myself there's no spark between August and me by the time he arrives for his portrait session that evening. One look at him with his wind-tousled hair and formfitting tee and it comes roaring back in full force. My heartbeat stutters the second he smiles at me.

He's not your boyfriend, I remind myself. *He never was.*

Some habits are hard to break.

Apparently, some feelings are too.

If things had worked out with Ren, I wouldn't be reacting to August this way. At least that's what I tell myself when he's close enough for me to see the angry red cut on his head that's thankfully devoid of stitches.

Ren is the dream. August is—has always been—just a decoy.

"Beach is a good look on you," I say. Because it's true, objectively speaking. I don't have to be attracted to him to acknowledge that.

Running a hand through his hair in a fruitless attempt to tame it, he says, "I did shower before coming over here. But now I'm thinking maybe this is a lot more formal than I initially thought."

"It's not. You're good just like this."

"I think I'm going to have to see the rest of your portfolio first before I'll agree with you."

I lead him through the side yard, conveniently avoiding Mom, who's holed up in the house working. She came to tell me about August's bike accident last night and how convenient the timing was. She didn't outright ask me if I had anything to do with it, and I was glad I didn't have to lie to her. Again. I've been avoiding her ever since.

The studio behind the house used to be a garage filled with all of Dad's things she wasn't ready to part with, but Mom cleaned it out and repurposed it a few years ago when I started getting serious about photography. It's big enough for a few couches and cushy chairs and a miniature kitchen alongside my worktable, stand lights, and backdrop setup. Mom likes for her clients to pick their preferred seat and backing color for their Soul Match profile photos, so we have multiple options to get them comfortable enough for their personalities to shine through.

For my portfolio, I keep it simple. Consistent. Light-gray backdrop. Square metal stool. I want my subject's love or heartbreak to be the focal point.

August gravitates toward the photos I have hanging from

a thick rope of twisted wire over my worktable. They're long since dry, but I hung them back up after my meeting with Mrs. Clemente to help inspire some creative thinking. He moves down the line, pausing at each one to really absorb it.

"These are amazing," he says when he gets to the end. "Like, if they were in a museum, I would think someone with decades of experience had done them."

I stop my smile while it's still forming on my lips.

"What's that look?" He circles his finger in the air inches from my face.

As I shift my gaze to the portraits behind him, my spark of pride ices over. "My adviser doesn't agree. She thinks it's too boring. Too safe. Hence these new heartbroken photo sessions. I'm hoping that'll give me the edge I need to get into this über-competitive summer arts program."

He rocks back on his heels and laughs. The sound fills the room. "Of course you're applying to Kinsey too."

"Unless there's another absolute dream of a summer arts program I don't know about. If so, I'm going to need you to tell me right now so I have a backup plan if I don't get into Kinsey." It takes a moment for the rest of his sentence to break through my fear-of-failure panic. "And speaking of backups. You said 'too'?"

"I submitted my application last week. The poem I sent you was the last piece in my portfolio."

"You're telling me I have an August Tate original?" I've only read that one poem, but it was brilliant. And definitely had the wow factor Mrs. Clemente is always pushing me to achieve in my own work. "Between you and Gemma, that's two spots fewer for the rest of us non-geniuses."

"Gemma's applying too?"

"Yeah. I'm doing the photos for her portfolio later this week. She makes these killer driftwood sculptures, and even though they're all gnarled hunks of wood, they're super intricate and detailed. It takes real talent to do something like she does. Like you do with your poems."

"Don't even try to pull that modest crap with me. You are crazy talented."

"What I see when I take someone's picture is so different from what's visible. With most people, their love or heartbreak only shows when they're actively thinking about the person they love. So when I can get them talking in front of the camera, I'm able to capture that raw emotion. But to get into Kinsey, I have to make others feel what I see even though they can't see it."

Am I setting myself up for failure by trying to do the impossible? Will my photos always be missing something because a key element is invisible to everyone but me and Mom?

"So how does this work?" August asks, walking to the stool set up in the portrait area. He sits like a child posing for picture day, all stiff and straight on, with a slight head tilt. "Do I just have to think about Shay for you to know what I'm feeling? Because I could use an objective opinion. And if you can make me see it too, even better."

I move in to readjust him. Grabbing both his shoulders, I shake out his posture to loosen him up. I lift his arms, trying not to notice the way his muscles flex under my fingers, and let them drop more naturally by his sides. He's biting back a smile when I lean in to straighten his head. I keep my touch light on his face, but his skin is warm and smooth, and my fingers have a mind of their own. They roam over his jaw and into his hair. When they find the cut on his temple, he sucks in a sharp breath, bringing me back to my senses. I don't know what it is about being close to him that hijacks my brain, but I need to get it together before I make things between us even more complicated.

Stepping back, I put some much-needed space between my hands and his body. "Right, so Shay. Thinking about her is good. Talking about her is better. Brings the emotions out more so I can get a more accurate read of things. But it's up to you."

"You say I have a choice, but I don't think you really mean it." The smile he's been holding back breaks free. He drags his hands through his hair, a perfect mess. Dropping his elbows on his knees, he looks up at me with his whole heart exposed.

I grab my camera and snap a quick photo of him while his guard is still down. His smile begins to fade once the camera shutter clicks. His expression turns so raw. A mix of loss and hope and desire. Each emotion does something different to his face in the span of a few seconds. I want to capture it all. The camera click click clicks as I snap a few more shots.

"What did you see just then?" he asks.

"Why? What were you thinking about?"

A blush blooms across his cheeks that has nothing to do with emotions I can see. "Wow. You went from *it's up to you* to *bare your soul* real quick."

"Fine, fine. Keep your secrets," I tease. "I'll just pretend you were thinking about me."

"What if I was?"

"You weren't."

Grinning at me, he says, "So you can read thoughts now too?" August wields his smile with such precision, he must know exactly what it does to me.

I walk to him and frame his face in my palms. "I can read *you*. You have a very expressive face." Then I put my thumbs on both corners of his mouth and firmly press down to keep his smile from growing deadlier.

"So I've been told."

"Shay?" I ask, attempting to steer the conversation back to safer waters. Namely, his heartache and how I can help him.

"Yeah. She doesn't find it as fascinating as you do though. She thinks I react the way I do to make her feel bad or something. Except if I could hide how shitty I feel when she starts in on me to 'be better,' there's no world in which I wouldn't do it." A watery-teal mist forms in the air around him as he speaks.

I only see it because I'm looking for it. After a few seconds it vanishes. But not before I manage to take a few pictures.

"From where I'm standing, there's not a single thing I'd change," I say.

Instead of perking him up, that only makes his gloom intensify. I raise my camera—part warning, part question—and start shooting again when he nods assent. He doesn't have to say much over the next ten minutes for his emotions to seep into the air, a riot of conflicting colors.

"Is this weird? Me talking about her with you?" he asks.

"Everything about our relationship is weird," I say. And statements like that are making it worse. I flap my hands in the air as if I can fan the awkwardness away. "Not that I think we're *in* a relationship. I swear I can tell the difference between what this is and what I've been pretending for the past year. I'm just going to stop talking now." My face flames hot enough to set the whole room on fire. But I'm not lucky enough for that to actually happen, so I have to stand here and endure the embarrassment.

"Are you sure? Because I'm kind of enjoying seeing you a little flustered. I didn't think Imogen Finch got nervous about anything."

"I'm not nervous. I just forget sometimes when I'm around you that we don't have the history everyone thinks." That what I feel for him isn't real.

"It might not be what everyone thinks, but we do have *a* history," he says.

"Spending half an hour together the day we met mixed with a year's worth of faked Instagram stories is not a relationship."

"Clearly, we made an impression on each other, or we wouldn't be here right now." August leans forward, the toe of one shoe balanced on the bottom rung of the stool, the other leg planted on the floor. All confidence and charm. With his eyes on mine, he says, "I know I should be more upset about what you did, but having someone see me the way you do—well, saw, I guess—that felt more real than most of my relationships."

I hold a hand up to keep him seated though he hasn't made a move toward me. There's a warm rose-gold tint to the air between us, and I don't know if his confession conjured it or if my own desire to be wanted did. "It's still present tense," I admit.

"It sucks that instead of taking a chance on the real me, you decided to make up a version of me that ticked all your boxes."

"The fact I picked you means you ticked a number of boxes all on your own."

He's still leaned forward, as close to me as he can get without touching me. His emotions cloud his aura again, that confused mix of love and heartbreak. A watercolor of rose gold and teal. "Just not enough of them, apparently."

"It's kinda hard for you to tick the box labeled *Ren*." Though if August had lived here, would he have gotten me over my crush on Ren? Or would I have still been waiting for the day he and Lana went their separate ways?

"What are you gonna do about him? Still thinking it's all over for you two?" August asks.

"I don't know how *not* to be half in love with him. That's basically my default setting. So even if I wanted to give up on him, it's not really a possibility."

"Have you tried? And, no, fake dating me doesn't count."

"I told you, nobody thinks about me like that," I say.

August dips his head, the curve of his smile just visible. "If someone did like you though, would you give them a chance? Or is it always only going to be Ren?"

The question is so unexpected, I don't have an answer ready to fire back. He chances a glance up at me. It's cautious but hopeful. And it frays another thread of my feelings for Ren.

"I want to say yes. I really do. But I honestly don't know."

I look away before my better judgment throws up a white flag, surrendering all control to my heart.

By the time August leaves, the sun's sinking below the horizon, streaking gold across the faded denim of the sky. The marsh grass guarding the dock out back whispers in the cool evening breeze. It sounds faintly like his name as I walk up the path to the house.

AugustAugustAugustAugust.

Like it's saying goodbye.

Like it's calling him back.

I shut the door on it and any lingering thoughts about how he surprised me tonight. How I enjoyed his company and the way his voice wrapped around the studio, making itself at home in the open rafters. I knew he would be trouble. I just hadn't counted on him being a problem for my heart.

Mom's abandoned her office for the comfort of the living room and waves to me from the oversize chair she likes to read in. It had been Dad's from before they got married. His sole furniture contribution to the household. I have a photo in my room of the two of us conked out in it together when I was a baby, me snuggled against his chest like it was the safest place in the world.

"Was that August sneaking away a few minutes ago?" Saving her place in the book with a finger closed between the pages, she uses it to point toward the front window. Through which she has a straight view out to the street where he parked.

I nudge the book back into her lap. "He wasn't sneaking so much as avoiding a parental smackdown. And, yes, it was August."

"I don't think a conversation about his actions toward you would devolve quite that far. Though after the stunt he pulled to get his mom and Jason out of our dinner, I can understand him not wanting to face me."

"What makes you think he got hurt on purpose?" If she's on to him, there's no way we'll be able to keep them from unraveling the truth for much longer. I'm surprised she hasn't talked to his mom already.

"Oh, sweet summer child. I, too, was once a teenager trying to hide things from my parents. I know the signs. And neither of you was very subtle. You tried to talk me out of going to dinner, and then he just so happened to get hurt, resulting in exactly what you wanted? That's not the coincidence you want me to think it is." She smiles into her steaming mug of hibiscus tea. "And now here he is, at our house, after everything he's done. I'm just trying to understand what's going on with you. I don't want you to get hurt again."

Her gentle mothering makes my throat burn with guilt. After sinking to the couch, I curl my legs under me and lay my cheek against the back cushion to look at her. "I'm okay. August just wanted to be part of my project for Kinsey. He knows what it means to me to get in, and one of the guys who said he'd help bailed on me, so August stepped in. Nothing more."

"Sounds to me like he wants you to see what he's feeling and forgive him. I know he made you happy before—"

"Mom, don't worry. There's nothing going on there." I mean it. So why does it feel like I'm still lying to her? "I don't see the point in holding on to all the sad stuff, you know? He broke my heart, so that means he wasn't the one. Now I can move on without worrying that I've lost something. You taught me that."

"There's no rush. Love will find you when you're ready."

"Says the woman actively avoiding finding love."

"Don't start that again, Imogen," she warns. Her nails scrape against the ceramic mug as she tightens her grip.

A shiver rolls through me. I pull the blanket from the back of the couch to drape it over my legs. "I just don't understand why Alex can't be a potential option. Not that you have to date him, but you won't even entertain the idea."

"He was your dad's friend. They were as close as brothers for a long time."

"Why have I never met him before?" I ask.

"After your dad's accident, our lives went in different directions. We lost touch," she says. There's a hitch in her voice. A piece of the story she's skipping over. Avoiding.

What doesn't she want me to know? The question nibbles at my brain, trying to locate a logical answer. "Is that why you haven't asked me to do his Soul Match photos yet?"

Mom lurches forward in her chair, nearly tipping out of it. Her tea splashes over the rim of her mug before she rights herself and it. "What?"

"If he's a client now, don't you need me to take his profile picture? Or are you purposely keeping me away from him because you think I'll be too sad to meet one of Dad's friends who left you to grieve alone? Or did something happen between them? You said they were like brothers 'for a long time.' Implying that stopped at some point. What happened?"

"Sometimes I forget how wild your imagination gets," she says. But she won't look at me. The dribbles of liquid on the floor between us claim the honor of her gaze. "I didn't ask you because you've got a lot on your plate right now. The breakup. The Kinsey application. Work. General being-a-teenager stuff. I can handle a few clients on my own."

On the surface, her excuse makes sense. In her current

state, pushing further will only make her mad. So I let it go. As much as I can let anything go.

"If there's nothing nefarious going on, do you think I could meet him the next time he's here? Not just a *hi, how are you* before you hustle him out of here, but like actually talk to him? I'd love to hear some new stories about Dad from someone who knew him well. I promise to keep the matchmaking to a minimum."

"I assume by 'minimum' you mean none?"

"You can assume that." As long as he's not glowing for her, it'll be true. But if he feels anything for Mom, all bets are off.

We are in the business of helping people fall in love after all.

Chapter TWELVE

Love Rule #27: You can't make yourself fall in love with someone. No matter how much you wish you could.

It's official. August can't take a bad photo. Of the fifteen pictures I took of him yesterday—including the first sneak-attack one—I cannot decide which is the best. Usually, there's one or two that stand out as the obvious choices. But with these, they're all equally good. When I sent the lot to Gemma to help me choose, she texted back an eggplant emoji. The opposite of helpful.

And maybe I am letting my feelings for August—whatever they are after last night—cloud my judgment. It doesn't change the fact I have to pick one. Or that my future rides on my photos being good enough to earn me a spot at Kinsey.

That's why I end up at August's rental house. Again.

"Three days in a row. We seem to be making a habit of this," he says when he opens the door. His smile is even more arresting in person.

If I spend much more time with him, I'll have to start lugging around a personal defibrillator for when my heart inevitably spasms out of control. Looking away from him for my own safety, I say, "I thought you might want to see the photos from yesterday. And maybe tell me which one you want me to use?" The pleading in my voice ticks up at the end like a question.

Pointing to the Yeastie Boys bag in my hand, he raises a challenging eyebrow at me. "Those don't look like pictures."

"These are cheddar, bacon, and jalapeño biscuits. And you can have them *if* you pick a picture." I hold up the envelope of photos and dance it around for effect.

"So we're the kind of friends who bribe each other for favors now?"

"If you don't want them, I can always give them to someone else."

He snatches the bag from my hand and steps aside to let me in. "Right this way."

"That's what I thought," I say, throwing a grin over my shoulder as I pass. But he's already moving to follow me inside, and our lips are seconds away from an accidental collision. For the span of a heartbeat, I let myself want it. Want him. Then reality gives me a little shove to remind me I'm supposed to want Ren, not August. I turn away too fast and stumble over a pair of shoes in the entryway. August wraps his arms around me to keep me from face-planting on the floor.

It's like the universe is torturing me.

Because kissing August, falling for him, is so not part of the plan.

Ren is.

Ren.

Ren.

Ren.

He's the one I'm doing all this for. Why August and I are spending time together this week. Ren may only see me as a friend right now, but I have to hope that'll change given enough time.

I extricate myself from August's grip before I can make this even more awkward. "Thanks."

"Anytime," he says. No hint of teasing in his voice.

In the living room, Owen's wrapped in a towel, bits of sand still clinging to his feet and calves that are kicked up on the glass-top coffee table. He scrambles up when he sees me. Though I suspect he's more excited about the bag of biscuits August took from me. "Mo! Are you coming to the beach with us?"

It's impossible not to smile at him and his instant excitement. "Looks like you've already been."

"And brought some of it back with him as a souvenir," August adds, shaking his head as more sand and shell bits flake off his brother's legs onto the tile floor.

"I'm not keeping it. That's why I didn't wash it off. I'm taking it back next time we go down," he says. Owen bounces on his toes—too much energy contained in such a small body. "Did you bring more biscuits?"

"Not the same as last time. But these are delicious too."

After opening the bag, August removes one and takes a bite. A trail of steam puffs out from the still-warm cheddar-and-bacon biscuit. "I can confirm that's true, Owen. Though one of them could be poisoned, so I have to eat them all and make sure you don't accidentally die. Sorry, bud."

Owen flies off the couch and launches himself at his brother, arms flailing to grab a biscuit. "They're not poisoned! You just don't want to share."

I step back to keep out of the fray.

"It's my duty as your big brother to protect you. But if you're willing to waive that protection, I guess your fate is in your own hands." August grabs a second biscuit and motions toward the kitchen.

"You say that every time, and I haven't died yet," Owen says.

"You better not start now," August says.

Owen runs to the counter and yanks three paper towels from the roll. When he holds them out to his brother, August gives him a look like, *What, no plates?*, and Owen shrugs like plates have ceased to exist. Compromising on napkins *at* the kitchen counter, they settle onto two of the barstools, leaving the one next to August open for me.

Watching these two is not helping me like August any less. Then he smiles at me and nudges the stool out with his foot, a tacit invitation to sit, and I'm dead. He's too perfect to be real.

"I feel like I should warn you that if you bring biscuits by one more time, I'll have to ask you to marry me."

I wave August's pronouncement away. Thankfully,

hyperbole is something I'm well equipped to deal with. Much more so than when he's being sincere. "You wouldn't be the first. Our biscuits have that effect on people."

"Seriously?"

"They don't say the way to a man's heart is through his stomach for nothing. But so far, the marriage proposals and profusions of love end as soon as customers walk out the door. So I promise not to hold you to anything," I say.

Mouth full, Owen mumbles, "If you did marry her, would we get free biscuits?"

"You're getting free biscuits now," I say.

August uses the last bite of his biscuit to point at me. "These are *bartered* biscuits. Goods traded for services rendered. Speaking of which, let me see those photos."

"What photos?" Owen asks.

I slide the stack of portraits out of the envelope and turn it toward the brothers. "Keep your greasy fingers to yourselves, please."

In identical movements, they both hold their hands up in front of them, fingers splayed. I flip the pictures, pausing on each one for a few seconds so they can let the image sink in.

"It's a picture. You should be smiling in more of them," Owen says. He tries to give his brother a stern look, but it comes off too adorable to have the desired effect.

It's nice to hear that phrase directed at a guy for once. Though August's smile is the bane of my existence at the moment. "I needed him to look sad," I say.

"Why?"

"Because I already have a lot of happy-people pictures."

August grins now just to spite me. "Imogen's applying to the same art program I did. Her art is photography, and I helped out yesterday by letting her take my picture to include in her application. And you know how her mom helped Mom and Jason meet?" He waits for his brother to nod. "Imogen takes a lot of pictures of people in love, and she needed to take pictures of other people to balance it out."

"Oh. You should've called Shay before she took your picture," Owen says.

I jolt at hearing August's ex's name. I check him for jumpiness as well out of the corner of my eye and am not disappointed. Fighting back a smile, I say, "Why's that?"

"Because she always makes him sad. Or angry. Or broo-something."

"Broody," August says in a pinched accent, which I assume is an imitation of his mom when Owen breaks out in a fit of giggles. "Our mom likes to call me that after I've been with Shay."

Owen peers up at me, biscuit crumbs clinging to his lips. His ability to attract a mess is apparently part of his charm. "He's not like that with you, Mo. When he got back last night, Mom asked him if he'd been out doing drugs because he was in such a good mood."

August lightly smacks his brother on the arm in the universal sign for *shut the hell up*. "Clearly, she's so used to seeing me in a bad mood that anything else is like a miracle."

"In that case, I have to give her this one," I say, holding up the first picture I took. It's pure August. Caught unawares with his playful smile and sparkling eyes. I try to ignore the fact *I* was the one who brought out that side of him.

"That would honestly make her whole year."

"Done." Setting it aside, I fan out the others. "Now, what about the rest of these? Which one says, *I had my heart broken by the girl I thought I loved but turns out she just made me broody?*"

August and Owen share a look. Whatever they're not saying out loud is communicated just fine with their eyes because they both nod and turn back to me.

"There's something about this one. It's darker or has more movement or something. I can't quite pinpoint what it is, but go with this one." August taps one of them with his knuckle to keep from staining the paper with grease.

The one he chose does have movement. Can he see the heartbreak and love warring around him? How the teal wraps around the rose gold, interlacing with it as it shifts in the air?

"Do you have some magical love-seeing abilities you'd like to share with the class?" I ask.

"If I did, at least I'd know if the girl I'm starting to like likes me back." His phone chimes on the counter. He silences it, barely glancing at the screen. It goes dark before I can see who the message is from. "You looked at that one longer than the rest. Like there's more to it than the others. And it makes your mouth do this cute little wobbly thing."

"Cute little wobbly thing?" He's baiting me. Luring me in with the promise of everything I've been looking for.

Everything I wanted with Ren.

"You know, like you're trying hard not to feel whatever it is you're feeling," he says.

I press my fingers to my lips to keep them from doing anything else where he's concerned. Leaving my hand in place, I release the pressure enough to say, "Nope. No feelings here." Definitely not ones that make me want to say to hell with chasing after a boy who doesn't want to be chased and see if there really is something happening with the one standing right here.

The smug look August gives me says he knows exactly what feelings I'm hiding. But instead of calling me on it, he says, "Wanna go for a walk? Or is that off-limits because someone might see us together?"

I look past him toward the window and the crowded beach beyond. Being seen in public together is suddenly safer than staying here where I am way too close to his mouth, which is still shiny with biscuit grease. "A walk never hurt anyone."

"I very much doubt that is true, but you already agreed, so you can't take it back now."

"I *implied* agreement. Not exactly the same thing as giving it outright."

"Oh, I get it. You just want an excuse in case someone catches us, and you need this to be all my fault." He smiles and wipes his hands clean on a paper towel, leaving the grease on his lips for his tongue.

Flirting with August is too easy. Too natural. Sometimes I forget—just for a minute—that we barely know each other. "You know me so well. It's like we've been dating a whole year or something," I deadpan. We could both use the reminder, even if I'm half joking.

"Or something."

It takes ten minutes to convince Owen to stay behind and play video games. A bribe of ice cream and an *Avengers* double feature that night finally does it. He invites me to stay for both. I tell him I'll have to see.

Who knows what that much uninterrupted time with August would do to me?

August and I head to the beach. Considering all that open space, we walk too close to each other, like the moon pulling the tide. His hand brushes mine, and our little fingers curl around each other for the span of two steps before we break apart. My heart is so full of longing and what-ifs it may burst in my chest.

It's probably what I deserve after all my lies. To finally find love—or the prospect of it anyway—and die before I can experience it.

"Do any of your friends know? About me, I mean," I ask. I angle my next few steps to put a safe foot of distance between us.

"Do they know you're this cool girl I met when my mom was getting set up with Jason? Yes. But anything past that, no. They would've given me shit for letting it go on for so long. And then they would've given you shit for making it all up in the first place. Until I talked to you and found out why you'd done it, I wanted to keep them away from you."

I stare at him from behind my sunglasses. Thank God he can't see the cartoon hearts that have replaced my irises. "You are quite possibly the nicest guy ever."

He mimes being stabbed in the heart. "Nice? Seriously? That's the worst letdown in the history of letdowns."

"Hey, nobody's letting anybody down here. It was simply a statement of fact. And I personally like nice guys. They're genuine and typically treat me like a person, not some magical matchmaking machine."

"Is that why you like Ren? Because he's the type of guy who would defend your honor from your heartbreaking ex?"

I've liked Ren so long, it's hard to remember a time when I didn't. Or why I started liking him in the first place. He's just always been there. A bright spot that dimmed everyone else in comparison.

Until now.

"He's always present. Fully in the moment, attention focused on the person he's with. Like nothing else in the world matters. Granted that's my thousand-mile view of seeing him with Lana, so I may be totally off, but whenever he talks to me, it's like there's this little spotlight on me for a few minutes, and I know he sees me." Granted, the rest of the time, his head is in the clouds—or, in his case, the waves—and any plans he makes get swept out to sea with him. Turning to look at August again, I bump into him, having drifted close again without realizing it. He steadies me with warm hands on my hips. A shimmer of rose gold forms in the air between us at the touch, a mist as delicate as sea spray.

He's got this look about him, like he's dying of thirst and I'm the rain.

What I wouldn't give for him to live here. For us to have this all the time. But he doesn't. And we can't. The most we can have is temporary. Part-time.

And I want it all.

"You deserve that. To be loved like that."

"Everyone does," I say. "Rule number seven: Don't settle for mild affection when true love is out there."

August stops at a patch of shells and scrubs his foot over the top layer to disturb what may be hiding underneath. Squatting to root among the broken pieces, he throws up a hand to shield his eyes and look at me. "Do you really believe in all that? Soul mates and everything?"

I crouch beside him, sifting through my thoughts. After a moment, I say, "I do. I'd be kind of a hypocrite if I didn't with Mom's job."

"That's your mom's job though. I know you help her out with the photography, but you don't have to agree with her. It's *nice* that you do, but it's not a requirement. You can support her and believe something different."

Mom's views are so ingrained in me, I don't think I could believe anything else. Even if I wanted to. "What about you? Do you believe in soul mates?"

"I want to. I mean, who doesn't want to believe there's someone out there just for them. But the world is home to billions of people. What are the odds of finding the one person you're meant to be with? And who pairs up soul mates in the first place? God? So what if you're an atheist? Does that mean you don't have a soulmate because you don't believe in God?"

I laugh. "So that's a no."

He shakes his head, focus still on the sand and shells he's displacing with his foot. "That's an *I want it to be true but need definitive proof*."

"Fair enough."

"I get the feeling that if I hang around you long enough, I just might get it," August says. Then, with an awed "look at that," he bends down and plucks a skinny black shark tooth from the broken shells.

I can't help but want him to be right.

Chapter THIRTEEN

Love Rule #24: If you have to chase it, it's not love.

It's halfway through the week, and I only have one heartbreak photo for my project. August's. I cannot go back to school on Monday with nothing to show Mrs. Clemente. On my break at work, I hide in the back booth with the No Sleep Till Brooklyn—a buttermilk biscuit drowning in espresso red-eye gravy—and my list of names from Saturday. I spend a solid twenty minutes shooting off emails to interested parties. And praying a handful of them respond.

Which is how Ren sneaks up on me.

He slips into the seat across from me, his arms stretched between us, a few inches from making contact. His smile is cautious, but for the first time since his breakup with Lana, it seems genuine. The teal aura enshrouding him is wispy, almost translucent. A bright contrast to the black of his wet suit. Day by day it will continue to fade as his heartache lessens. And he's back here again, so maybe I have something to do with that after all. Even if he doesn't want his friends to think I do.

"You didn't tell me you had a thing for surfers," he says.

Taking a deep breath to reset the nerves going haywire at his implication, I ask, "Who said that?"

"I was doing a private surf lesson this morning. Spring break family. And your boy August spent as much time hounding me about what's going on between us as he did falling off his board. Dude is not a natural. He didn't give up though, I'll give him that. But the way he was talking about you and trying so damn hard to just stay upright made it seem like there was more to it. Like he was doing it to impress you. So I figured you must like guys who surf, which is funny when you think about it since you don't swim."

"I do swim! Just not well."

"So do you? Like surfers?"

It's a harmless enough question, but I don't know how to answer it without all my crush-y feelings giving me away. Though maybe I should let them. Show Ren I'm interested in being more than friends. Once he's ready. I say, "I do. Even when they like the ocean more than me."

Ren shrugs, looking out the window to the sliver of water we can see from the café. A puff of rose gold rises around him. "What can I say? The ocean's a jealous mistress."

Our knees press together under the table, sending a current of heat buzzing through me. "Then I guess I have to be grateful she shares as much as she does."

"I totally thought she might take August as a sacrifice today." He drags his damp hair back from his forehead, looking up at me. Is he waiting for a reaction? To see how I'd feel if August were gone? "He's not what I pictured."

I don't even try to fight my smile. Ren spent time thinking about what the guy I was dating is like? That's a fantasy I never thought would come true. Yet... "How so?" I manage.

"You just seem like you'd go for a guy who's a bit more polished, you know? You're always so"—he motions to all of me—"put together, I guess. And absolutely crushing it. You know what you want. I didn't think you'd be into someone who's a little rough around the edges."

He sounds hopeful. Like maybe he's not talking about August. My heart does a little happy dance in my chest. Then a rush of guilt sweeps through me like a tidal wave, washing that good feeling away when August pushes his way into my thoughts. After his photo shoot on Monday, my feelings for him—the real August—are muddled. But if Ren's even a little bit interested, I have to see if it can grow into something more. He's the one I want to be with. The one I've wanted for so long. A few days with August can't change that, right?

My sudden mood change must show on my face because Ren says, "Hey, I hope I didn't offend you. That's not what I meant at all. The opposite actually."

"No, you're good," I assure him. It's not his fault I can't get a handle on my emotions today. "I'm flattered that that's how you think of me. I don't think anyone's ever described me like that before. As for my taste in guys, I think you might be pleasantly surprised."

"Yeah?" he asks.

"Yeah." I flash him a quick smile then leave him there to contemplate our exchange while I finish my break by grabbing an order from the pass-through kitchen window. I make a quick round of the tables, refilling coffee and tea and generally making sure they're all good. Gemma throws me a what-the-hell-is-going-on look as she scribbles down an order. I do a little shimmy, and she rolls her eyes. When I circle back to Ren, he's moved to the counter like he can't decide if he wants to stay or go. "Are you eating, or did you just come in to tell me about August's lack of surfing skills?"

Ren drums his hands on the table and straightens. A sheepish smile curves his lips, almost as if he forgot where he was. That we weren't alone. "Oh, right. Food would be good. A regular biscuit, I guess. Honeysuckle butter on the side. And a coffee."

"You got it." I turn to grab the biscuit, but he reaches out to stop me. His hand is warm on my wrist. My pulse races at the unexpected contact.

"Mo, wait. August was just an excuse to come see you. I feel terrible about bailing on you the other day and was hoping you'd maybe want to hang out tonight? There's supposed to be a meteor shower visible at like ten thirty, so I was thinking we'd go to the north end of the beach and camp out for a while. See if we get lucky."

Ren Kano just asked me out.

Ren *freaking* Kano.

I abandon all hope of getting my heart rate back under control. "That sounds fun." And super romantic. Beach. Blanket. Shooting stars. It's the kind of first date I've always wanted to have with Ren. Though I'm not even sure this is a date. It may just be two recently single friends going to see a natural phenomenon together because one of them feels guilty. "But you know you don't have to make up for what happened the other day, right? We're good."

"Yeah, no. I know that. I *want* you to come."

"Oh. Well, in that case, I'm in. If you want to grab dinner beforehand, let me know. Or I could always pack some food to bring out too."

"Cool. I'll text you later to coordinate."

"Sounds good. Do you still want the biscuit and coffee?"

He squeezes my arm twice then lets go. "Definitely." His heartbreak still swarms him, half a dozen different shades of teal and copper pulsing as his aura moves around him. But it's a touch lighter now.

Or maybe I'm just hoping it is.

If I am affecting his heartbreak—if I'm the one who can break him out of it—we may have a shot at something real.

"Give me just a second, and I'll have it right up," I say.

Gemma follows me into the kitchen and leans on the doorframe, blocking the path back out front. "Bad idea, Mo."

"What?" The innocent act won't work on her. We've been

friends nearly our whole lives, and she knows every one of my tricks. But I try it anyway. "I'm getting him a biscuit."

"No, you're flirting with trouble. Normally, I'm all for that sort of thing, but you're so far past desperate, you're no longer in the same time zone with it."

"It's not like it's a *date*-date. We're just hanging out." But maybe, by the end of the night, it will be something more.

She rolls her eyes. "He's not the one you should be hanging out with."

"August is not an option." I slide past her into the kitchen. We go through enough biscuits in a morning that there's always a fresh batch right out of the oven. Gabe is a one-man biscuit-making machine. After picking up the tongs, I transfer a perfectly golden biscuit into a clamshell to-go container. Heat seeps through the compostable material and would've burned my fingers if I hadn't burned them a million times before. Stopping at the counter, I write a receipt on the pad from my apron pocket then pause long enough to scribble my phone number on the closed container lid. Then I grab a plastic knife and a to-go ramekin of our signature honeysuckle butter on my way back to Ren.

"You're all set. And I figured you might need that," I say to Ren, tapping the top of the container so he doesn't miss my number.

He nods like this is some covert op then slides his thumb strategically over the ink in case anyone glances at his food on the way by. "Yeah, that is definitely helpful. See you tonight."

I wave him out and don't relax my shoulders until the bells on the door stop chiming. I finally have a date with Ren. And I have August to thank for it. Who knew him being in Portree would actually work in my favor?

If I can make things work with Ren, then I can let go of August—both versions of him—and finally put it all behind me. And I'll never have to tell Ren—or anyone—that I lied. Taking one deep breath after another, I calm my racing heart. After eight, I'm back under control, but I do two more for good measure. I can't let my emotions get in the way. Not tonight.

Tonight I need to see if there's anything more than friendship between Ren and me.

He texted around seven thirty to say he was heading over to stake out a good spot before the beach fills up and he'll let me know exactly where I can find him.

I forgo a dress and settle on a full-length navy romper with thin crisscrossing straps across the back. It's fun and flirty but still casual enough that I hopefully don't look like I'm trying too hard. I pull my hair into a high ponytail and spritz on some perfume. Even though I've showered since my shift this morning, the smell of baked dough and fried chicken tends to linger. After one last check of my makeup, I'm ready to go.

When I find Ren at the beach half an hour later, it takes all of two seconds to realize a) I'm underdressed and b) not only is it not a date, it's a full-on meteor shower–watching party for all his friends. Blankets and sleeping bags are spread over the sand so they overlap, forming a patchwork of color and patterns in the fading light. A handful of pop-up tents are staked into the sand a little ways away from the main cluster for the semblance of privacy. The thin fabrics shiver in the cool breeze coming off the water.

Ren jogs over to me before wrapping me in a quick hug. "Hey, you found us!"

"That I did. Thankfully, the group is hard to miss."

"Don't worry, you're not the last to make it. There are at least ten more who said they'd be here. It's weird to think that a few weeks ago I was planning to watch this from the top of a mountain. But the beach is gonna be so much better." His voice is overly chipper, the fakeness of it ringing hollow.

So this isn't so much a step forward as an attempt to forget he was supposed to be snuggled in a sleeping bag with Lana, making wishes on each star that streaked across the sky. There's enough sunlight left to make out the heartbreak rolling off him, as dark and steady as the ocean waves. He went out of his way to invite me though. And he came over the second I arrived. So maybe it's not completely hopeless.

I steer the conversation away from Lana. Tonight is supposed to be about moving on, opening ourselves up to something new. I need the reminder just as much as he does. "I've never actually seen a meteor shower before, so I'm really glad you invited me."

"How have you not seen one before? This one happens like every year."

"I guess I've never been that into astronomy. With my mom's job, she's into science but not the woo-woo hippie stuff like astrology, so the stars are kind of off-limits in our house."

"Well, we are fixing that tonight. Real star science, I mean. Lana's super into horoscopes and when certain signs are in retrograde and everything, so I know some of that too. But tonight is all about meteors. No woo-woo hippie stuff, I promise."

I laugh. "Sounds good to me."

He wraps his arm around my shoulders, pulling me in close. He smells like pine and citrus. All earthy and warm. "Come with me. I'll show you where my stuff is, and we can make space for you to set up next to me. I tried to save you some room, but things got out of hand while I was building the bonfire."

And he means it. When we get to his spot, he walks right over the other blankets butted up to his and instructs me to lift the one on the end so we can shift them out. All we manage to do is get sand on all of them. Scratching that idea, Ren gathers them all, shakes the sand off once he's far enough away that it won't just blow back on the rest, and lays them back down again with a few feet of space carved out just for me. Everyone watches him, but no one protests. Maybe they're all just happy he's not moping over his breakup tonight and will put up with his shenanigans if it means keeping him in a good mood.

"I've got extra blankets. You look like you're gonna need them later. It gets cold out here."

"I'll take you up on that. Clearly, I took the *spring* part of spring break to heart."

Ren's eyes roam over my body, taking their time to catch every detail. "You look good. But the second you start getting cold, let me know. I've got you covered. Until then, we can hang by the fire if you want."

The air's already turning cooler with the setting of the sun. Before long, it will be downright chilly. I'll never understand the people who live in Scotland or Scandinavia where seventy degrees is a heat wave. Once the temperature drops below seventy-two, I'm reaching for long sleeves. But with Ren's promise to keep me warm, I leave my sweatshirt hidden in my bag, which I drop onto my blanket before tiptoeing back across the rest to keep from kicking up too much sand.

His friends' eyes skim over me, assessing, categorizing. Writing me off as a random tagalong at best or as a rebound at worst. Not that either is preferable.

To be honest, I don't really know what I am.

I just know I'm here because Ren invited me. And because this is what I thought I wanted. A chance to show Ren there could be happiness on the other side of Lana. With me.

Now though, I hear Gemma whispering in my head that Ren isn't the one I should be with. And all I can think is that August would have saved a spot for me no matter how many people showed up to take my place. Despite the version of him

I've built up in my head, I know it's true for the real August too. I've spent enough time with him in the past few days to understand he doesn't do anything on a whim.

Ren, not so much.

Within ten minutes, he's abandoning me to play a game of touch football with his friends. He doesn't even ask if I want to join. I don't, but that's not the point. He's made it clear this isn't a date, so I have no reason to think he'd spend the whole night with me, especially since I was only one of dozens of people he invited out tonight. But it doesn't stop me from wanting his undivided attention. At least for a little while.

I can't even blame it on good waves this time. He's not surfing. He's just not into me. And the harder I try to make him see me differently, the more it's becoming clear that no amount of wishing will change his feelings.

I make small talk with the group around the bonfire and utter obligatory comments when phones are passed to me with pictures of everyone who's off on vacation somewhere more glamorous than Portree. A few people are bold enough to ask me about August. Ending that relationship was also supposed to stop my lies. But here I am pretending like I haven't seen him again after he came into Yeastie Boys on Saturday morning. Like I haven't had to stop myself half a dozen times from messaging him tonight to see what he's up to.

After an hour, everyone makes their way back to the blankets to settle in for the meteor shower. Even Ren. He sits next to me but still manages to avoid me like it's his job and he's up for a promotion. I could stop breathing less than a foot away from him, and he'd never even notice.

Shivering, I wrap myself in one of the blankets. When my phone chimes, it takes me a minute to untangle myself and dig it out of my pocket.

TheRealAugust: Short notice, but do you wanna come meet me to watch a meteor shower tonight?

MoGlows: I'm actually at the beach with someone to do just that.

MoGlows: If only you'd asked me first.

TheRealAugust: Ditch them. Come hang with me instead.

MoGlows: Can't.

TheRealAugust: Tell me where you are and I'll come to you.

It is so tempting. And Ren would have to be paying attention to me to even realize August was here. But I can't risk anyone finding out the truth about us.

MoGlows: Can't do that either. I'm with Ren.

MoGlows: And a dozen other people.

MoGlows: Too many witnesses.

It hits me too late that I shouldn't have sent the last two

messages. Let August think I was out here on some romantic date with Ren. Because August and I are already too comfortable with each other. If anyone saw us together, they'd never believe our year-long relationship ended in heartbreak. Hell, I'm not sure I could convince anyone we aren't *currently* in a relationship.

TheRealAugust: You don't seem like you want to be there with him though.

MoGlows: Why do you say that?

TheRealAugust: Because you're still talking to me.

TheRealAugust: Put Gemma on. She'll tell you I'm right.

MoGlows: She's not here. And stop corrupting my best friend. She's supposed to be on my side.

TheRealAugust: She is on your side. It's not our fault you can't see what's right for you.

TheRealAugust: In case that wasn't clear, it's not Ren.

TheRealAugust: You know I'm right. In more ways than one. 😉

The laugh bursts out of me, and I press the back of my hand to my lips to keep the sound from attracting too much attention. Too late. Me having fun with someone else is all it takes for Ren to remember I exist.

He turns back around, his knee bumping mine. "You know

you've got to look up to see the meteors, right?" he asks, with a glance at the phone in my hand.

"I've seen a few." I turn off my phone screen before he catches me messaging August.

"Did you make a wish?"

"Not yet." I don't even know what I'd wish for anymore. After tonight, pursuing a relationship with Ren is not something that's going to happen. He's not over Lana. But more importantly, I'm not over August. And wishing things could be different with August—that we could date and fall in love—feels futile. As much as I'd like to, I can't erase the lies I told, and I don't know how to start a real relationship with him with our fake past hanging over us. As long as I'd rather sit here virtually chatting with him than talk to the people almost within arm's reach, I won't be ready to date anyone else either. "Did you?"

"Yeah. We always—I always wish on the first one I see. With a meteor shower, you'll always get more than one. But in life, there's no guarantee, so you've gotta shoot your shot when you have the chance, you know?" It's too dark to make out Ren's expression, but his voice is distant, contemplative.

"I'll wish on the next one. Promise."

"Nope. I'm not taking your word for it. Scoot over, I'm coming in."

He shuffles closer, slipping underneath the blanket with me. A chilly blast of air invades my little pocket of warmth, and I shiver. Wrapping both arms around me in a bear hug,

Ren tugs me to his chest and fits his chin on top of my head. I'm locked in place against him, my cheek pressed against the steady beat of his heart. No view of the sky. If I could see the stars, I'd wish this moment could be the start of something more. That I weren't thinking of August, and he weren't thinking of Lana, and our current closeness were a direct result of undeniable desire. But I am warmer now, so the situation's not all bad.

"Better?" he asks.

"Much. Thanks."

"Good." Then, arms still tight around me, he lies back on the sand so I'm half sprawled over him. He releases me a few seconds later and eases out from under me so we're lying side by side. "Sorry. I didn't mean to...I wasn't trying to...just sorry."

I laugh to let him know it's all good. It's *more* than good. That if he wanted this, I would too. "I'm surprised by how few meteors there are. I guess I just thought *shower* meant there would be more action."

"How many shooting stars do you see on a normal night?"

"None."

"And how many have you seen tonight?"

"Maybe like ten," I say.

"That's your action. Just because it's not what you expected doesn't mean it's any less impressive." Ren is looking at me when he says it. His face is inches from mine.

And I can't help but wonder if maybe he's talking about

me. Not that he's given any indication he's remotely interested in me, but there's a huskiness to his voice. A subtext to his words. If I turned my head, met his gaze straight on, would he kiss me? Would I want him to?

I'm frozen with indecision. Then a flash of light streaks across the inky sky. "Ooh, there's one!" I point toward it, grateful for the distraction. From his words. From my thoughts. From his lips.

"Quick. Make a wish," he says, his breath teasing my neck.

My eyes trail the meteor as it cuts through the dark. The only thought in my head is not so much a wish but a person. August.

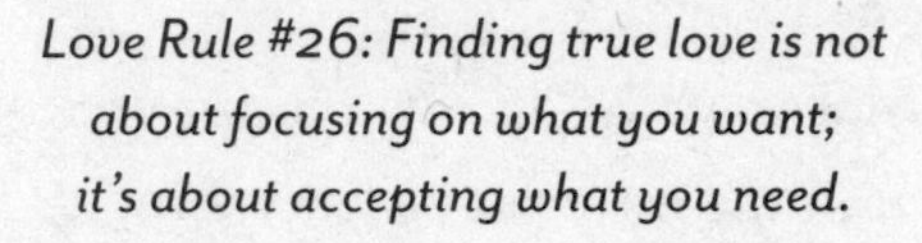

Chapter FOURTEEN

Love Rule #26: Finding true love is not about focusing on what you want; it's about accepting what you need.

It's close to midnight when the group finally starts to break up, people stepping over each other to collect blankets and bags. Ren and I keep lying here. His arm is under my neck, a makeshift pillow. The rise and fall of his chest is as steady as the waves. I could fall asleep right here given a few more minutes and a little less noise. We're both pretending we're with someone else, and as long as neither of us acknowledges that out loud, we can stay in this little bubble of make-believe.

Ren threatens to pop it when he asks, "I saw you texting earlier. Was it August?" He stares straight up, like he's talking to the stars. But maybe he just doesn't want to see the look of longing on my face when I answer.

I tug the blanket tighter around me as if that will keep all my lies from spilling out. "Why would you think it was him and not Gemma?"

"You look different when you talk to him. Like everything about you lights up. And with as much as he talked about you this morning, it seems like maybe he doesn't want to be broken up."

"Things with August are complicated. After so long apart, he's finally here, and neither of us knows how to deal with that after the way things ended. He messaged me to come watch the meteor shower with him, but I told him I was already doing that with you."

Ren turns to me, and I'm just able to make out his smile in the dark. "Is this going to turn into one of those fake-dating situations, where we pretend to date to make him jealous but end up falling for each other instead?"

The fake-dating scenario hits a little too close to home. Now it's my turn to avoid eye contact. "That's just a rom-com movie device. It doesn't happen in the real world."

"You don't think you could fall for someone like me?"

"I think it's only been a week and some change since you and Lana broke up. And I'm clearly having some letting-go issues where August is concerned. But doing something with another person tonight was a lot of fun. At least once you stopped avoiding me." I poke my finger into his ribs, making him squirm.

Laughing, he tries to defend himself. "I wasn't avoiding you."

"You were."

"Okay, I was. But in my defense, you're the first girl I've gone out with in forever who wasn't Lana. As soon as I asked you to come tonight, I freaked. I wasn't sure if you thought it was a date, so I thought if I played it cool and gave you a little space, you'd know it wasn't *that* kind of date."

His honesty makes my lies sit even heavier in my chest. I can't do anything to lighten the load, but I can ease his conscience. "For the record, you played it arctic. But when you didn't pick me up, I figured it wasn't a date. Plus, my mom's a matchmaker. I know it takes way longer than a week to get over a three-year relationship."

"What about a one-year relationship?" he asks, nudging me.

"It would go faster if I stopped talking to him every day." I hate the words as soon as they're out of my mouth. It's like some part of me wants to get caught.

Ren's arm twitches under my neck as he rolls onto his side to look at me straight on. "You still talk every day? Lana hasn't said a single word to me. Like, if she hit me with her car, she wouldn't even reflexively say she was sorry. She'd probably just get back in and drive away."

"She'd at least call the paramedics first," I say, which manages to pull a laugh out of him. "Seriously though. Lana's just as upset about the breakup as you are."

"Doubtful. She's the one who broke up with me."

I sit up, shivering as the cold nips at me. But I can't be all cozy with Ren while talking about Lana. Not when part of me still hopes I have a future with him. "That doesn't mean she's not hurting too. That she doesn't miss what y'all had. And if anyone would know how other people are feeling, at least when it comes to love and heartbreak, it's me."

"Do you think you and August will get back together?" Ren asks. He shakes out his arm now that I'm no longer lying on it and restricting his blood flow.

Get *back* together? Not possible. Get *to*gether? That's a possibility I'm not ready to think about yet. Not when Ren is so close. Most likely, once August goes back home, that's it. This week of #mostloved live and in person will become some funny story he tells his next girlfriend.

Oof. Just the thought of his next girlfriend sends my heart into spasms.

I've got to get it together. Here I am wasting my shot with Ren by thinking about August. Ren is here. No amount of liking August will change the fact he's not. "I don't think so," I finally say. Hopefully, he'll think my inner freak-out was just me giving the question proper consideration.

"Yeah, I think Lana and I are done too." His whole demeanor changes. The aura around him grows darker and almost tangible. A black hole of emotions.

I'm captivated by it. My fingers itch to have my camera in my hands, to document this in its purest form. "I know it's late, but would you want to come home with me so I can do your portrait for my project?" The question is out before I can think it through. He's hurting, so my timing is the worst, but this right here is exactly the kind of mood I need to capture on film.

Readjusting the blanket around my shoulders, Ren says, "Like right now? Won't your mom have a problem with you sneaking a guy into your house in the middle of the night?"

"The studio's behind the house, so it's not like we're going anywhere near my bedroom. But she knows how important this project is to me. She won't be mad."

"Yeah, okay. I've just gotta check in with my parents to let them know I'm good and give them an ETA. As long as it's not more than an hour or so, they'll be cool."

"It should only take about half that. That's how long it took with—" I almost say *August* but catch myself in time. "With the couple of others I've done so far."

It takes us ten minutes to pack our stuff—and more sand than if we'd taken our time to shake everything out—and make our way back to our cars. Ren walks me to mine, waits to make sure I'm safely locked inside, and then heads to his to follow me back to my house. I check my phone for the first time in hours. No new messages from August. Not that I really expected any. He put the ball in my court, and I basically kicked it into a corner when I didn't ditch Ren for him.

It's probably for the best. He's leaving in a few days anyway, and whatever game we've been playing this week will end. No winners. All losers.

I shove my phone back in my bag, burying it beneath my sweatshirt as if that will magically hide my disappointment too. As much as I don't want to have feelings for August, I do. I need to kick some sand on them before they flare up into something I can't control.

By the time we get to my house, I've almost got my emotions back in check. Ren, on the other hand, is so tense, you'd think I asked him to do the photo shoot in the nude. Mom left the porch light on, so his nerves are on full display as we walk to the front door. I lead him down the hall and out the back door, not slowing down for him to get a proper look at the inside of my house. Then we're back outside, the moon illuminating the stone path leading to the studio. The water lapping softly at the dock and the ornery call of frogs hidden in the dark fill the silence between us. I unlock the French doors and go in first to turn on the lights.

"Whoa. This place is legit professional," he says, turning in a circle to check out the full space.

"You were expecting a dungeon darkroom?" I ask.

Ren drops to the sofa, letting his head loll back as he laughs. "I don't know. When a cute girl invites you over to take pictures in the middle of the night, your mind goes to some dark places."

Not dark, just *sex* places. I haven't had sex, but there's no way my first time will be as a meaningless rebound booty call. Not even if it's Ren Kano.

"I'm sorry to disappoint, but I did tell you you wouldn't be seeing my room," I say.

"You did. I swear I wasn't actually thinking about that. And I'm not going to try anything. Tasteful photos only." He holds up his hands where I can see them as if to prove his intentions are pure.

Rolling my eyes, I grab his hand and drag him to his feet. "I appreciate your restraint."

"So what exactly are you looking for with these photos? I mean, I've seen some of your stuff when the school does student art shows, but what do I have to do?"

"You don't have to *do* anything besides sit on that stool," I say, pointing to it, "and talk about Lana."

"Can't we talk about something else? Like, literally anything else," Ren says.

"Not for the pictures I need. If you don't want to do this, you don't have to. But if it helps, I took August's picture the other day, and we both survived." And we had a moment where I was momentarily tempted to kiss him, but that's so not the point here. And definitely not something Ren ever needs to know.

He veers away from the stool, detouring to the worktable as if I'd leave pictures of August just lying around. "Can I see it?"

"August's portrait?"

"Yeah, might help to know how intense talking about the girl you love—*loved*—gets."

August's photo is right on top, but I shuffle through the photos in my portfolio case like it's not the first one I see every time I open it. "Here." Holding it out to him, I look at everything but August's face staring up from the glossy eight by ten.

Ren studies it for a moment then walks to the light table. After grabbing a black marker from the cup, he draws devil horns emerging from August's head.

"What are you doing?" I ask, making a grab for the marker and missing as he moves it out of reach.

"If he's stupid enough to cheat on you and then show up in your town to win you back like it was nothing, he must be some kind of devil spawn. I figured his portrait should reflect that."

Is he flirting with me? Or does he just feel bad about my supposed situation? We've shared enough tonight that it could easily be either one. And I have no clue which one I want to be true. "While I appreciate the sentiment, I do actually need his photo for my portfolio."

"Nah." He tosses the doodled photo in the air, and it floats to land facedown on the floor. "You don't need him. You've got me now."

I should kiss him. There won't be a more perfect moment than this. So what if I'm not all tingly with anticipation? I've wanted to know what kissing Ren Kano would be like for so long. If I don't do it now, I might not have another chance. And then I'll be left with a big, fat what-if in its place.

As I lean toward him, the words *this is what you want, this is what you want, this is what you want* play on repeat in my head.

But if it were really what I want, I wouldn't have to try so hard to convince myself of it. Ren's hand curls around my wrist, warm and strong, whether to pull me closer or to stop me, I can't tell. I'm not sure he knows either. My eyes lock on his, and I try to find something in them that says he wants this. Some spark of attraction or encouragement to close the gap between our lips.

He decides before I do and releases me.

A flash of disappointment cuts through me. There and gone before I've really even noticed it. Not too long ago, a single smile from Ren could sustain me for hours. Now he's close enough to kiss, and we're both hesitating.

"Ren..." Not sure what to say, I let his name stain the air between us.

"Lana's going on a date," he says, the pain manifesting in a deep teal cloud around his chest.

The disappointment from a moment before doubles down. "Oh."

Ren backs away and drops to the stool like the weight of that fact is too much to bear. Even with sadness swirling around him, he's beautiful. All soulful eyes and heart on his sleeve. He's so easy to read, I wonder if that's part of why I've always gravitated toward him. Because I know his kindness is genuine. I never have to question his motives.

"Yeah. But I knew if I went out with you tonight, I wouldn't think about it. You've been so cool about helping me not drown in all of it, I've got to be straight with you. It's hitting me now. Please don't take anything I'm doing personally, okay?"

"I won't," I say and hope he believes me.

Chapter FIFTEEN

Love Rule #7: Don't settle for mild affection when true love is out there.

I make Ren cry. Rather, talking about Lana makes him cry, and he's only talking about her because of me. His heartbreak is so thick, I'm surprised he doesn't suffocate from the weight of it. The whole experience is raw and intimate, leaving us both feeling a little too exposed. His photos are some of my best yet. Though he makes me promise not to show anyone outside the admissions office. Because while he doesn't seem to mind being vulnerable around me, the rest of the world seeing photographic proof that he cried is unacceptable.

Before he leaves, he pulls me into a hug and insists we take a selfie to show Lana and August we are doing just fine without them.

The epitome of Instagram life versus real life.

But I can't say no.

Which is why a few hours later, there's a comment on my

Instagram post from TheRealAugust: Is this what they call the morning after glow?

I send him a direct message within seconds.

MoGlows: You can't comment on my photos as the real you.

TheRealAugust: I don't exactly have access to the fake August account to comment from there.

MoGlows: You shouldn't be commenting at all.

MoGlows: Everyone thinks we broke up.

MoGlows: If you keep popping up everywhere, they're going to start asking questions and I can't tell them the truth.

TheRealAugust: I thought the point was for me to try to win you back?

MoGlows: Yes. And then admit defeat.

TheRealAugust: That doesn't sound like me.

TheRealAugust: The real me or the fake me.

TheRealAugust: We could just get back together and date for real this time. No one would have to know the truth.

He throws the idea out there like it's simple. Something we could do without any consequences. And he could be right. *If* I hadn't claimed he cheated on me. Because how do I "take him back" after that when it goes against everything I believe about love? Then there's Ren. He might not be emotionally available yet, but last night brought us so much closer. I'm not sure I'm ready to give up on him yet. Even for August.

MoGlows: Let's just get through the rest of the week first.

Maybe by then I'll know what to do about August *and* Ren.

Running on three hours of sleep, I'm on my third cup of coffee by 8:00 a.m. Luckily, we've had a steady stream of customers, so my body's been in constant motion, but the regular caffeine hit keeps me from mixing up orders. Though the thought that August might come in this morning is enough to keep me alert all on its own.

Every time the door opens, ushering in a new group of customers, my head swivels to see who it is. I keep expecting it to be August. I keep *wanting* it to be him. Every time it's not, the stupid smile that crept onto my face falls.

Gemma walks by after dropping off an order for one of her tables and knocks her shoulder into mine. "If you want to see him so badly, just message him."

Clearly, I'm about as subtle as a New Orleans funeral. "Can't do that."

"No, *won't* do that. You can and you should. You said you had a great time with him the other day, so what's the problem?"

"Aside from the obvious?" I bump her shoulder back. We've already had this conversation multiple times. She conveniently forgets—or more likely, she just doesn't care—that I've backed myself into a corner where August is concerned. It's a catch-22. No way out. Despite August's solution that we start dating now and pretend like we got back together.

Gemma is fully on board with that option, while I'm still one foot on the fence. Tempted but still safe on my side.

Leaving her, I do a round of refills and check-ins on my tables. I linger at each one, chatting up the tourists and regulars alike. I keep it up for almost fifteen minutes, but there's only so much stalling I can do before I'm actively interrupting their meals. And before Gemma knows I'm avoiding her.

She's waiting for me when I return, unpausing the conversation to pick up where we left off. "Couples break up and get back together all the time. Granted, your case is a little bit different, but no one besides the three of us ever needs to know that."

Love rule number fourteen: Don't go back to a relationship that wasn't working the first time around.

Technically, we haven't had a first time, so the rule shouldn't apply. But Mom still thinks he's my ex, which means he's off-limits. Unless I fess up and face disappointing her on multiple levels. I shake my head, wishing the idea of dating August weren't so appealing. "What about Ren?" Can I really give up on him after everything I've done to get him to notice me?

With her hands on her hips and a scowl wrinkling her forehead, Gemma's doing a spot-on impression of her dad Gabe when a batch of biscuits aren't rising properly in the oven. "What about him? You said he's still hung up on Lana. And last night was *not* a date. He wants a friend to make him feel better, and you fit the bill. August wants *you*. How is this even a question?"

"You didn't see Ren last night. There were moments between us that could be something more given time," I say.

"How much more time are you going to waste on him, Mo? I love you, but you cannot seriously tell me you'd still pick him. I want you to be with someone who makes you happy, that's all."

The implication hangs heavy between us. August makes me happy. And we both know it.

Her silent disappointment follows me out into the dining room. It's my constant companion for the next hour, refusing to let thoughts of August stray too far from the forefront of my mind.

But the universe sends me Ren instead. I can't help but see it as a sign.

Last week, he would have been the person I was hoping to see. Not that I'm unhappy he's here now. It just takes my heart a couple of seconds to recalibrate after a few days with August. He and his friends clog the doorway as Astrid saunters away from them, hips swinging in a calculated sort of way to make sure all eyes are on her as she leaves. And all eyes are. Ren's friends extend fist bumps to each other without looking. While they're appreciating the view, Ren is all wide-eyed, open-mouthed shock.

Tapping his shoulder to snap him out of his daze, I ask, "You okay?"

He jerks back from my touch, but he visibly relaxes when he turns and sees me. "I think Astrid just asked me out. Well, no, she told me we were going out. I didn't get the impression I really had a say in the matter."

After their encounter last week at the beach, how did he not see this coming? A laugh bursts out of me at his naivety.

"What's so funny?" he asks.

I pat his shoulder to both comfort and placate. "Sorry. I don't mean to laugh, it's just that girl is on a mission, and nothing is going to get in her way. It's kind of impressive."

"Impressive? If I tried anything like that, I'd be blacklisted by every girl at school."

His friends finally accept Astrid is not coming back and regain partial brain function to add their own versions of "yeah" and "can you imagine if we pulled that shit?" One tells Ren not to look a gift horse in the mouth. They all laugh. Except Ren. He reverts to his deer-in-headlights look.

"Rightfully so. No one should ever force anyone to go out with them against their will." I loop my arm through Ren's and drag him away from his friends so we can talk without their commentary. "It would be against your will, right?"

The distance seems to calm him, his jaw relaxing enough to let a smile sneak through. "Yeah. Absolutely. Not that there's anything wrong with Astrid. I'm just not ready."

He's not ready.

Not for Astrid. But maybe with the right person—maybe with me—he could be.

I ignore Gemma's voice in my head saying I'm making the wrong choice.

"You might not be ready, but girls certainly are. You being single after so long is opening a door for so many of us who thought we'd never have a shot with you." When I move to grab a stack of menus and silverware to show his group to a table, he steps with me, keeping me pinned to his side.

"Like you?" he asks.

"Yes, like me." I look up to make sure he sees my eye roll, despite my honest answer. A few weeks ago, the prospect of someone else swooping in on Ren before I could show him I'm the right choice would have sent me into a tailspin. I should be fighting for Ren. That's partly why I broke up with Fake August in the first place. But now there's Real August throwing a whole lot of complication into the mix.

"If anyone else asks, maybe you could tell them we're sort of together. You know, just to give me some time to get my head back on straight as far as dating goes. We could even hang out some so it wouldn't really be lying." Ren's expression is so open, so vulnerable, like he's depending on me to save him. Again.

It might be closer to the truth than my relationship with August, but it's still dishonest. I don't know how many more lies I can tell before they consume me. "That's not a good idea."

"Oh, yeah, okay. If you don't want to do anything, I totally understand." A tendril of teal aura curls around his collarbone as he looks away.

Catching his attention, his friends shout at us from the table they commandeered when I took too long to seat them. I shake the menus at them so they know I haven't forgotten them. But I'm not done with Ren yet.

"I do. I just don't want to purposely mislead anyone about what we're doing. We can be friends, and if people think it's something more, I won't go out of my way to correct them. But if anyone asks me directly, I have to tell them the truth."

Ren dips his head, shaking it slightly. "Yeah, I get that. I don't know what I was thinking asking you that. I don't want you to compromise your morals or anything for me."

If only my morals were still squeaky clean. I give him an apologetic smile. "You're not wrong about us spending time together. My mom always tells her clients that to get over someone, they have to put themselves out there and try again with someone new. It might not happen right away, but it'll never happen if you don't try. Fake it till you make it, right?"

"Is that one of her official love rules?"

"It is. It also doubles as a heartbreak philosophy. And if we want to move past being sad, our best shot is to do it together. Keep each other company without any of the pressure that comes from dating. Commiserate when we run into our exes and need someone to vent to who understands how much it sucks. I know you were joking with Evans the other day about us being a broken hearts club, but we could be. We could help each other."

"No, I like that. The two of us keeping each other going until we're ready to move on."

Or until he sees we've moved on to each other.

My heart throws a tantrum at the thought, beating hard and fast against my rib cage. It no longer wants Ren. Maybe it never really did. Because all I can think about is August and how spending time with Ren feels a little like cheating on him.

Chapter SIXTEEN

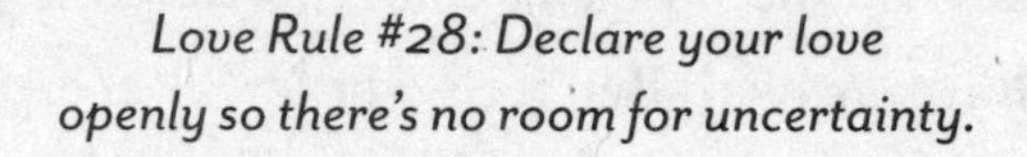

Love Rule #28: Declare your love openly so there's no room for uncertainty.

With spring break almost over, Gemma and I spend Friday morning working on her Kinsey submission. She's been tinkering with a new sculpture for days. It's a life-size human body, currently headless. After three failed attempts to get the face to live up to what she sees in her mind, Gemma's given up and decided to leave it as is. I jump on taking pictures of it before she changes her mind again.

She plays on her phone while I work. "August posted a photo of you," Gemma says.

"What?" I whip my head around, but she's not holding it out for me to see.

"It's a photo of the beach, but you're very much in the frame. It's a really good picture of you too. He captioned it *the most beautiful thing I've ever seen.*"

I shouldn't find that post or the sentiment so charming. But I have to turn my back to keep Gemma from seeing my smile and never letting me forget it. "Why are you even looking at his posts?" Better yet, why is August even posting things like that? His normal accounts are locked down, but this one—TheRealAugust—is out there for anyone to see. Is this part of our plan to get Ren to notice me, or has he thrown that out the window because we somehow caught feelings for each other?

"Why *aren't* you?" Gemma grabs one of her balled-up sketches from earlier and lobs it at my back. When I cut my eyes to her, she says, "Don't you want to know if he decides to out you and your fake relationship to everyone?"

"August wouldn't do that." If that were his plan, he would've done it the second he walked into Yeastie Boys for my portfolio casting call, not spent the past few days pretending to want me back to keep up appearances.

"Seriously, you're not even going to react to him calling you beautiful?"

"I'm sure he was talking about the ocean view."

"God, you're an idiot." Gemma groans and flops back on the floor like the stress of dealing with me is too much to bear. "I was going to let you find it on your own, let it be a nice little surprise, but at this rate, you'd probably miss it altogether. Come with me."

I take a few more shots of her sculpture before relenting. "Where are we going?"

"I'm taking you to see something from one of his other photos. It's also about you." After latching on to my wrist, she marches me out to her car. "No, don't get out your phone to look now.

You'll just have to wait and see it in person," she says when I try to do just that. She takes my phone for good measure and tucks it beneath her thigh so I won't go grabbing for it while she's driving.

"You could've just shown me the photo instead of taking me on a field trip, you know?"

"Where's the fun in that? And besides, you're still on the fence about wanting Ren. Maybe seeing this in person will push you to the right side."

Whatever's in this photo, the last thing I should be doing is seeing it in person. I don't need any more reasons to like August. But I can't tell Gemma that, or she'll never lay off. Not until August and I are officially in a relationship. At which point I'd have to spend the rest of my life living a lie. No thanks. One year of lies was enough.

"And what side is that?" I ask.

Gemma takes her eyes off the road long enough to roll them at me. "For someone who claims to see love, you are surprisingly unobservant."

Rolling down the window, I let the cool morning air wash over me. There's no question August and I are attracted to each other. And there have been sparks of something more with him this week. But just because he thinks he likes me now doesn't mean those feelings will stay once he's back home. How would that even work? Would he tell his friends the truth about how we got together? Would I keep lying to all of mine, pretending we reconciled even after I told Ren August cheated on me?

Love rule twenty-five: Don't confuse attraction for love. Attraction is surface level and wanes over time, whereas true love becomes a part of you forever.

The bigger problem? I don't want a boyfriend I barely see. Who's nothing more than a voice on the phone. A text. I want someone who's here. Like Ren.

"You went quiet over there. I wasn't trying to be mean," Gemma says.

"I know. And I'm not upset, not at you anyway. It's just pointless to want something that can't happen."

"Do you really think you have a future with Ren?"

There was something with him the other night. Not a spark exactly but an understanding. A sense that we could each be what the other needed. I don't know if it's anything more than friendship, but I'd be lying if I said I don't want to find out. "Maybe. We had fun. Once he actually started paying attention to me. And taking his picture was oddly intimate. He opened up to me in a way no one ever has."

"Does he make you happy?"

"To be determined," I say.

"Does August?" she asks.

My smile is immediate. I couldn't lie even if I wanted to. "You know he does, or you wouldn't be trying to prove to me why I should give him a chance."

"This is what you've wanted. A guy who likes you for you. And August clearly does. You picked him to be your fake boyfriend for a reason. Maybe it's because he's supposed to be your real boyfriend and you were just too scared to put your feelings out there. This is your chance to fix that, Mo."

She pulls up her falling-in-love playlist and cranks up the volume. We sing along to "This Feeling" by The Chainsmokers at the top of our lungs. We're nowhere in key. Everyone we pass stares. We don't care in the slightest.

By the time she stops in front of the Wishing Wall—a community chalkboard where passersby can write their wishes for all to see—I've forgotten why we came here in the first place. Then I see it. A blackout poem made from all the messages on the board. The words are too small to make out from any distance. There are just blocks of colored chalk stretching across the board with small breaks for the words he left behind. Gemma's already smiling her I-told-you-so smile when I open the door to get a closer look and a quick photo of it.

"I can't believe he did this," I say. What I want to say is, *I can't believe he did this for me.* This poem is more romantic than anything I could've ever dreamed up. And he didn't even tell me about it. So maybe it's not for me at all. "We don't know it's about me though. It could be about Shay. Maybe talking about her to me the other day made him realize he does still love her. Or maybe it's not about anyone specific and just his wish that he'll find that with someone someday."

Gemma claps her hand over my mouth, forcing me to stop the excuses. "Don't ruin this. If ever there was a hashtag most-loved moment, this is it. Enjoy the hell out of it. Please."

Greer Latimore lowers their phone after snapping a picture of the poem too. "Wait. You know who did this?"

"August." His name is out of my mouth before I can stop it. That one word is so full of longing and hope and want. Everything his poem evokes.

"It's genius," Greer says. "I wish I'd thought of it."

"I didn't know you were an artist," Gemma says, eyes bright and interest piqued.

"A writer, actually. Mostly fiction, but I'm trying to make myself understand poetry. And this kind of poetry, I can get behind." They smile as if at any second the poem will reveal all the secrets of love and poetic genius.

Gemma moves closer to them, pulled by an invisible gravitational force. "Oh, in that case, you need to check out his Insta. August has hundreds of poems on there. Most aren't to this scale, but the words are the important part anyway. And if you tell him you're Mo's friend, I'm sure he'll be more than happy to talk to you about it."

I grab her arm to pull her back to reality. "Gemma," I warn. The last thing I need is anyone here talking to August.

Greer looks at me, confusion clouding their expression. "Didn't you guys break up?"

"We did."

"It's not going to last. The breakup, I mean. Clearly, he still has feelings for her," Gemma says. She sweeps her arm up and down in front of the poem as if its mere existence is proof it's about me.

"That's why I'm trying to figure out poetry. It's so freakin' romantic. Like, how do you evoke that much passion in so few words? And then have the balls to put it out there for the world to read?" Greer says. Their focus is trained on Gemma, a half smile tugging at their lips.

Gemma, never one to shy away from any situation, goes all pink in the cheeks. "I know what you mean. I can't even tell the person I like that I like them." A delicate rose-colored cloud builds around her. It's not a full-on love glow. Not yet. But her feelings toward Greer are well past friendship.

How did I not see that it was more than a crush sooner? And more importantly, why didn't she tell me? I nudge my elbow into her ribs. "Ahem. I do know a thing or two about matchmaking. So, if you need some help in that department..." I trail off, skimming my gaze over to Greer. Their shark-blue hair dye makes the blush blooming on their cheeks appear even more intense. Maybe my services won't be needed after all.

I wait until we're back in the car to call Gemma out. "I'm sorry. What was that?"

She busies herself with checking her mirrors, though I suspect it's as much to get one last glimpse of Greer as it is to avoid my stare. She waits until she's pulled onto the road to ask, "What was what?" She would have been able to pull off the innocent act if not for the slight tremor in her voice.

"That atomic bomb–level glow that just burst out of you when Greer smiled at you."

"You're seeing things."

"Technically, yes, I am. And what I'm seeing is that you're this close to being in love with them." I hold my forefinger and thumb so they're almost touching.

She swats my hand away. "I am not in love with them. I think you're projecting your love for August onto me. You're so full of love glow, it's blinding you to the real world around you."

Not true. I'm fully aware of my feelings for August and how chaotic they are. "While I may have a small crush on August, I'm not—"

"Nope. I'm gonna stop you right there. You've spent all week flirting with him. This is way beyond a crush. I don't need to have your magic to see how you feel about him."

"Okay, fine. If I admit I have feelings for August, will you own up to yours for Greer?"

"I already told you I don't have any feelings for them."

"I don't believe you," I sing, stretching out each word. "Seriously though, of the two of us, I'm the one with a legitimate reason not to get into a relationship with the person I like. Why are you fighting it so hard?"

Gemma spares me a glance while we're stopped at a light, then returns her eyes to the road. "I don't want to be the Republican poster child for how gay marriage shouldn't be legal because it's turning kids gay."

That might be the most ridiculous thing I've ever heard come out of her mouth. And she's said some out-there stuff over the years. But if she's serious, I don't want to dismiss her worry. "Do you think that's what's happening? That your dads' relationship is why you like Greer?" I ask.

"Of course not!"

"Good because I was about to slap some sense into you. You have two of the best dads on the planet, and you should consider yourself extremely lucky to be like them."

"No argument here. But not everyone sees that. Some people are assholes and won't see past two gay dads and their queer kid. I don't want to be the reason anyone piles more hate on them or thinks for even a second they're not the absolute best fucking parents. You know, when they're not driving me batty."

"You would never be that reason. Assholes, remember? You're not going to change their minds, so you may as well live your life the way you want and be happy to spite them."

"Ah, spite-induced happiness. Why didn't I think of that?"

"Your brain's too full of Greer to think straight. Love has a way of doing that to people."

"Which brings us right back to you and August. Don't think I missed when you said you like him earlier," Gemma says.

I groan, letting my head fall back onto the headrest with a soft *thunk*. "I also said I shouldn't date him. You're conveniently ignoring that part."

She reaches over and taps my phone awake. The photo of August's poem fills the screen. "Now who's being the idiot?"

It's hard to argue with her when she's right. It's even harder when I want to agree with her.

After Gemma drops me off at home, I touch up the pictures I took of her sculptures and email several options to her so she can pick the ones for her portfolio. I only look at the photo of August's poem once every five minutes or so. It's cued up on my phone, ready to post a story on my Insta, but I can't. If anyone knows he's the artist behind it, there'll be questions.

Questions I can't answer.

The smart thing to do is pretend like I didn't see it at all. But if I've proven anything with my decisions lately, it's that I'm not smart when it comes to August. There's something about him that makes me want to be reckless. To throw away everything I've been building with Ren and give us a chance instead.

I've been chasing love for so long, what if August's it and I'm too wrapped up in old feelings for Ren to see it?

Then there are Ren's feelings. Not for me but for Lana. He may never love me the way I want. One thing's for sure though. If I post this picture of August's poem, he'll know I'm having second thoughts about our broken hearts club pact and about wanting to get over August.

I discard the draft post, the artist in me crying at having to keep the poem to myself. It's too beautiful to go unacknowledged though. I type out a message to August.

MoGlows: Gemma showed me your poem. It's incredible.

TheRealAugust: Thanks. I'm glad you like it.

TheRealAugust: I was worried someone would erase it before you got to see it.

MoGlows: Even if someone had, there are gonna be so many pictures of it popping up on socials that there's no way I would have missed it.

TheRealAugust: Shame I didn't sign it then. A viral art project would move my Kinsey application to the top of the pile.

August's viral moment would most likely trigger my own. But a fake-dating scandal is not likely to impress the admissions committee. I drum my fingers over my heart to make sure it gets the message that this thing with August could ruin everything if not handled correctly.

MoGlows: That reminds me. While we were there, Gemma and I ran into someone from school who might reach out to you to talk about poetry. Their name is Greer. And they were appropriately awed.

TheRealAugust: Is it just me or are you trying to set me up with someone else?

MoGlows: It's just you.

TheRealAugust: Good.

MoGlows: Good?

TheRealAugust: In case it's not clear, I like you.

TheRealAugust: And before you say I shouldn't or that I can't, it's too late.

TheRealAugust: I already do.

TheRealAugust: I like you, Imogen.

TheRealAugust: And who cares what anyone else thinks?

I care. I don't want to, but caring what other people think is what made me lie about dating August in the first place. And he says he doesn't care now, but what happens when everyone finds out? Will he still like me when his friends realize how messed up I am and tell him to run as fast as he can in the opposite direction?

Chapter SEVENTEEN

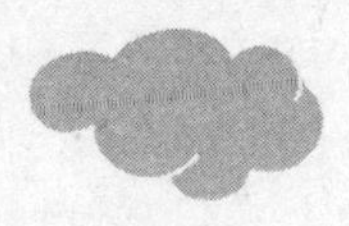

Love Rule #17: Denying your feelings will only make them grow more insistent.

I'm normally a morning person, but not today. Today August leaves. And once he's gone, I'll have no reason to keep talking to him. At least with him in town, I've been able to justify spending time together as a way to make sure he keeps my secret. But that threat disappears when he does. I shove the coffee carafe back into place with more force than necessary, and Gemma glowers at me for the millionth time since our shift started. I think she would have sent me home to brood in peace, but we're busy with all the tourists filling up before hitting the road.

"I didn't break it. It's fine," I say, holding the intact pot up as proof.

"That's not what I'm worried about breaking," she says.

"You don't need to worry about me either. I knew what I was getting into this week and that it had an expiration date." I just didn't expect to care that it would end. Not that I can admit it out loud.

Gemma walks over and practically mauls me with a hug. "Oh, I totally read that wrong."

"Read what wrong?" I ask. Gemma when she's in a hugging mood is like quicksand. The harder your struggle, the worse you make the situation. So I stay still, letting her comfort me.

"I thought you were angry that things with August were going well and you didn't want to like him so you were throwing a little fit to snap yourself out of it. But you're sad he's leaving. You want this to go somewhere with him."

I shake my head, pulling back far enough to meet her eyes. "No, *you* want this to go somewhere."

"Of course I do. He's perfect for you."

"That doesn't matter."

She releases me, laughing. "Look at that. You agree with me."

Only Gemma would take my logical acceptance of my fate as agreement. It doesn't matter what I want. Or if I like August or not. He'll be gone after today. My feelings, not so much.

"I didn't say that. You're inferring feelings that aren't there." Grabbing an order from the pass-through window when the cook, Saint, slides four plates up, I motion with my elbow for Gemma to take the remaining two. Thankfully, work takes precedence over talking about crushes—real or nonexistent.

"They are most definitely there whether you want to acknowledge them or not." Gemma loads up. She pauses next to me and says, "And because the universe knows I'm right, it's about to throw some proof right in your pretty little face."

I don't have to turn around to know August is here. The victorious grin lighting up Gemma's features says it all. There's no way I'll be able to hide my feelings for him—or convince her they don't exist—when he's standing right in front of me.

I take my time delivering the food. Not only does it give me a few minutes to wrangle my heart back into working order, but by taking care of all my customers' needs, I'll be able to stay with August a little longer before having to check in again.

"I thought y'all would be on the road by now," I say when I make my way back to the counter where he and Owen found seats.

"We couldn't leave without one last biscuit," August says.

Gemma slides behind me, making a kissy noise right in my ear. To August, she says, "Right, it's the biscuits you'll miss."

"Are you gonna miss us?" Owen asks, all innocence and hope. He has no idea things between his brother and me are so precariously balanced. One light breeze and my lies will all topple down to crush this fluttering feeling in my chest.

I will miss them. My public relationship with August is fake, but what we shared this week has made a comfy little nest in my heart, and nothing short of hurricane-force winds would dislodge those feelings. He could have blown this whole lie up in my face. Instead, he played along and reminded me why I picked him for my perfect fake boyfriend in the first place. "Of course, I'm going to miss one of my favorite customers." I don't mean to look at August when I say it, but my emotions have a way of hijacking my brain without me knowing until it's too late.

August catches me. He dips his head, a shy smile sneaking onto his lips.

Owen lights up at the idea, blissfully unaware he is not the brother I meant. "I'm really your favorite?"

"Sorry, kid. You can't be her favorite," Gemma says. She leans on the counter next to me, checking me with her hip.

"Why not?" Owen's chest puffs up like he's ready to fight to prove his worthiness.

"Because you're *my* favorite. Mo here's just going to have to settle for your brother."

My cheeks burst into flames like I'm standing in front of an open oven blasting me with three-hundred-and-seventy-five-degree heat. "Don't you have other tables to serve?"

She makes a show of scanning the crowded dining room and rolls her eyes when they land back on me. "And give you a chance to try and steal my favorite customer? I don't think so."

Gemma's enjoying this way too much. Did she forget August is not a viable boyfriend option? Even if part of me wishes he were, he can't be. Not after everyone thinks he cheated on me. How would it look if I took him back after that? Apparently, I need the reminder just as much as she does. "You know what, it's probably better if you take these two anyway. Don't want anyone to see us talking over here and start asking questions."

August frowns, his whole face tightening. "Yeah, we wouldn't want that, now, would we?"

"Oh, right." Gemma straightens and pours two glasses of water for them. "I kinda forgot about that."

"Liar," I say, laying menus in front of them.

"Forgot about what?" Owen asks.

August spins the menu on the counter. "It's just this game Imogen and I have going where she pretends she doesn't like me when other people are around."

"That doesn't sound like a fun game."

"It's not," August says. He looks right at me, the soft coppery-teal glow lighting him up.

I can't tell if the heartbreak is because of me or if he's thinking about Shay and how she played mind games with him. Made him think he wasn't good enough. And I hate myself for not being honest with either of us. "Did I forget to mention you get a free biscuit just for playing?"

Owen's eyes go wide, like a free biscuit is the best possible prize. "Is Gemma playing too? Is that why she's trying to get you to be Mo's favorite to make her lose?"

"No, Gemma's not playing." August gives her a look I can't interpret. Is he telling her to back off because he's got this or begging her to rush in with reinforcements to make sure he doesn't lose? Turning to me, he says, "About that free biscuit? I know what *I* want."

"For breakfast?" I clarify, biting the inside of my cheek to keep from smiling.

"In that case, no. I do not know what I want. If you were eating breakfast, what would you get?"

"The Sabotage, which is the biscuit made of cheddar, jalapeño, and bacon with buttermilk fried chicken, sweet pepper jelly, and goat cheese, or the Time to Get Ill, which is a buttermilk biscuit with bacon, avocado, fried pickles, cherry tomatoes, and chili mayo," I say without having to think about it. They're my go-to biscuits, though there's nothing bad on the menu.

He laughs. "Do you have anything that won't kill me?"

Gemma pauses on her way to deliver an armload of plates to a table. "If that's what you're after, you may be in the wrong biscuit joint."

"Ignore her. I promise, it'll be a good, honorable death," I say. Leaning over the counter to point at the menu, I continue, "But if you're looking for something lighter, you can always go with the Egg Man. The choice of biscuit and egg style is up to you."

"These names are so weird," Owen says, looking up from the menu.

Clapping my hands over Gemma's ears, I whisper to him, "Don't let Gemma or her dads hear you say that!"

"If you think that's weird, just ask Mo about the weekly special," Gemma says.

"Imogen, would you please tell us about your weekly special?" August asks like this is a three-star Michelin restaurant.

I point to the chalkboard on the far wall. "This is the one biscuit on the menu that's not named after a Beastie Boys song. It's called the Frankenbiscuit. Gemma and I take turns Frankensteining biscuits out of all sorts of wild ingredients."

"So what is the Frankenbiscuit this week?"

Gemma cackles, startling a handful of customers into looking up from their meals. She ignores them and gives August a glee-filled smile. "Oh, I'm so glad you asked. This one's all yours, Mo. You're not off the hook quite yet."

I cross my arms over my chest and glare at her. "You're going to pass this to me all day, aren't you?"

"That's what you get for creating the monstrosity. You need to see the look of horror on every customer's face when you tell them all the random things you Frankensteined into a biscuit this time." She must decide it's safe to leave me alone with them now and moves off to refill coffee for the other customers at the counter.

"It's not that bad," I tell August when he gives me a skeptical look. "So, it's a bacon, cheddar, and jalapeño biscuit with a buttermilk fried chicken breast topped with a fried egg and sriracha pimento cheese."

"You forgot the hash puppies!" Gemma calls.

I don't bother to acknowledge her, instead keeping my focus on Owen. He's safer than August, who's laughing quietly at Gemma's utter disgust. "They're on the side so not technically part of the Frankenbiscuit."

"What are hash puppies?" Owen asks, voice full of wonder.

"Cheesy tater tots on steroids," I say.

His eyes roll back in dramatic anticipation. "I *need* those in my life."

"Obviously." August taps his fingers on the counter like he's seriously deliberating. "You know what? I'm gonna go for it. Your Frankenbiscuit. I'm trusting you on this, Imogen, so don't let me down."

With August, I'm always Imogen. Never Mo. And the way he says my name, it sounds like poetry. There's a rhythm to it. A subtext. It's easy to forget he's not the version of August who's been in love with me this past year.

"You will not be disappointed." This week's Frankenbiscuit is delicious, despite Gemma's very loud, very frequent assertions to the contrary. But if August doesn't leave with egg yolk or pimento cheese staining his formfitting V-neck, it'll be a miracle.

"I'll take one too," Owen says.

"I thought you wanted the one with honeysuckle butter?" August asks, arching one skeptical eyebrow.

"I'll get that one to go. That way I'll have a snack in the car so when Jason doesn't stop, I won't starve to death like on the way here."

My heart pinches as I laugh. I really am going to miss them. "Looks like you made a quick recovery if you've already died once this week."

Owen shrugs. "I was only mostly dead."

"You and the Dread Pirate Roberts," I say. August gives me a fist bump at the *Princess Bride* reference. I make a note to bring Owen a honeysuckle-butter biscuit to go and force myself to walk away. The last thing I need is one more reason to like August.

Then he has the nerve to smile at me over his little brother's head. It's all charm and playful challenge. My own mouth betrays me and smiles right back.

Determined not to go back over there until their food is ready, I become the most attentive waitress ever to my other customers. One of them, Walter, is a regular who, at eighty-five, has zero filter. He asks me point-blank about "that boy who's flirting with you." I don't lie exactly, but I keep August's name from spilling out of my lips by saying he's a spring breaker who's on his way home today. Short and sweet. And effectively puts a pin in any follow-up questions Walter might have had.

He bows his head in disappointment and mumbles something about not knowing a good thing when I see it. Gemma whistles not so innocently from a few tables over. There's no question she put Walter up to it. Or at the very least pointed out August to Walter so he could come to his own conclusions about my love life. Every week for the past year, he asked when he would get to meet "that boy of yours" and gave me a hug and an extra five-dollar tip the day I told him August and I broke up.

Guilt prickles my skin like hot oil splashed from a pan. Walter has done nothing but support me, and all I've done is lie to him. To everyone.

I scrub my hands up and down my arms as if that will wipe my slate clean. But there's no going back. No starting over. I either have to let August go today—for good—or do what Gemma keeps insisting and tell everyone we got back together so we can date for real. I should go with option one and be done with it. But I make the mistake of looking over at August and realize it was never really a choice.

It was always going to be August.

When Saint calls "two Franks up" and passes the plates out of the kitchen, I'm on them before August even looks up to see if it's theirs. As soon as I'm back in front of him though, his eyes lock on me, a smile catching in the corners of his mouth. Owen's giving his food the same look of reverence. There's still an inch of space between Owen's plate and the counter when he goes to grab the fist-sized biscuit drowning in thick cheese with his bare hand. August nudges the fork toward his brother without a word.

Retracting his hand, Owen side-eyes August before returning his focus to his breakfast. "Are you going to use one?"

"Have you seen this thing? Trying to use a fork would be an insult to its honor."

My laugh pulls out of me as if August summoned it with a spell. It's like I have no control over what I do or say or feel when he's around. And I can't say I mind it. But I shouldn't encourage him either. So, instead, I plop a handful of napkins in front of him. "It wouldn't do any good anyway. There's not a non-messy way to eat it."

August nudges the forks away and sighs when Owen pumps his fists in victory. "Just don't tell Mom."

August doesn't say anything after his first bite, just closes his eyes and tilts his head back like he wants to savor every second of flavor. I can't help but think that's probably the same look he gets when he's kissing someone.

I throw a cold bucket of water on my imagination before it takes that little fantasy any further.

"See that, Gemma?" I call to her, dragging my mind away from unproductive thoughts. "Frankenbiscuit for the win."

Wiping excess pimento cheese from his lips, August looks right at me. There's a pinkish aura building in the air around him that gives him an unmistakable glow. "You don't know how to be bad at anything, do you?"

Oh, I am failing at containing my feelings for August. Big time. A week with him and my heart is ready to stow away in a to-go container alongside Owen's biscuit. Turning toward Gemma, I send up an SOS flare. She pretends not to notice my distress and continues chatting with customers, a devilish twinge to her laugh. If she's not going to save me from this mess, I'll have to do it myself. "I wouldn't say that. Clearly, I'm bad at breaking up with people."

"Maybe that just means it was the wrong decision," August says.

"It was the only decision, and you know it."

Owen pauses with his fork halfway to his mouth. A dollop of cheese plops onto the counter. "Is that why you're pretending to not like August? Because you already have a boyfriend?"

"No, she doesn't have a boyfriend," August answers for me.

"Good." Noticing the mess he's made, Owen wipes the cheese up with a napkin and adds it to the growing pile littering the counter around him. "I like her way better than—" He slaps a hand over his mouth like he has to physically keep August's ex's name from spilling out. His eyes slide toward his brother, guilt flushing his cheeks.

August scrubs his hands clean on a napkin then ruffles Owen's hair, resulting in a fit of giggles from the younger Tate. Leaning down toward his brother's ear, August stage-whispers, "I do too."

How was I ever supposed to resist the August-Owen combo? If August hadn't won me over on his own, seeing him with his brother would have sealed the deal. Their obvious love for each other would melt even the coldest heart. "That's cheating," I say, pointing at them each in turn.

The biscuit slips from August's grip and drops onto the plate, splattering a soupy mix of cheese and hot sauce across his chest. His expression is an adorable mix of confused and embarrassed. I have an overwhelming urge to hug him. Thank God there's a counter between us, or I'm pretty sure I would wrap my arms around him and never let him go.

To keep from even attempting it, I toss him a clean bar rag from the stack beneath the counter and pour a fresh glass of ice water for dipping. I leave him to clean up without an audience and take a few orders from recently seated diners.

"Just so we're clear," I say when I come back to him, "wearing your breakfast doesn't mean you're not also trying to flatter me so I slip up and forget I'm not supposed to like you."

August continues to dab at the growing wet splotch on his

shirt. "Right. You caught me trying to cheat my way into winning." His voice is the tiniest bit gravelly, like there's something stuck in his throat.

Owen perks up at the mention of our game. "What does the winner get?"

It's a fake game with fake rules. We don't have a grand prize. Unless you count being in a state of romantic limbo, and that's more of a side effect than a prize.

"Bragging rights," I decide on the spot.

At the same time, August says, "A date."

It's a dare and a wish rolled into one.

I go all gooey in the center. Holding on to the counter so I don't puddle onto the floor, I say, "You want to go on a date with me?" I should be annoyed with him for going so far off script. Instead, all I want to do is say yes before he's even answered the question.

August throws up his hands and leans back on his stool. "Whoa, who said anything about *wanting* to? I can't help it if those are the rules." He struggles to keep a straight face and looks away.

"Yes, you can. You made up the rules," Owen says. His hand goes flying to emphasize his point and knocks over August's glass of cleaning water. It cascades across the counter, making a waterfall over the edge.

Swiveling out of the way, August catches the brunt of the spillage with the rag before it soaks his pants. Almost like he was expecting it. Then, as if nothing happened, he says,

"Well, in that case, yes, I want to go on a date with you, Imogen."

I add another rag to soak up what's left. Owen's used napkins are now a sopping pile of mush but served as a dam to keep the water from rushing off the other side too. "Refresh my memory. Do the rules say how a winner is determined?" I ask August, following his lead of not making a big deal of the mess. It was an accident, and the fact he doesn't even seem to think about getting mad at his brother for it is a solid case for sainthood. Even the most mild-mannered moms lose their cool when their kids spill drinks on them.

"If I can get you to publicly admit you like me, I win. If you don't ever tell anyone—Gemma excluded, of course—then you win. Either way ends in a date, just so we're clear. But the winner decides what happens on said date," he says.

Owen plucks an errant ice cube from his plate and drops it in the empty cup. "You should let August win. Shay never lets him plan their dates. All she wants to do is hang out in his room. Alone." The way he snarls "alone" makes it seem like he thinks they're in there playing video games and just won't let him join, not getting each other into various states of nakedness.

I shut my eyes and attempt to mentally censor the image of August in bed with another girl. It's immediately worse. My imagination fills in all the unknowns in the few nanoseconds before I open them again.

"Owen!" August barks. Apparently, Shay has a direct link

to his anger button. Or Owen unknowingly divulging details of August's sex life with Shay to the girl August is trying to impress does. I take a step back, hoping he didn't notice my momentary freak-out.

"Sorry!" Owen flinches, knocking the edge of his plate with his elbow.

August's hand flies out to catch it before it flips too. "It's fine. You just need to watch what you're doing, okay?" Though the admonishment sounds more like Owen should watch what he *says*. "Ignoring the part about my bedroom, what my brother meant is I was always trying to plan romantic dates I thought would be fun. Things I saw on this one Instagram account I follow, for instance. But you can't take dates meant for one girl and expect them to work for someone who's basically her opposite."

Part of me wants to be mad that he wanted to use my #most-loved dates for his then real-life girlfriend, but most of me is happy dancing because the ideas were something the real August would have liked too. "See, to me that sounds like I need to win this so at least I know the date will be something *I* like."

"I think I know you well enough to do something hashtag worthy," he says. His phone lights up on the counter with an incoming text. He's ignored it so often when we've been together this week, I'm surprised when he not only checks it but responds. "Looks like I'm about to turn into a pumpkin. My mom and Jason are waiting in the parking lot for us."

"Did you write back already, or can you pretend you didn't

see it so we can stay longer?" Owen asks, looking out the front window at the dark-cloud skies and wall of rain coming down.

"I already said we're heading out."

Even knowing the end was coming, I feel like I'm trying to breathe underwater now that it's here. My chest burns with the pressure of goodbye. All the things I want to say to August keep building and building until I think I might pass out if I don't release them soon.

August beats me to it, saying, "This week has legitimately been one of the best weeks of my life."

"Mine too." It's an inadequate response. True but inadequate. We're out of time though, and to be honest, I don't really know what to say to him that would contain everything I'm feeling. For him. For the possibility of us.

He pulls out his wallet before extracting more than enough cash to pay for breakfast. I wave his money away, but he catches Gemma's attention and slips it to her instead. Turning back to me, he looks like he wants to say more. But all he says is, "Bye, I guess."

"Bye, Mo! Bye, Gemma!" Owen says, breaking the tension.

There's nothing to say after that except: "Goodbye, Tate brothers."

And then they're going.

Going.

Gone.

I remember Owen's to-go biscuit seconds after they leave. They're not yet halfway across the parking lot. I should have just enough time catch them. Once I grab it, I run outside into the rain and call August's name. He turns, and a burst of rose-gold aura explodes around him. I squint against the brightness. August motions for Owen to keep heading to the car then jogs back to meet me.

Up close, his glow is almost blinding. But I can't look away. Who needs the sun when I have August Tate as my own personal solar system?

Taking my hand, he pulls me under the shelter of the roof's overhang as fat cold raindrops pelt us. He stands so close, I feel each quick intake of breath.

"For the road," I say, lifting the rain-soaked biscuit bag between us.

"Looking out for my brother's survival?" He drops his head so our foreheads press together. So our breaths and anticipation are inseparable. "Don't tell me you're picking him over me. He'll never let me live that down."

"If I were, I would have put more than one biscuit in there for him."

August shakes the bag. "I don't even rate a biscuit?" His voice is a whisper, but the disappointment comes through as if he'd yelled it.

I reach a tentative hand up to stroke the side of his face. "I thought you might want something else to tide you over."

"If that's your way of asking if you can kiss me, Imogen, the answer is yes."

"Way to steal my thunder," I say. As if on cue, the storm

gets in on the joke with a flash of lightning followed by a slow rumble of real thunder.

"Go on then. Ask me." He steps back directly into the rain, careful to keep Owen's biscuit under the cover.

I close the distance again. "August, can I kiss you?"

"You already know the answer."

The world stops when our lips meet. There's no rain. No family waiting to take him away. No customers glancing around impatiently for an AWOL waitress.

It's just August and me.

Our hands grasping. Our breaths gasping. Our hearts glowing.

His lips linger as if my mouth is new territory to be explored and mapped. The last of my walls come crashing down, giving him free rein. My fingers curl into his wet hair to keep him with me for as long as possible.

Not nearly long enough later, a car horn bleats three times in rapid succession. A friendly reminder that the rest of the world exists and he's holding things up rather than an angry get-your-ass-back-to-the-car-now honk. It's still enough to have us jumping apart.

August waves over his shoulder to let them know the message was received. Then he kisses me one last time. "See you, Imogen."

"See you, August," I say.

There's no spoken promise of when. For now, it's enough to know we both want there to be a next time.

Chapter EIGHTEEN

Love Rule #6: Love can be conveyed in as little as a look or a touch.

Love does not like being ignored. Once it's in your system, it interrupts your thoughts. Disrupts your routine. An ever-present reminder that your heart is no longer yours alone.

That's what August's done to me.

We didn't make any promises to each other or even say out loud that we want anything more than that epic kiss this morning. But part of me—okay, a very large part—is hoping he does.

If the car in my driveway after I worked a double is any indication, Mom is having the same effect on Alex. That or she worked some literal magic to find him a match this quickly. I send a little prayer up to whoever is listening that Mom has decided to stop fighting her feelings for him.

Love rule seventeen: Denying your feelings will only make them grow more insistent.

Alex lives a few hours away, and his job keeps him from coming to town during the week, but not all long-distance relationships are doomed to fail. Absence makes the heart grow fonder, right? I have to believe that for both Mom's and my sake. And really, out-of-town boyfriends make the most sense for both of us. It's just been mom and me for almost as long as I can remember. Who knows what adding another person into the everyday mix would do? That's something we should ease into. Like buying a new brand of cat food or adopting a cat to feed with said food.

I sneak up to her office door, careful to keep out of sight so I can listen undetected. The walls are thin enough in our house that even with the door shut, I can make out everything they're saying as if I were in the room with them.

"You seem awfully confident that my soul mate's in here," Alex says, a hint of skepticism rippling through the deep rumble of his voice.

"I have an exceptional record. One of the highest in the country," my mom says.

"I'm not doubting your skills, Claire. But you and I both know that's not why I came to you."

That's the perfect setup for a confession of love if I've ever heard one. I hug the wall, trying to contain my swoon.

Mom's chair squeaks, and I imagine she's standing to throw herself into Alex arms, finally giving in to her feelings for him. She ruins that fantasy while it's still forming when she says, "You came to me because I know you." Another protest from the chair makes it clear she was only shifting her weight to switch into no-nonsense mode.

I mime beating my head against the wall. I'd do it for real if Mom wouldn't hear the thudding and come run me off.

"There was a time you knew me better than anyone," he says.

"That was a long time ago."

"A connection like that, that's not something you forget."

"Then trust me to know the kind of woman who will be right for you," she says. Her voice is all business—confident and coaxing.

But the hint of reluctance softening her words gives me hope. Does Alex hear the difference too?

Shifting to have a clear view through the glass French doors, I peer inside. If they're going through the profiles of potential matches, Mom will be watching and evaluating his reaction to each. If he glows for any of the women, even the slightest glimmer, she'll narrow the options until they're down to one. The one. Sometimes it happens in the first session, but often it takes a few rounds to make a successful match. And then it's not 100 percent confirmed until the first date when they meet face-to-face for the first time. But Mom's instincts are rarely wrong.

With the way they're love glowing all over each other though, there's no way she'll be able to tell which women he reacts to in the pictures. If he reacts to any of them at all. He's so smitten with my mom, it's a wonder they don't set the room on fire with all those smoldering looks they're exchanging. Mom soldiers on, dutifully revealing each potential match with a carefully drafted bio designed to make them shine. Alex nods along. He smiles, asks follow-up questions. But his eyes never leave Mom's face.

Watching Mom resist love this ardently sends a trickle of doubt through me. What if August isn't the right choice? Just because we like each other doesn't mean it will work out. Or that I'm even what he wants. He kissed me when I asked—and kissed me like he meant it—but if I hadn't stopped him, he would have left without acting on whatever feelings he has for me.

I can't exactly ask Mom for advice without telling her I've been lying about August from the start. But if I can find out why she's so opposed to dating Alex when they clearly like each other, I might be able to piece together what to do about August.

Usually, after mom makes a successful match, she celebrates with a glass of champagne. After Alex leaves fifteen minutes later, it's scotch, no ice. I used to think it was the only hard liquor she kept in the house because she knew I'd never touch it if it smelled like drinking a damp, mossy forest, but it's her go-to drink when she's had a shit day.

I'll take a bowl of mint chocolate chip ice cream, thank you very much.

She sent Alex home matched to one of her pickiest clients. Delaney Richards is the last person Mom should have matched him with. Unless her failing to find him a match is her plan. Mom's good at her job. She's never failed to match someone, even if it took her the better part of a year. And she's never manipulated clients before. Not that I know of anyway. So she can tell me there's nothing going on between her and Alex all she wants, but I won't believe her. Not after this.

She's taken her drink back into her office. The glow she emitted earlier has gone dark, tendrils of teal aura now weaving through her hair and curling along her slender shoulders. With each sip, her heartbreak grows a little more. And I can't stand it any longer.

After walking in to take the seat Alex occupied earlier, I pull my feet up onto the seat and hug my knees. "Why did you lie to him?"

"I didn't lie." She drains the rest of the glass and looks at the bottle on her desk. Then she turns her attention to me, apparently deciding a second drink would be a dead giveaway that she's lying to me too. "Alex and Delaney are a good match."

"But he's not interested in her. He's interested in you."

"How many times do I have to tell you to drop this, Imogen? There is nothing going on between Alex and me."

"But there could be." Dropping my legs, I lean forward to make her look me in the eye if she's going to keep lying to me. "I've never seen you like this with anyone. Not since Dad."

She picks up her drink again and stares into the empty rocks glass, whispering, "Not then either."

I freeze, my muscles turning to stone. The words turn over and over in my head as I try to fit them into an order that makes sense. Because "not then either" cannot be true. If it is, she means she never felt that way about my dad. But she loved him. Still loves him. Her love for him is what defined her rules. What makes Soul Match such a success.

Before I can ask what she means, she looks up. Realization that she said it out loud—that I heard her—flushes her face. "You were so young when we lost your father, you can't possibly remember that."

"Young or not, I do remember," I say, like I have to prove what I just heard is a lie. "You were wearing this long yellow sundress with fluttery cap sleeves. Your hair was braided over one shoulder, and it tickled my cheeks as you danced me around the living room. You were glowing so brightly, I kept pulling your hair over my eyes to peek up at your face. Dad had been somewhere, I don't know, but he was coming home from a trip or something, and you were so excited to see him. You were so happy. So in love with him. It's one of my first memories, and I remember feeling so awed by your glow. By how it transformed you. I want you to have that again."

I want me to have that too.

But how do I know if I'll find it with August?

Alex's file, with his picture stapled to the front, still sits on her desk. After opening the top drawer, she sweeps it in as if she can make the real Alex go away as easily. "That was the night he died."

"What?" How do I not remember that was the same night? Reaching my hand across the desk, I curl my fingers around Mom's.

"He cut his trip short and was coming home early to surprise us."

"No, you knew he was coming home. You were waiting for him because you'd made him a special dinner. There were candles on the table. I remember the candles because you were already so bright."

She squeezes my hand once then pulls away before folding her hands in her lap. "You must remember that from another night and your mind has fused the two together. There were no candles that night. No romantic dinner because he was supposed to be gone for another night. He came home early. If he'd just stayed that night like he was supposed to..." Her voice gives out, her eyes glassy with unshed tears. One drink isn't enough to have her drunk crying, so the tears must be for Dad.

Way to go, Mo. You made your mother cry.

Backtracking, I say, "I'm sorry, Mom. I didn't realize it was that night. You're right, I was probably too young to remember it properly. But I really do want you to find that kind of love again. You deserve to be happy."

"I am happy," she says. But her heart's not in it. She's already given that to Alex whether she wants to admit it or not.

And I'm afraid August might have taken mine when he left too.

August and I messaged all night until our phones died. Which was probably for the best since I had to get up for work well before it could be called *bright and early*. Gemma's not scheduled until midday, so my customers get my full attention for the first time in a week. If Lee and Gabe noticed my slacking off, they never called me on it. Though Gemma probably covered for me with them as well as the tables I neglected.

I try to make up for it by not checking my phone once during my shift. When I finally do, the second I clock out, my heart drops. No new messages from August. He knows I have to work, so it's possible he doesn't want to distract me. But what if the magic of what we had over spring break is gone? Worn off with the distance? After gathering my bag and jacket, I get out of there before Gemma sees me and decides I can't leave until she cheers me up.

I don't need cheering up. I need to get my head back on straight. To focus on my portfolio. The application window closes in two weeks, and I'm still nowhere near ready to submit mine.

Yesterday's rain is long gone, replaced with a perfect spring afternoon. When I get home, I leave the studio door open to bring the fresh air in. The breeze flutters the photos I have strung up over the worktable, August's smile catching my eye and sending my mind daydreaming about our kiss the day before. The opposite of productive. Just as I reach to pull it free, a knock sounds on the door.

August.

It's not him. I know it's not. But he's still my first thought.

Ren leans his head through the open doorway. He smiles

when he sees me, his heartbreak contained or temporarily forgotten. "I hope it's okay that I just stopped by."

If anyone can make up for not being August, it's Ren. "I'm always happy to see you," I say.

We walk out to the dock and stretch out on the sun-warmed wood. The water's still too cold to put our feet in, but we sit on the edge anyway, dangling our legs just above the rippling surface. Leaning on my hands, I tip my head back, eyes closed, soaking in the perfection of the moment.

"So you and August, huh?" Ren asks.

My heart rate spikes, shooting a hit of panic straight to my nerves. I meet his gaze and fight to keep my voice as disinterested as possible when I say, "No, not me and August."

"Really? That's not what it looked like yesterday when I pulled up for breakfast and saw you two outside."

"I don't know what you're talking about."

Unsurprisingly, he doesn't buy my lie. His laugh wraps around me like a warm hug, no hint of malice or jealousy. "No, it's cool if you're back together. You shouldn't have to hide that it worked out for you just because my situation with Lana hasn't changed. I promise I'm not the type of guy to hold something like that against you."

"I know you're not." Sitting up, I turn to face him and fold my legs beneath me. "And I'm not back together with August. That thing you think you saw between us—"

"By 'thing' you mean you kissing August like he would disappear if you stopped?" Ren grins at me.

My face bursts into flames. Too bad the fire of embarrassment can't consume me and leave me a pile of ash so I don't have to finish this conversation. "Yes, that. Well, it shouldn't have happened. We got caught up in the moment and forgot ourselves." We forgot everyone else too, and what they would think if they saw us kissing.

"That's good though. Right? I mean if you forgot all the shit that broke you up, maybe that's a sign you should try again." He sounds so earnest. So hopeful. Like if there's hope for August and me, there's hope for him and Lana too.

Part of me hates to take that from him. And part of me hates he's still thinking of her. "That kiss didn't magically erase everything else standing in our way. If anything, it made it all that much bigger." Because now my lies about August are the very thing keeping me from being with him.

He reaches out and taps my knee. Leaving his finger pressed there, he asks, "Can I ask you something?"

"Sure."

"If August wanted to get back together, would you?"

I may not be able to tell Ren the whole truth, but I can at least own up to how I feel about August. "I wish I could say no. I really don't want to have feelings for him, but I do. Being with him this week, I had moments when it felt so right. If it could be like that between us all the time, it would be perfect."

"Yeah, I know what you mean. That was basically me and Lana our whole relationship. At least that's how I thought it was. She obviously didn't."

"Would you take her back if she said breaking up was a mistake?"

He bites his lip and side-eyes me, as if debating telling me the truth or what he thinks I want to hear. "The answer stays between us?"

"Of course."

"Cool. My friends have already threatened me with bodily harm if I so much as look in her direction, but yeah, I would risk that if she wanted to give us another chance."

I shouldn't care. Not after kissing August yesterday. But disappointment burns bitter on my tongue. Ren may be here with me, but his heart still belongs to Lana. "And if she doesn't? If you two really are over, are you okay with that?"

"I kinda have to be, right? You can't force someone to have feelings for you."

Ren's hand falls away, but he leans in closer. His eyes drop to my lips for a fraction of a second. It's so quick I'm not even sure it happened.

He's not wrong. That's love rule twenty-seven: *You can't make yourself fall in love with someone. No matter how much you wish you could.*

Chapter NINETEEN

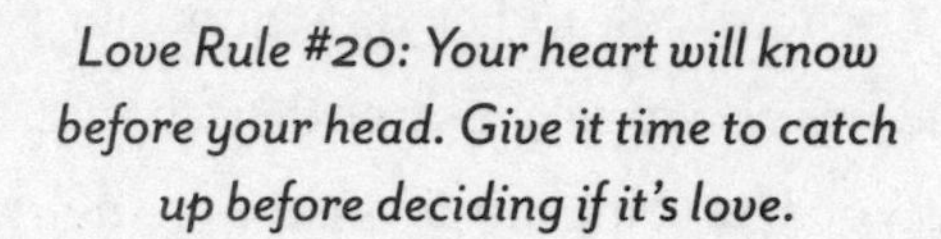

Love Rule #20: Your heart will know before your head. Give it time to catch up before deciding if it's love.

Spring break was supposed to be my time to eat, sleep, and breathe my Kinsey application. And while I've met my goal of working extra shifts to pad my bank account, my progress on the portrait front is lacking. In addition to August's and Ren's photos, I got just one other done thanks to two no-shows. Constant distraction in the form of August is also to blame. So three heartbreak photos will have to do for now.

Gemma and I have a check-in meeting with Mrs. Clemente over lunch break midweek. As we're arranging our photos on one of the worktables in the art room, Gemma keeps picking up August's photo and making kissy noises at me. She's lucky we're artsy artists and not martial artists, or she'd have a throwing star sticking out of her neck by the time Mrs. Clemente joins us. I snatch the photo from Gemma and place it as far from her as possible.

"Hello, you two. I trust you both used the break to refill your creative wells and be artistically productive."

It's like she knows I slacked off. Got distracted. I smile at her to hide my guilt. "You could say that." She doesn't need to know it's not an accurate statement yet. As soon as she looks at my photos, she'll see how little progress I made last week. I'd like to prolong that disappointment as long as possible.

Gemma swoops in to save me. Or maybe she's just proud of how on track she is. "I think I'm almost there. I just need to decide which one to cut."

There's a lot of "I love it" and "this one is so brilliant" thrown around over the next few minutes as Mrs. Clemente goes through Gemma's work. Not that Gemma doesn't deserve it—she absolutely does. But maybe doing this review together was not the best decision for my self-esteem because the only place to go from enthusiasm like that is down.

When they're done, I explain my updated concept to Mrs. Clemente. Her face is neutral, unreadable. All her smiles have already been used up. Though when she gets to the photo of Ren, she nods, as if she can sense the magic of that shot and all the feelings swirling around him. Then she moves on, the moment gone.

I hold my breath, awaiting the verdict.

Mrs. Clemente leans back on the table, crossing her legs at the ankles. She folds her hands together as if praying for patience and levels me with a look so full of dashed hope, she could almost be one of my heartbroken subjects. "While Mr. Kano is very photogenic, I'm still not seeing anything different. It's great that you have a theme for your submission, but it's not coming through enough in these photos. We talked about trying a different subject matter before the break. Have you given any more thought to that?"

Of course, I'm not lucky enough for her to drop that. Not willing to compromise my artistic integrity, I hold firm. "I did think about it, but I don't want to take pictures of objects. My passion comes through in people. In *faces*."

"Okay. So maybe you can try different angles or distances or settings. There are so many options out there to add some variety to your work. That's all I'm advocating for here. I would never want to stifle your creativity or passion, but you came to me and asked for my help. And this is my advice: try something different."

"But to convey what I'm trying to with my work, they need to be portraits so you can have this side-by-side comparison. If there's no commonality, the point will be missed." Or removed entirely. And if there's no point to the photos, there's literally no point in submitting anything.

"Gemma, do you mind if I use you as an example since you're sitting here?"

She glances at me, a quick *I'm sorry* flashing in her eyes. "I guess not."

Mrs. Clemente feathers out the photos I took of Gemma's

sculptures. "While Gemma's work is some variation of a wooden sculpture, each piece is unique. There's movement to them. Different shapes and sizes. And she subverts expectations. Here she's got a three-foot bee. And then there's a five-inch shark. And the weeping willow tree held together with wire so the branches drip from the top of the trunk and sway." She points out each one as if I didn't take the photos myself. As if I don't know my best friend is an artistic genius and will therefore likely be going to Kinsey without me. But Mrs. Clemente is too nice to say that outright.

Turning her attention back to me and my work, she continues, "If you want to show love and heartbreak in your work, I'm all for it. But give me something more with your photos. Even if you end up tossing them out afterward. I'm guessing you'll be pleasantly surprised once you give yourself the freedom to explore. Just do it quickly. Today's the tenth. You only have until the twenty-sixth until your application has to be in for the summer program. I don't want to see you miss out on this opportunity by playing it too safe. Really push yourself here. I know you can do it."

Her cheerleading feels more like a conciliatory pat on the head. Something to satiate my need for validation without actually validating a damn thing.

"I'll take another pass," I say more to end the conversation than because I want to change anything about my photos.

"Well then, I look forward to our final check-in before it's go time." Her smile is so genuine, and I hate myself a little for thinking she's not 100 percent supportive.

Now I just have to find a solution that works for us both.

As if that verbal takedown weren't brutal enough, Lana's waiting for me in the hall after I pack up. Whatever she wants with me, it can't be good.

"You have a free period now, right?" she asks.

"Yeah, I was going to get a head start on my homework," I say.

Translation: *I'm going to sulk in an empty classroom, where if I cry, no one will see.*

Gemma shoots me a look, raising one eyebrow and tilting her head in the opposite direction to silently ask if I need her to save me from this conversation. When I shake my head, she throws a wave over her shoulder and heads to her next class.

Lana hikes her backpack higher onto her shoulder. "I wasn't trying to eavesdrop or anything, but I overheard you talking to Mrs. Clemente about your project. It sounded like Ren was part of it?"

"Yeah, it took a little cajoling, but I eventually got him to let me take his picture."

"Was that where the photo y'all posted of you two came from?"

Warning bells go off in my brain. The accusation in her

voice promises to be lethal if I don't talk her down. She may have broken up with Ren, but she is nowhere near over him. Smiling like it's all some big misunderstanding, I say, "All his photos were pretty serious. We took that one just to lighten the mood. It was nothing."

"I heard you watched the meteor shower together. From the sound of it, y'all were very cozy." Lana's voice is pure ice. All cold and sharp and ready to stab me right in the heart, leaving no trace of evidence behind while I bleed out.

Someone conveniently forgot to tell her about the half of the night where he ignored me. Or the photo shoot he missed. But he keeps finding his way back to me, and I don't know what that means, if anything, now that August and I may be working our way toward something real. "I forgot my jacket. He was just keeping me from being too cold. The wind at the beach was no joke."

"I wouldn't count on that kind of attention lasting if I were you. You're used to a boyfriend who made sure you knew how much he cared. Maybe it was because he wasn't physically here, but you never had to question it. With Ren, you'll always wonder. Good waves will always come first. And after so long, that feeling of being an afterthought to the person you love will eat its way into your life until the only option is to get out before there's nothing left you recognize."

Ren adored Lana. Even without my ability, I could have seen it. Granted, I'm sure it felt different being inside that relationship, but from the outside, his feelings for her were never in question. But I'm trying to diffuse her anger, not wind it up, so I ask, "Why did you stay with him for so long?"

"Because I loved him. And I didn't want to lose him." Tears fill her eyes. Lana looks up at the ceiling, furiously blinking them away before they spill over. After a moment, she straightens like her emotions were nothing more than a momentary inconvenience. "Turns out losing yourself is way worse. I am *so* much happier now that we're not together anymore. I was worried there'd be this massive hole inside that Ren used to fill, but it's like now that he's out of my life, there's room for me again."

I don't know if she believes what she's saying or if she's just really good at faking it. But despite her outward confidence, her broken heart tells a different story. Her aura is all dark teal, not even a hint of copper or rose gold to lighten it. It folds around her, an impenetrable cloak of sadness.

"Can I tell you something?" I ask.

She shrugs like whatever I have to say will be as interesting as picking lint from a sweater.

I press on despite her disinterest. "If you're projecting this not-at-all-affected-by-your-breakup persona to get Ren's attention, I don't think it's going to work the way you want. He *will* believe you."

"Oh, you know him so well after one night on the beach?"

"No, but I know he loved you, whether you felt it or not. And if he thinks you'll be happier without him, he won't try to win you back."

"Good. I don't want him to," Lana says.

"So all this dark and gloomy heartbreak literally pouring out of you like smoke at a five-alarm fire is all for show?" I swirl my hand in a circle to indicate the air—and heartbreak—around her.

"I can be sad for what I've lost and still not want it back." She purses her lips, stained a delicate shade of matte ruby chocolate, as if she's trying to keep from saying more. "It's the same with you and August, right? He was here for spring break. Here *in person* for the first time in who knows how long, and you didn't go running back to him. No, you showed him you don't need him or his apologies. That you're better off without him."

So much for Gemma's theory that I could quietly "get back together" with August and no one would care.

I don't know where August and I stand after our kiss, but I want us to have a chance at something real. Even if I have to keep lying to everyone to get it.

My phone vibrates on the nightstand, waking me from a hazy half sleep Friday night. August's face flashes on screen. He usually messages before calling. Though to be fair, he might have and I slept right through it since I have to be up early for work tomorrow. Pulling the phone under the covers to retain heat, I answer. "It's the middle of the night. Everything okay?"

"Can't sleep," August says, his voice breathy. "And I was thinking how much better it would be if I were there. With you."

My skin warms at the thought. Three sentences—not even full sentences at that—is all it takes from August for me to melt. Ren never had a chance. "Too bad you live so far away, or I'd invite you over."

"Then maybe we just pretend I'm there?"

"How will that help you fall asleep?"

"You have a really soothing voice. And I have a very active imagination," he says.

"I'm sure you do." Curling on my side, I tuck the sheet underneath my thigh and wonder how he's imagining me right now. "Okay, how is this gonna work?"

"Are your eyes closed? 'Cause my eyes are closed. I'm lying on my side, and you're next to me with your back pressed against my chest. And I've got my arms wrapped around you like that's exactly where you're supposed to be. Your heart's beating too fast for you to be asleep yet. And I'm pretty sure it's because of me, which is making it hard for me to fall asleep."

"Oh, it's not you. Or at least not how you're thinking," I say, deciding to play along. If he's going to imagine us spooning and then blame me for his inability to sleep when he's the one who woke me up, I'm going to play dirty. "I'm claustrophobic, and with you holding me down, I feel trapped."

"Then why haven't you tried to push me away yet?" he asks.

"Paralyzed by fear?" I say.

His laugh booms through the phone, sending a wave of

goose bumps racing along my skin. "You didn't seem to mind so much when we were kissing outside Yeastie Boys."

That kiss might have been the best few minutes of my entire life. Not that I can tell him that. "The key word there is *outside*. Fresh air and all. Plus, I had full range of motion."

"So you're saying you don't like our current position because it's too restrictive?"

"Seriously, August, you've got to move over. You're about to push me off the bed."

"Sorry. It's not my fault your bed's so damn small."

"I wasn't expecting to have to share. I'll get a bigger one for next time."

"God, yes, please. If I have to spend the whole night with your frozen toes against my calves, I'm going to rethink this whole arrangement. I mean, really, put on some socks," August says. His voice is low, almost gravelly, playing his part too well.

I press the back of my hand to my mouth to keep my laugh from waking Mom. We're still in PG territory, but just barely. My mind conjures images of him curled in next to me, our legs tangled. Opening my eyes, I stare at the empty pillow next to me and let reality reclaim my senses. I take a steadying breath and say, "Why do I need socks when I have you to warm them up? I've got to get something out of this, right? Having you as my personal heater would do it."

"I'm shocked you would use me so blatantly, Imogen." His voice shakes with mock annoyance.

"You're the one who called me, remember?"

The line goes quiet for a minute. I hold the phone away from my ear and blink against the electronic glow emitting from it. The timer continues to count the length of the call. He's still on the other end. Closing my eyes again, I let the silence continue.

"Imogen?" He says my name the same way he did before he kissed me. So much longing and affection packed into three little syllables.

With my eyes closed, I can almost feel his breath on my neck and the way his hands would roam my skin, sneaking under my shirt to leave a trail of heat everywhere he touched. If he were actually here tonight, who knows how far things would go?

I stick my legs out of the covers to cool off. "Yeah?"

"Your elbow is digging into my ribs." The barest laugh escapes him, crackling through the phone.

He must know what he's doing to me. That this whole conversation—as innocent as he's pretending to be—will leave us both aching for more. Well, two can play that game. "Oh, I'm sorry. Would it be better if I just lie on top of you?"

"Now that you mention it, that might be best," he says. "I'm never going to get to sleep with you the way you are right now."

"We could always—"

My bedroom door flies open so fast, it smacks against the wall with a deafening crack. I jerk up, clutching the covers to my chest, and drop my phone somewhere in the tangle of sheets. "Shit."

"Imogen Eliza!" Mom's voice precedes her into my room but only by a second. Then she's snapping on the overhead light and searching the room with a steely narrow-eyed glare. I keep my eyes trained on her so I'm not caught off guard if she starts shooting laser beams out of her eyes. When her gaze lands on me, I flinch. Being sliced in two by my mother and her overprotective anger is not on the agenda tonight. "What is going on in here?"

"Nothing. I'm just talking to August," I say.

Mom snatches up a handful of covers and whips them back, nearly throwing me to the floor. She stares at the empty bed as if she's expecting him to materialize out of thin air. After a moment, she releases the comforter, and it pools on the floor. Then she moves on to the closet, shoving hangers back and forth like her life depends on finding him there.

"Where is he?" she demands.

Fumbling for the phone, I check that August's still on the line before holding it up for my mom's inspection. She ignores me. Turning on speakerphone, I say, "August, please tell my mom you're not actually in my room."

"Hi, Mrs. Finch." His voice is tinged with amusement like he's holding back a laugh as it comes through the speaker, whisper soft. "I swear I'm not under the bed, so you don't even need to check."

Mom drops to the floor, tossing the comforter she'd heaved there back onto the bed.

"Not funny," I say to August. His laugh fills the room in response. "I'm hanging up. Good luck getting to sleep now."

"Good night, Mrs. Finch. I really am only on the phone," he says. Like that will help me now. "Good night, Imogen Eliza."

I run my fingers over the phone screen after it goes dark.

"Care to explain?" Mom asks. Her eyes still search the room, not ready to believe me.

When her gaze finally lands back on me, I meet it straight on. "August couldn't sleep."

"So you thought phone sex was the way to go?"

I toss the phone to the end of my bed, my face flaming. I may have had one or two errant thoughts of a sexual nature, but the conversation was 100 percent aboveboard. Well, 99 percent anyway. "God, Mom! No. It's not like that. We were just joking around. Fully clothed. The only body parts discussed were my feet. And not in a fetishy way, in a normal cold-feet way."

"What I heard didn't sound like joking."

"You shouldn't have been listening in the first place."

"I'm not sure you should be talking to August anymore. You two did not end on the best terms, and it worries me that you've forgotten that so easily. Since you saw him over break, it's like you're a different person."

"Yeah, because before he showed up, I had to fake our relationship so everyone didn't know the daughter of a matchmaker was so much of a loser, she couldn't even get a boy's attention. Is that better?" I spit out the words without thinking. The admission steals the life from the room faster than any incantation could.

Mom sinks onto the bed next to me, smoothing the covers around us. "What are you talking about?"

"August and I weren't really dating. That's why we didn't want you and his parents to go to dinner. So you didn't find out. But I'm done with that now, so we don't need to rehash it. Lesson learned. No more fake boyfriends. I promise."

"That's not going to cut it. You can't just tell me you've been lying to me, to everyone, for a year and shrug it off like it's not a big deal. It is a very big deal. What possessed you do something like that?"

"Because no one wanted to date me. And I just wanted to feel lovable. For other people to think I was. I'm sorry I lied to you, but I couldn't handle being alone, and I didn't see another way out of it. August knows now, and he's not mad at me. Miraculously. And I like him, Mom. Please don't be mad at me for this."

"I'm reserving my right to be mad but will let it go for tonight because I'm too tired to fight with you right now. I hope you know you never needed to fake anything. If you haven't found love yet, it's because it hasn't found you. And I promise you, you don't want to think you're in love and then realize you're supposed to be with someone else. You're smart to wait." The sharpness has left her voice. In its place is a sadness that stabs at my heart.

I never wanted Mom to know what a failure I am at love. She's built her life around it, and here I am falling for a boy I never saw coming.

"What if it is love with August? Or it could be, at least." My eyes drift to the poem he sent me that's now taped to the wall beside my bed. If that's really how I make him feel, I can't give up on us. Not without at least trying first. "Things with August aren't that far yet, but I like him. And he likes me. And for some reason being around me seems to make him feel better, more like himself. So, if I can help him, I'm going to."

"Do you think you can help him while keeping things below an R rating?"

"I think I can manage that."

She strokes a hand down my hair and flicks a finger over the tip of my nose. "Be careful with August, okay? You don't want to have to add your own broken heart to your project."

"I am being careful."

But for the first time, I don't want to be.

Chapter TWENTY

Love Rule #23: Following the whims of your heart when the feelings are fleeting will only end in pain.

It takes me forever to fall back asleep, so when my phone buzzes again with an incoming message, it takes my brain a few seconds to register it's morning rather than the middle of the night. It's still dark out, but years of getting up before the sun for work make me more attuned to the different shades of predawn skies. Judging by the hazy blue peeking through my blinds, my alarm's going off any time now.

I check my phone. August beat it by two minutes.

Either he was never able to fall asleep last night, or he purposely woke up early so he could talk to me before work. Even the thought that he might have done that sends my heart into free fall. I dismiss my alarm before it goes off, then click on his message.

TheRealAugust: Are you still alive after last night?

TheRealAugust: Do I need to send an anonymous

tip to the authorities to check the water around your dock for your body?

TheRealAugust: Mrs. Finch, if you did kill Imogen and are reading this, I was just joking about the cops.

TheRealAugust: Your secret's safe with me.

MoGlows: WOW.

MoGlows: You got over my supposed death quickly. Guess I know who I'll be haunting first.

TheRealAugust: Promise?

MoGlows: You're not getting rid of me this easily.

TheRealAugust: I'm gonna hold you to that.

MoGlows: Promise?

TheRealAugust: Cross my heart.

TheRealAugust: And if you get bored at work today, I had an idea for a Frankenbiscuit while I couldn't sleep last night.

TheRealAugust: Have you ever had a Monte Cristo? It's basically a deep-fried ham and cheese sandwich.

MoGlows: Never had one. Sounds intriguing though.

I look up the recipe online, and my stomach grumbles in response.

TheRealAugust: Intriguing? Try fucking delicious.

MoGlows: I'll take your word for it.

TheRealAugust: I'm serious about the Frankenbiscuit.

TheRealAugust: Try it.

TheRealAugust: And then try and tell me I'm not a culinary genius.

MoGlows: You're already a poetic genius. How many genius titles do you really need?

TheRealAugust: I've gotta do something to convince you to want to date me.

It's not a matter of want. I'm already convinced. I just have to let go of the vision of Ren and me together that I've been clinging to for so long. But for August, it might be worth it.

MoGlows: This must be some sandwich if you're hanging the fate of our relationship on it.

TheRealAugust: I wouldn't have to resort to such high-stakes tactics if you'd just agree to a date.

TheRealAugust: I just want to be worth it, you know?

TheRealAugust: Because I think being with you would be worth doing just about anything no matter the cost.

That's easy to say when being together is a fantasy. Real

life be damned. But damn if I don't want everything he's promising me.

When I tell Gemma about Mom's freak-out at work a few hours later, she laughs so hard that she scares a customer into dropping their drink. Claiming it was my fault, she tosses me a rag to go clean it up. I apologize to them, get them a refill, and offer them a complimentary cinnamon biscuit for their trouble. They happily accept all three. Then Gemma and I burst out laughing again, this time in the privacy of the supply closet, where no customers—or their breakfasts—will be harmed.

"August had an idea for a Frankenbiscuit. I thought we could test it out," I say after the breakfast rush finally dies later that morning.

With the back of her hand pressed to her forehead, she fake swoons against the counter. "Damn, you have it bad for this boy. We have customers who have been eating here almost every week for years and we don't let them do that."

"They also order the same thing every time, so their taste buds can't be trusted."

"Fair point. So what's this recipe we just absolutely have to make right now?"

I mime strangling her. "Remember when he was my fake boyfriend and you went along with everything I suggested without question or commentary?"

"Nope. Neither of those things rings a bell."

"Okay maybe it wasn't *that* easy, but I still miss those days when you were *slightly* more open to my ideas without the constant ridicule."

Gemma's smile softens. "There's no ridicule here. Just a little best friend teasing. It's cute seeing you legitimately happy over a real boy." Throwing her arms around me, she hugs me hard enough to crush bone.

"It feels good being this happy." My heartbreak pact with Ren flares in my mind, refusing to be ignored. I told him I was done with August. That I was ready to move on. In the moment, I meant it. But the more I let myself think of dating August as a real possibility, the more I want it. "Are you going to help me make this thing or not?"

"Depends. Is it going to be edible, or are you just making it because August said you should?"

I shove away from her, mock offended. And a little actually offended if I'm being honest. I take biscuits very seriously. "I'm going to pretend you didn't insult me like that and tell you what his idea is. Then you can apologize. And then I *might* let you try it when we're done."

"I like how you assume I'm going to help you without the option of tasting this work of staggering genius at the end. Now tell me what it is already," Gemma says.

"Basically, it's a breakfast Monte Cristo but in biscuit form. So it's a fried biscuit with ham, Swiss cheese, and a fried egg. Then it's dusted with powdered sugar and accompanied by raspberry jam for dipping."

Licking her lips, she says, “That’s not a bad idea. It might clog our arteries instantly, but it sounds delicious.”

“Right? How have we not thought of that before?”

“Probably because my dads took the fried biscuit balls off the menu after the rancid grease incident of 2018.”

My mouth twitches, but I know better than to smile. The biscuit balls had been her favorite, and no amount of begging had swayed her dads to bring them back. “Oh, shit. I forgot about that.” But really, who asks two twiggy tween girls to carry five-gallon vats of old grease to a recycling receptacle on their own? “They won’t say no when it’s for a Frankenbiscuit, right?”

Gemma says, “Depends on how many vetoes they get.”

“Let’s not tell them until we’re done, just to be safe.”

In the kitchen, she sweet-talks Saint into letting us work on a new creation while divulging as few details as possible. I steal a few rounds of biscuit dough off the tray waiting to go in the oven. Then we take over one of the gas burners on the stove and a five-inch swath of the griddle and get to work. And by *we* I mean Gemma. She’s the one with the cooking skills. I bring the outlandish ideas and the appetite. Since the deep fryer is off the table, she panfries the biscuit dough until the biscuits puff up and turn a gorgeous golden brown. In between flipping them to cook both sides, she cracks two eggs onto the hot griddle and lays out slabs of ham that curl at the edges as soon as they hit the heat.

My mouth is watering before the biscuits touch the plate.

After slicing them open, I lay the tops to the side for Gemma to pile on the rest of the ingredients. When we're done, we carry them out front and stage a quick photo on the counter with the Yeastie Boys menu strategically displayed beneath the plate. Emphasis on *quick* so we can dig in while they're still hot. Posting the picture can wait.

I bite in and nearly die from sheer taste-bud euphoria. The outside of the dough is perfectly crispy while the inside is like a cloud, all fluff and lightness. I may have to petition the dads to bring the fried dough balls back. I forgot how much I loved them. But this biscuit sandwich takes them to a whole new level.

"Oh God. So good," Gemma says around a mouthful.

"I think the jam needs to go on the biscuit, not on the side. It should not be an optional flavor when we introduce this to the masses."

"Hard agree."

I make it three-quarters of the way through mine before I shove the plate away, too stuffed to finish. Wiping the grease and jam from my fingers, I let out a satisfied groan. Then I pull up the photo on my phone and apply a halo filter, framing the biscuit in an angelic ring of light. Since the idea was August's and I can't exactly give him credit publicly, I caption it **I died and ate heaven.**

Gemma reads over my shoulder and barks out a laugh. "Is that some new sex euphemism I'm not up on?"

"Gross. No. It's what August's little brother said the first time he had one of our biscuits. Now I have to change it."

"Don't you dare. I want that on a T-shirt."

"That's what I said."

My phone pings with a new notification.

TheRealAugust: You made it!

TheRealAugust: Why hasn't anyone invented smell-o-vision yet???

MoGlows: In this case, I think it would be smell-o-pic. Or Taste-a-gram is maybe more accurate. And yeah, you're missing out.

TheRealAugust: If it's even half as good as it looks…

TheRealAugust: Do you think I can make it there and back without my mom noticing I'm gone?

MoGlows: That's a long drive for a biscuit.

TheRealAugust: Worth it.

TheRealAugust: If I didn't have Owen's soccer practice today I'd so be there.

August might not be able to come to the biscuit, but the biscuit can absolutely go to him. And that *is* a euphemism.

When my shift is over, I look up August's address in Mom's files. Then I leave a note in my room in case she comes looking for me. It says where I'm going, the route I'm taking, and roughly what time I should be home. If all goes well, she'll never even read it. If not, then I'm probably grounded for the rest of my life, but at least she'll have some idea of where I am and won't freak out as much as if I just left town without any sort of explanation. Better to ask forgiveness, right?

I sneak past her office, where she's working hard to convince Delaney that Alex is a match. Based on Delaney's pinched expression, I'm guessing they'll be there for a while yet. Then I'm out the door and on the road, hours of energizing driving music keyed up on my phone to keep me awake. Plus a thirty-two-ounce thermos of coffee Gemma insisted I take. She was torn when I told her my plan. On one hand, she was swept up in the romantic gesture of it all. On the other, she didn't want me to fall asleep behind the wheel and die in an accident on the interstate.

In the end, romance won out. Like it always does.

I stop once for gas and a pee break, and make it the four hours to August's house in what feels like half the time. Only now that I'm here does this seem like a bad idea. Maybe I should have told him I was coming. Or arranged to meet him somewhere where his mom won't see me and immediately call mine and land me in trouble. Or worse, what if our kiss and everything after was all an elaborate joke to get back at me for roping him into my fake-dating scheme and I'm about to be the punch line for all his friends to get a good laugh?

There are so many ways this could go wrong.

He said he would've come to see me, I remind myself. And he's been messaging me as much as I've been messaging him. I shake off the sudden doubt. There's no place for it in my life.

Just as I get out of the car, his front door opens. August steps out, followed by a petite blond with a messy pixie cut who's wearing cutoff black shorts and an oversize flannel shirt, the sleeves rolled up to her elbows. The perfect emo girlfriend. Shay. She's just as he described her. And she looks every bit a current girlfriend, not an ex. Taking his hand, she commands every ounce of his attention. From my distance across the street, their conversation looks serious, but that could just be the intensity of their eye contact. Like they're the only two people in the world. She's cocooned in warring feelings of love and heartbreak. The longer she stares at August, the darker the cloud gets.

But August, he's all rose gold. Love lights him up like a nuclear freaking reactor.

Shay stretches up on her toes and captures his mouth with hers. Wrapping their joined hands behind her back, August pulls them closer together. And whatever heartbreak doubts Shay had about him vanish in a burst of renewed love.

My heart forgets how to beat. Or maybe it's checked out altogether, going dormant in my chest and leaving a vacancy sign in its place. My body finally remembers how to move, and I fumble with my keys, pressing buttons to unlock the car so I can get the hell out of here. I manage to hit the Panic button in my, well, panic. Fitting, but the opposite of helpful. My car's horn blares to life, and the lights flash on and off. I mash the button again to make it all stop, but it's too late.

August is pulling away from Shay.

Calling my name.

Jogging toward me.

"What are you doing here?" he asks, still a few feet away.

I hold up the Yeastie Boys bag, unable to put words to my stupidity.

"You brought my Frankenbiscuit? Because I said I would go there if I could? I wish you'd told me you were coming."

You and me both. Better yet, I wish I'd stayed home. At least then I wouldn't have the image of him kissing Shay burned into my retinas. "Is that Shay?" I can't look at her. Or him. So I end up asking the question to the empty air next to him.

He looks over his shoulder at the girl abandoned on his porch who is trying to set fire to us with her eyes. "Yep."

Thrusting the bag at him, I stammer, "Enjoy the biscuit."

And by that, I mean, *Enjoy your life because I'm out.*

I don't want to be part of this triangle. Or hear his excuses.

I retreat a step, still facing him. Turning would take too much time. Plus, I've heard true friends stab you in the front, so I may as well make it easy on him.

"Imogen, wait." He matches my step back with a forward one to keep us close.

"It's a long drive. I need to get going."

I need to get away from him. From *them* and whatever I'm interrupting.

Shay calls his name, all frustration and possession.

August stiffens but doesn't respond to her. Instead, he reaches for me, stopping short of touching my arm. "You just got here. Stay for a few minutes, give your legs a break from the car. Let me explain. Please."

When he doesn't run right back to her, she storms into the yard, a cloud of teal heartbreak following in her wake. It's clear from her death glare that August told her about me. "Are you serious right now? After everything you've done, you're just going to show up here and what? Steal my boyfriend? I guess pretending he was already yours wasn't enough anymore?"

"I didn't know you'd be here," I say.

"And that's supposed to make what you're doing okay?"

"No, that's not—"

"This isn't her fault," August says.

For a moment, I think he's defending me. That maybe I've read the whole situation wrong and I'm the one he'll choose. But he's staring at Shay, his rose-gold love brightening the air as it overtakes him. The intensity of it knocks me back a step. It was never going to be me. Not when his love for her is that strong. "Looks like Shay's the one who needs an explanation, not me. I understand perfectly."

He shakes his head, and the rose-gold mist around him churns, a vein of coppery teal weaving through it. Lowering his voice, he says to me, "You really don't. And if you'll just hang on long enough for me to get her to leave, we can talk. And I can fix this."

He's so earnest, I almost believe him. Almost. But I don't want to hear his excuses. I don't want him to say he's sorry.

That he's choosing her. I've seen how he feels, so there's nothing more he needs to say. "There's nothing to fix, August. I shouldn't have come. I shouldn't have let things get this far to begin with."

August opens his mouth, presumably to argue, but Shay shouts his name again. Conflicted, he looks from me to her. He doesn't follow when I take the few steps back to my car, and it's clear he's made his choice. And it's not me.

The second he showed up at Yeastie Boys two weeks ago, I should have sent him packing. A relationship between us was never going to go anywhere. Nowhere good anyway. If I'd followed Mom's rules, I would have seen it before I was stupid enough to let him break my heart.

Chapter TWENTY-ONE

Love Rule #16: You can fall in love in an instant, but heartbreak will linger until you're ready to let go.

My phone chirps with a message before I've made it back to the highway. I stop at a gas station to fill up. And to give my hands time to stop shaking before I drive home. August is so not helping with the latter as he bombards me with messages.

TheRealAugust: It's not what you think.
TheRealAugust: Please just give me a chance to explain.
TheRealAugust: I don't want to do this over DM.

My phone rings. I don't answer.

TheRealAugust: Pick up.

Ring. Ring. Ring. Ring. Ring. Ring. Ring.

TheRealAugust: Pick up.

Ring. Dismiss. I would turn off my phone if I knew Mom wouldn't try to call and lose it if she went straight to voicemail.

TheRealAugust: Pick up.
TheRealAugust: I'm taking your silence as you're driving and can't check your phone.
TheRealAugust: Because you have to talk to me and give me a chance to fix this.
TheRealAugust: At least let me know when you get home safely. Please.

Like you let me know you were still in love with Shay? Sure thing.

I think about August the whole drive home. I analyze every moment we were together. Every smile. Every look that made me think he was who I wanted, not Ren. I try to find some clue I missed that would have predicted this is where we'd end up. That he was using me or setting me up for this final humiliation. All it does is make me cry so hard, I have to pull over onto the shoulder until I can get myself under control.

When I get home, I don't respond to any of his messages. Not even the last one, despite Gemma's protestations that he at least deserves to know I didn't die in a fiery road-rage crash on the interstate. Since I arrived home and found her waiting for me, I've gone over what happened no fewer than ten times. She's hoping my story will change. That I'll suddenly remember some vital piece of information that will exonerate August so I'll be forced to call him and talk this through. I hide my phone so she can't message him behind my back.

If I were smart, I would block him. I try to, but I can't make myself follow through. What if he does have a perfectly good explanation for being with Shay today? What if it really was a misunderstanding and I'm blowing it way out of proportion?

No. I will not be that girl. This is real life, not a fairy tale.

Whatever he has to say wouldn't change what I saw. August in full love glow for *her*. The small sparks of attraction I saw from him over spring break were nothing in comparison. I can't compete with that kind of love. And even if I could, I wouldn't want to.

His heart's already made its choice, whether or not his head agrees.

Gemma doesn't understand what I saw. Or how I can be so sure everything he's said to me has been a lie. August's photo that Ren doodled devil horns on catches my eye from where I tacked it up in the studio. And I know what I have to do. Ripping the photo free of the clip, I ignore the needles in my chest. Mom's choice to redecorate the studio in shades of rose gold and pale teal comes in handy—I grab the sample paint cans from the shelf and spread everything out on the light table.

"What are you doing?" Gemma asks. Wanting to keep her hand attached to her arm, she's smart enough not to attempt to save the photo from what I'm about to do to it.

"I'm going to show you what he looked like with her. I thought when I took this photo that maybe the love I saw was because of me, but it was all her. Just like today. She may have broken his heart, but he still loves her. And I need you to believe me."

Without paintbrushes, I'm forced to dip my fingers into the cool pinkish paint and smear it over the photo. I'm sure there's a better kind of paint for this. Something thicker, opaque. But I'm not making art. I'm just trying to make Gemma see.

I follow the swirling pattern of love emanating from him with my fingers, over and over until it's thick and pillowy. Then I open the pale teal and trail a few streaks through the rose gold. I do the same with the darker teal. Despite the photo being in black and white—or maybe because of it—August's smile appears even brighter with his emotions clouding around him.

The result is chaotic and messy and beautiful.

Just like love.

Just like heartbreak.

Gemma hands me a wad of paper towels she rips from the roll. "That's what you see? Like all the time?" Her voice is awestruck, impressed.

"Not all the time." Wiping my hands clean, I nod to the other photos hanging on the line. "And everyone's looks different. From each other but also every time I see it manifest for the same person. It's always changing. Growing lighter and darker as their feelings lessen or intensify. Like, this is what August looks like in *this* picture. But the one for my portfolio that shows his heartbreak, it's mostly teal with only hints of the rose gold peeking through."

"What did he look like today?"

"This," I say, picking up the jar of rose-gold paint.

She stops me before I upend it over his photo. "Okay, okay. I get the picture." Thanks to my impromptu painting party, my phone is free for the taking. Gemma dances it back and forth. "Okay if I send him a message?"

"You can respond to let him know I made it home."

She types out her message, which is much longer than *Mo's not dead*, and hits Send. Only then does she let me read what she wrote.

MoGlows: Gemma here. Mo needs some space. I know you want to apologize or explain or whatever, but she's not in the head space to listen right now.

August writes back within seconds. Like he hasn't put his phone down since he first started messaging me hours ago.

TheRealAugust: How long does she need?

MoGlows: Too soon to tell.

TheRealAugust: Tell her I'm here whenever she's ready?

MoGlows: Just start working on your apology. I'll make sure she listens.

I read over the texts, my heart wringing out like an old dishcloth. "You shouldn't have done that," I say.

"You said I could respond."

"Respond, yes. Give him hope that I'll forgive him after today, no. That was not part of the deal."

Gemma holds my phone in front of my face as if I didn't read it all already. "He's clearly sorry."

"Yeah, that he got caught." I take the phone away from her before burying it in my back pocket for good measure.

"You don't mean that. You're just mad he took your whole fantasy relationship and threw it out the window so you'd want something real with him instead."

After recapping the paint jars, I return them to the shelf, the rose-gold sample considerably emptier than when I started. Luckily, Mom only needs a small swatch to decide if she's going to go through with the full paint job or not. When I turn back to Gemma, she's leaning over the painted photo, just staring at it. Like his love is hypnotic.

"Of course I am," I say. "Because it was just as made up as our fake relationship. He was using me to get back with Shay."

"I'm sorry, but I'm not going to believe that until you hear him out. If he truly is an ass, I'll help you deface every picture of him in existence. But I don't think he is."

"You have an awful lot of faith in some guy you barely even know," I say.

"No, I have an awful lot of faith in how easy it is to love you."

It's a nice sentiment, one I know she believes. But if it were true, I wouldn't be on the verge of tears again because the boy I like is in love with someone else.

Mom's in the kitchen when I come inside. She pats the stool next to her, an invitation to join. "I haven't seen you all day. Does that mean you got some good work done on your project?"

After sliding onto the stool, I let the rest of my body melt onto the counter. Emotionally spent, I'm almost depleted of energy as well after eight hours in a car and then my impromptu painting session, all on top of my shift this morning. "It was more an exorcising-some-demons kind of day."

"Oh, no. You and Gemma didn't decide to paint the studio without me, did you?"

Only then do I notice my paint-splattered hands. Resolidifying into some semblance of a human, I sit up and pick at the paint crusted under my nails. "No, but we may need to buy more samples. I kinda used some of what we had to give Gemma a visual tutorial of what someone in love looks like."

"And what exactly did you do this demonstration on?" she asks, passing me a paper towel to collect the flecks of dried paint instead of dropping them on the counter.

"The walls. The floor. The ceiling. Oh, and the outside too. She's a slow learner."

"So none of those then?"

"It was one of my pictures. But don't worry, not one of the ones I need for my portfolio." At least not if I'm going to take Mrs. Clemente's advice and scrap my heartbreak idea. No matter which way I go with it, August has no place in my portfolio or my life. Not after today.

She runs a soothing hand over my hair. "Did it help?"

"Gemma finally understands what I'm talking about when I say someone glows, so there's that."

"I meant with the demons, but good for Gemma too," she says.

"The demons are a work in progress." Getting rid of feelings is much harder than catching them in the first place. Though to be fair, I did have a head start with August. After a year of pretending, it was way too easy to transfer that attachment to the real August without even realizing it. Now I have to figure out how to untangle those feelings and leave them behind. Leaning into Mom's touch, I ask, "How did you know you were in love with Dad?"

She sighs, her hand stalling. Swiveling her stool to face me, she says, "It wasn't one thing. I don't think I noticed at first. Most people don't. And then one day, I looked at him and just knew. I could see he loved me, and this rush of warmth filled me. I was so full of it, I thought I would burst, and I knew if I looked in the mirror, I would be glowing as brightly as he was."

That glow is gone now, at least where my dad is concerned. Her feelings for Alex have taken over, replaced it. Not that she'll admit that to me or to herself.

"How do you stop feeling that way about someone?" I refuse to say *being in love with*. I am *not* in love with August. But I was definitely in the falling stage before seeing him with Shay. "Do you just have to live with it until you feel that way about someone else?"

"Love doesn't work like that, honey. It's not that orderly, that linear. Love is messy and confusing, and as much as I like to say otherwise, it's unpredictable. You can't control who you fall in love with. Or when."

"But let's say I want to. How do I reverse those feelings or stop them from getting stronger? There must be a way when the person those feelings are directed toward is already taken. When they're not the person you thought they were."

"This is why I wanted you to be careful with August. Something about him didn't sit right with me. Even after you told me the truth about your relationship. Maybe especially then. What happened?"

I nod, dropping my gaze so I don't have to see her I-knew-he-was-trouble look. I don't need a lecture. I just need her to tell me how to get over him. "I saw him kissing his ex-girlfriend—or I guess girlfriend—today. And I could see how much he loved her. He wanted to explain things, but there's nothing to explain. He loves her. Not me."

"Love is messy, remember? You can love more than one person at a time," she says. Her voice stays even, but there's a sharp edge to it that I can't place.

"Not when it's love like that. When it's all-consuming and fills you up to bursting. That's what I saw from August today. Like what you and Dad had. You don't fall in love with someone else when you already have that."

She tips my chin up, forcing me to look her in the eye. "I don't presume to know what's in this boy's heart or yours. But I do know love. If you have feelings for August, real feelings, they're not going to disappear just because you want them to or because he hurt you. They're going to stay with you for a while. Maybe forever. And that's okay because whatever you feel for him is part of you."

That's all well and good in theory. But in practical application, being *almost* in love with someone who doesn't love you back is like slowly dying from the inside out. And I'll do anything to get this feeling to stop.

Chapter TWENTY-TWO

Love Rule #5: A good kiss can't make up for what's lacking in your heart.

August's Frankenbiscuit is a hit. At least if my Insta notifications are any indication. Dozens of comments ask when it will be on the menu so they can come in and try it. Just the thought of it turns my stomach, though that's more to do with August than the biscuit itself.

I have a new notification from him, too. Not a message, thankfully, but he's tagged me in one of his photos. I've avoided clicking on it since I woke up an hour ago and saw it, but I'm going to have to check what the picture is before I see Gemma, or she'll ambush me with it. She told him to apologize, so if this is how he's chosen to do it, she will make sure I pay attention to it. To him.

No more stalling.

I open it, and a poem fills the screen. It's not like the others he's posted. Those are true blackout poems, all dark and broken, black ink filling the page so only a few words are left. This one is all rose gold—bright and full of promise. The printed ink bleeds through the rose-gold marker in places. Ghosts of words refusing to move on now that they're no longer needed. What's left—what I'm meant to see—is this:

His color choice is not lost on me. It was deliberate, just like the words he chose to show. It's not an apology so much as a clever appeal to my ruthlessly romantic heart. It could have worked on another girl. Or even me if I hadn't seen the way he glowed for Shay yesterday. He can say whatever he wants—what he thinks I want to hear—but that won't change how he feels about her. And hoping it will is about as useless as wishing on stars.

What I need is to get August out of my system. To remember why I started all this in the first place.

Before their breakup, Ren and Lana could always be found in the quad before first period. The spot went to Ren and his friends in the split, while Lana and hers got their customary lunch table. He's there Monday morning, sitting at the cluster of lawn chairs the administration gave up on removing years ago when students kept multiplying the number of chairs every time the existing ones were put in storage.

There are no empty seats as I walk toward Ren's group. Which is fine. I'm not here to chat. He notices me when I'm still ten feet away and says something to Evans next to him. Evans checks me out, scrunching his face in an are-you-serious kind of way when he turns back to Ren. It's almost enough to make me rethink this. But I'm done letting what other people think about me control my life. Then Ren grins at me, all straight white teeth and perfect dimples. My heart responds in kind, somersaulting in my chest at what I'm about to do. Evans jumps out of his seat with a sweep of his arm to offer it to me.

"Recruiting more people for your love-slash-hate project?" he asks.

He's trying to distract me. I don't take the bait. "Here to see Ren, actually. But if anyone here wants to help a girl out, I won't say no." I'm another subject down now that August is with Shay. His heartbreak was fleeting and has no place in my project. Just like he has no place in my heart. Refocusing on the goal, I turn to Ren and say, "Can I steal you for a few minutes?"

Ren shoves up from the chair so fast, it wobbles on two legs before one of his friends rights it. "Steal away." He slings his book bag over one shoulder and throws a two-fingered wave to his friends.

"How it'd go with Astrid on Saturday?" I ask when we're far enough from his friends for them not to overhear.

"Two words: yacht club."

"So you stole a boat?"

He drops his head forward, moaning. "I wish. At least then the cops would have come and put an end to the night much sooner."

"That bad, huh?"

"Her parents were there. I had to wear a sport coat and was expected to know the difference between, like, three different forks. Let's just say I'm much more of an ice-cream-for-dinner kind of guy."

I smile up at him, inviting him to lean into those feelings and into me. "No utensils required."

"Plus, the company wasn't so bad either," he says, nudging my shoulder. There's no explosion of color around him when he says it, but at least I don't have to see how strong his heartbreak still is either.

"Maybe we can go out for real? And not just because you

need me to save you from Astrid." I ignore the jolt of guilt at the word *real* and how it feels like that word belongs to August now.

"I kinda thought after you kissed August that you weren't into me like that anymore."

Does he sound a little disappointed? Or are my residual feelings for him making me hear things that aren't there? Gripping the strap of his backpack, I pull us both to a stop. I step in front of him and tip my head back to meet his dark eyes. "Well, you're wrong. In fact, I almost kissed *you* the other night when you came over to let me take your picture."

"But you didn't," he says. "Was that because of August?"

"August is very much out of my life," I say.

To prove it to Ren—and to myself—I stretch up on my toes and capture his mouth with mine. His inhale of surprise sends a rush of panic coursing through me. Threading my hands into the hair at the nape of his neck, I silently beg him to kiss me back. To make the world and all our feelings for other people disappear. His lips move against mine almost robotically. Like a reflex rather than a desire. But he doesn't pull away. Almost as if he needs this as much as I do.

The kiss changes then. Deepens. His fingers dig into my hips, pulling me hard against him. We pour everything we're feeling—the loss, the heartbreak, the desperate need for physical connection with someone who needs it just as badly—into this kiss.

The world doesn't stop, but for a moment, it feels really damn good.

Someone, probably one of Ren's friends, yells, "Just bone her already!" and ruins everything.

Ren jerks back, thumb wiping away all traces of our kiss from his mouth. "Sorry," he says like he's the one who kissed me without permission first. He doesn't stick around long enough for me to set him straight. Or to make sure he knows I'm more than okay with what just happened between us.

A chorus of booing from his friends follows him as he jogs away. From them. From me. From our very public kiss.

Before I can follow him to see if *he's* okay, Lana blocks my path.

With her arms crossed over her chest, she digs her nails into the cream-colored fabric of her long-sleeved shirt. "So much for it not being like that between you and Ren, huh?" she says.

"You said you were over him. And that you were only trying to warn me that dating him was a bad idea."

"That warning did a lot of good, I see. But I guess you didn't really care what I had to say if you were planning to throw yourself at him the first chance you got. You were probably thrilled when you found out I was over him. Honestly, I'm surprised it took you a whole week to move in on him."

I hadn't thought about Lana when I set out to kiss Ren this morning. I knew she wasn't over him no matter how much she claimed to be. Her heartbreak piles on her shoulders like fresh snowfall, a thick blanket of cold-teal aura that adds ice to her words. But if she's not willing to own up to her true feelings,

I'm not about to apologize for kissing Ren. He may be my one chance at eradicating my feelings for August, even if I felt nothing when we kissed.

"Well, you might want to get used to it," I say.

"I knew you wanted to date him," she says, vindication lighting a fire in her eyes. "There was something about that photo of the two of you, the way you were looking at him. It was so obvious."

"He's a great guy. Just because he wasn't the right guy for you doesn't make him bad for everyone. He was always going to move on. Date someone else. I'm sorry if it's sooner than you'd like, but you broke up with him. His life doesn't revolve around you anymore."

"Wait. Are you saying we never had a chance? Could you see our relationship was doomed the whole time we were dating? 'Cause if there was always going to be someone after me, then I basically just wasted three years of my life on a guy who only ever sort of loved me. And you stood by and watched it happen. Were you letting me break him in first? Or do you enjoy watching people's hearts break over and over?" Lana asks.

This is exactly why I don't get involved in people's love lives. Somehow, they always blame me when things don't go the way they want.

Not backing down, I say, "It doesn't matter what I saw. Your feelings—or anyone else's for that matter—are none of my business. You have no idea how badly I wish I couldn't see what I do." I never would have made up a relationship with Fake August if I were normal and could have gotten a date on my own. And I sure as hell never would have had to see him kiss Shay like the sun rose and set just for her.

"I would kill for a gift like that. Being able to know instantly if the person you love loves you back."

"Yeah, until the answer to that question is always no."

Lana taps her lips, contemplating. "You must have seen something different with Ren though. Or maybe you just sensed he's vulnerable right now and decided to make him feel sorry that you both got yourselves dumped."

"Why? Because you don't think Ren would like someone like me?"

"No, but I refuse to believe I meant so little to him that he'd rebound with the first person who threw herself at him."

I don't get a chance to talk to Gemma until lunch. By then, practically the whole school knows about my kiss with Ren. Half of them probably witnessed it firsthand since I wasn't exactly worried about privacy this morning. Their speculation nips at me as I weave through the tables to the one Gemma and I usually share.

"Get it, Mo!"

"Think they hooked up over break?"

"If I'd known Ren was open for business, I'd have made damn sure I got to him first."

"How long do you think she's been planning to do that?"

"Lana said Mo basically admitted to stealing Ren from her."

"Maybe she's *the real reason Lana broke up with Ren."*

Despite the deafening chatter in the cafeteria, the whispers about Ren and me are somehow the loudest. Like they're hoping I'll hear and validate their theories. Give them something juicier to feast on. I keep my head down, not making eye contact with anyone, pretending I don't hear them.

I slide into the seat next to Gemma. "So I'm guessing you've heard."

"That you and Ren were making out in the quad this morning? Oh, yeah. That topic has been covered once or twice today," she says. Her tone is light, but there's something dark lurking beneath the words. Something that cuts deeper than everything anyone else is saying about me.

"I'm sorry I didn't tell you. I knew if I did, you'd wave around your Team August flag, and I didn't want you to make me feel guilty for kissing Ren."

She points at me with one of her carrot sticks, hummus dripping from the end. "If you're feeling guilty, that's all on you."

"I'm not." I have nothing to feel guilty for. No matter what people are saying, I didn't have a hand in breaking up Ren and Lana. And whatever I thought I had with August was all a lie. I don't owe him anything. Not after finding out he's still with Shay. I open my lunch bag and pull out my turkey, apple, and cheddar sandwich and bag of potato chips. "But I know you want me to talk to August, so me kissing Ren is not exactly something you'd be happy with."

"If I thought you kissed him because you wanted to, I'd be happy for you."

"Really? You wouldn't insist I give August a chance to explain?"

"I do think you should ask him what was going on with Shay. I just don't believe he'd want to be with her after what I saw over spring break. He's so into you, Mo. But," she says before I can interrupt and tell her she's wrong, "if he was lying and really is a piece of shit, I will fully support you dating someone else."

"But not Ren?" I ask.

"You can't honestly tell me that's what you want anymore."

I look around to make sure no one else can overhear. "You sound like Lana. Do you know she basically accused me of being a sadist before saying the only reason Ren likes me is because he's desperate?"

Gemma jerks one shoulder up in agreement. "Can you blame her? She walked in on the guy she dated for years kissing some other girl. You were crushed yesterday when you saw August with Shay, and you two are...whatever you are. So I'm kinda with Lana on this one."

"Me ending up with Ren was always part of the plan," I remind her.

"Initially, yeah. But then you fell for August, and the plan changed. You kissing Ren today was out of spite, not because you want to be with him."

I recoil from the truth in her words. Just because I'm mad at August doesn't mean I don't care about Ren too. "I *do* like him."

"I might believe you if you had maybe done it a little less publicly."

"It's not like I jumped him in the middle of class."

"You were trying to make a point. Prove August didn't hurt you," she says. "Or you were using Ren to make yourself feel better, which is even worse. Either way, it's not a good look."

I throw my untouched food back into my lunch bag, my appetite gone. "That's rich coming from the girl who won't admit her feelings to the person she likes because she's scared of what other people will say." It's the worst possible thing I could've said to her. Never mind that it's what I did with August before I realized he was still with Shay. I regret the words before they're even fully out of my mouth, but there's no way to stop the avalanche once it's started. "I'm so sorry. I didn't mean that."

Gemma bites into a carrot, the resulting snap like a shot fired, and pushes her chair back from the table. "No, you did. And that's fine. If you want to blow up your whole life within twenty-four hours, don't let me stop you."

"Gemma, c'mon. Please don't be mad at me."

"If you don't want people to be mad, maybe you should stop acting like the world revolves around you. Because some of us have more important things to do than hold your hand while you obsess over your fake boyfriend kissing his actual girlfriend. Maybe instead of dragging others into your mess, you could talk to August like I suggested last night. It's not my fault you don't like that option. It's certainly not Ren's. So either talk to August or don't, but leave the rest of us out of it."

I grab her arm to keep her from leaving. "You're right. I'm sorry, okay?"

"Okay," she says and sits back down. But the bitterness staining the word says she doesn't mean it.

"I mean it. I'll fix things with Ren. Promise."

Whether or not I want to fix things with August is still to be determined.

Chapter TWENTY-THREE

Love Rule #19: Give out the kind of love you want to receive.

My apology tour starts with Ren.

Not wanting a repeat of yesterday's very public display, I get to school early and wait for him in the parking lot. I wave when he gets out of his car, and he veers toward where I sit on the trunk of my car with two steaming cups of coffee and a to-go bag from Yeastie Boys for him.

Holding out my peace offering, I say, "Got a minute?"

"Hey," he says, his smile immediate but low-key. "I was gonna call you last night, but I wasn't really sure what that was yesterday. I mean, obviously it was a kiss. A good one. I just haven't kissed anyone but Lana in a really long time, so I started to second-guess myself and got all in my head about what you thought it meant. Did you want me to call you?"

As if this weren't awkward enough, Ren's nervous rambling takes it to a whole new level. I would say just about anything to put an end to his self-inflicted torture. But what he deserves after my behavior yesterday is the truth.

"No, I should have called you. To apologize. I'm so sorry for the kiss and for stressing you out about it. I had this theory that the best way for me to get over August was to move on with someone new. Which is why I kissed you. And it was a shitty thing to do to you, especially without warning or making sure it was something you wanted too. It was selfish and a mistake I promise I won't repeat."

"So I'm your rebound guy?" His face scrunches in hurt—or possibly relief—that the kiss wasn't entirely about him.

Whatever he's feeling, I rush to clarify. "No. Not at all. *Rebound* implies it's temporary, unimportant. And you are neither of those things. I kissed you because I've liked you for a long time, but kind of like how I got in your head yesterday, August got in mine. I thought I could get him out for good if you and I were more than friends."

He takes a big gulp of his coffee, not caring if he burns his mouth. It's the same thing he's done with every cup I've ever seen him drink. Like the second this thing he loves is in front of him, it commands his full attention. And what Lana considers being in a rut is actually Ren being content. He's found what he likes, and he sticks with it. That's how I knew what biscuit to bring him this morning without even thinking about it, but it didn't dawn on me until just now why Ren is so steady, so predictable.

"So you did want me to call. I'm such a jerk," he says.

"You are the furthest thing from a jerk that exists. Whatever that is, it's you. I'm the jerk in this scenario. That was a lot of pressure to put on you when I know you're not ready for a relationship this soon after Lana. And I clearly have my own August issues to work through. None of this is on you though. I really am sorry for dragging you into my mess."

"I don't know how long it'll take me to get over Lana, but you're right, I'm not there yet. I may not be there for a while because just thinking about her makes me feel like someone's trying to cut out my heart with a dull butter knife. Which is about as ineffective and painful as it sounds. It's not fair to ask you to wait for that stop, but when that does happen—and I have to believe it will at some point—if we're both in a place that we want to see where this goes, I'd be down for that."

"I would too," I say, resting my head on his shoulder. If nothing else, at least Ren and I became friends out of all this. I don't know what he's going through firsthand, but I can still be here for him. Do what I can to help him be happy again. Even if it's never going to be with me. Straightening, I realize something else about Ren. "If not being with Lana is that miserable, don't you think maybe that's a sign you should try to fix your relationship instead?" That flies in the face of everything I know about love. It *shouldn't* be true love if Lana could break his heart. And yet here I am rooting for Ren and Lana to prove me wrong.

"Not if being with me was as bad as she says. I want her to be happy, and I wasn't doing that for her. Not lately anyway." The paper bag crackles as his fingers tighten around it.

"She's miserable without you too."

"Lana told you that? Is that what y'all were talking about yesterday? I saw you together after, you know, but figured if it was about me, I was safer staying out of it."

I shake my head. "She didn't tell me, but I can see people's heartache, remember? While she may seem fine with everything, she's not. She was really pissed that I kissed you."

Ren's heartache flares around him, a teal so thick, it must feel like a hundred pounds weighing on him. "I wish I could believe her being jealous means something more, but it was probably a knee-jerk reaction after being together so long. I'd lose my mind if I saw her kissing someone else. But she made it clear she was done with me when we broke up. Even if I did think there was a chance I could get her back, it'll never happen because she won't even be in the same room with me long enough for me to try."

"Keep trying. She'll come around," I say. Though that's the tactic August is deploying with me, and I'm still holding firm in my decision to pretend he doesn't exist. So if Lana's half as stubborn, Ren will be waiting a while.

"Why are you trying to convince me there's still a chance for Lana and me?"

Looking him dead in the eye, I admit, "Everything with August has made me reevaluate my views on love. Maybe I didn't have it all right. Maybe the rules don't always apply."

"Maybe he just didn't know a good thing when he saw it," Ren says.

Ren wouldn't think that about me if he knew my whole relationship with August was made up. Or that me kissing him yesterday had less to do with him and more—okay, all—to do with seeing August and Shay together. "Maybe," I say, so far into this hole I've dug for myself, I can no longer see the light on the surface.

Apology stop number two: Gemma. I try to catch her in the couple of classes we have together, but she must have taken a master class in avoidance since yesterday, because she manages to evade me all morning. She sits with Greer at lunch. On a normal day, I'd be throwing her a one-person parade for making a move like that. Today it feels like a message: *I don't have the energy for your bullshit.*

There's space at the table, so I could join them—it's not like she's completely cut me out. But I'm not in the mood to sit there and pretend like everything's fine. And I can't exactly apologize with an audience.

Taking my lunch to the art room, I decide to focus on my portfolio instead of my imploding life. I don't have anything new to show Mrs. Clemente. Other than defacing the photo of August on Sunday, I haven't touched my project in days. I haven't even thought about it. If I don't get it together—*it* being both my shit and my portfolio—I'll have nothing to submit for the summer arts program in ten days.

Which might be for the best. Mrs. Clemente wasn't exactly

enthused about my portraits anyway. I don't want to find out they're not good enough with a rejection from my dream school. First impressions stick. It's smarter to skip the program this summer and put that time and effort into my portfolio for Kinsey's college submission instead. Maybe by the fall, I'll have an idea for how to give my work the wow factor it needs to stand out.

Now I just have to get Mrs. Clemente to agree. I find her in her office, the windows open despite the misty rain outside. The smell of acetone permeates the room, and her choice of natural air circulation makes sense. Looking up from her own lunch, she waves me in.

I dump my bag on the floor, careful to keep it away from the water accumulating under the windows. "I need you to be honest with me. Don't worry that you'll hurt my feelings. I know I don't always take criticism with the most open mind, but I really do value your opinion. So if you tell me I'm not good enough and I'm wasting my time and yours with this project, I'll scrap the whole thing and let it go."

Mrs. Clemente wraps her half sandwich so it doesn't dry out, her eyes narrowing in concern as she looks me over. "Where is this coming from? I know you don't want to do that. The Imogen Finch I know would do whatever it takes to prove me wrong about her work."

"What if you're *not* wrong?" I ask. I've been wrong about so many things in the past few weeks alone that I have to question everything now.

"What if I am and you believe me? I would have failed you as your teacher, and that's just unacceptable. So, I'll ask again, where is this coming from?"

I slump in a chair across from her and unload. "My judgment has been...questionable lately. Liking things I shouldn't like. Making rash decisions that end in disaster. Emotionally speaking." Remembering August's photo I painted for Gemma, I pull it out of my art bag as evidence of my bad decisions. "And some actual disaster too. Don't worry, no boys were harmed in the making of this monstrosity."

She takes the picture-painting from me, the look of awe she usually reserves for Gemma's work brightening her face. "What do you think is bad about this?" She runs her fingers over the layers of paint, literally feeling the emotion pouring off August.

"It's not so much the picture as the boy in it that riles me up enough to do that to one of my portraits."

"Well then, I think you need to be spending more time with him. This is stunning work, Mo. It's maybe a bit raw technique-wise, but the idea is fascinating."

I stare at her for a full five seconds as the words sink in. Then I'm still not sure I heard her correctly. "Wait. You like it?"

"I love it. Is this what you see when you're taking your photos? What you've been trying to convey in your pieces the whole time?"

"Yes to both."

Mrs. Clemente goes back to studying the picture, analyzing every swirl and dot of color. "And this is someone in love?"

"Yes," I say again.

A boy in love with a girl who isn't me.

"This is what you should be submitting as your portfolio. The colors and the paint add another layer of depth and movement that is exactly what will set you apart from the other photographers." She turns the picture to face me as if it's suddenly a work of art meant to be admired and not artistic catharsis.

I snatch it from her before August's smiling face can charm her any more than it already has. He has that effect on people. Muddles their thoughts until they think something's a good idea when it's not. "But it's no longer photography if I do that. I'm not a painter."

"No, you're an artist. And artists work with what they've got," she says. Sorting through the stack of photos, she handpicks a few shots and sets them aside. "Heartbreak is a different color, right? It's strange—now that I know what you're seeing, it's easier to pick up on the differences in the photos themselves. I'm guessing here, but these five seem like they'd provide the most contrast if you were to paint them. Side by side with your black and white portraits, these will make people stop and really look—really think—about your work and the message you're conveying."

This wasn't supposed to be part of my portfolio. And definitely not turn into my *entire* portfolio. "I think our wires got crossed here. I was showing you this as an example of my bad decisions, not as what I'm proposing to do."

Mrs. Clemente lays a hand on my arm, comforting yet firm. "You just said you trusted my opinion. Now I am telling you *this* is next-level art, bad decision or not. Just because it's not what you planned to do doesn't mean it's not what you should be doing. So, as an experiment, I'd like you to do this to one of your heartbreak photos. Let's just see what it looks like, okay?"

"My application is due in a week and a half. Isn't it too late to change it now?"

"It's only too late when the deadline passes. Until then, I want you to put every ounce of yourself into this project. I, for one, cannot wait to see what you end up with."

I should have known suggesting it was too late wouldn't fly with Mrs. Clemente. I hadn't expected her to let me back out of submitting something either, but painting over my photos feels a little like blasphemy.

Damn August for ruining this too.

Chapter TWENTY-FOUR

Love Rule #14: Don't go back to a relationship that wasn't working the first time around.

By Saturday, most everyone's forgotten my momentary lapse in judgment. Even Ren. He comes into Yeastie Boys with one of his friends, sits at a table in my section, and smiles at me like I didn't blow up his life for a few days this week.

"Morning, Mo. You're looking particularly resilient today," Evans says.

Ren leans across the table and punches Evans on the shoulder. "You said you'd be cool. That is the opposite."

Evans rubs his arm, his mouth quirking into a half smile. "She knows I'm just messing with her. Plus, not cool would have been to tell her if she wants to ambush kiss anyone today, I'm free. So I think I deserve a little credit for my restraint."

I back up a step in case he takes my proximity as an invitation. "Restraint, you say?"

He grins at me. At least he doesn't wink. I could not be

held responsible if he had and I dumped this pot of sizzling coffee on his lap. Waitressing rules.

"I'm sorry," Ren says to me. He shoots Evans a knock-it-off glare, and Evans's smile vanishes. "If you want us to go, just say so."

"You're good. But thanks," I say. And I mean it. Ren has every right to hate me after the past few weeks, but he's still here. Still treating me like a friend.

Which is more than I can say for Gemma. She called in today. Or rather she gave her dads some story about how she needed a few days off—for what, I don't know—and they agreed. She's taking avoiding me to a whole new level if she's ditching work.

If Ren can forgive me, I know Gemma will come around. The longest fight we've had was almost a month back in fourth grade when her dads took her to Colorado for a ski trip over Christmas. She begged them to take me too. I went behind her back and told them I didn't want to go. I didn't want to be away from Mom for the holidays. So they told her no, but she found out what I'd done and didn't talk to me until well into the new year.

Fingers crossed she lets go of this thing with Lana much quicker.

After taking their orders, I check on my other tables. We're in a bit of a lull, with fewer than half the tables filled. Normally, I'd chat up the customers or talk with Gemma as we took our time wiping down the empty tables or sweeping the front walk. Lee's favorite thing to say at work is, *If you have time to lean, you have time to clean.* Gabe stays on brand with, *You can't, you won't, and you don't stop.*

I ignore both this morning and sip a cup of cream-and-sugared coffee while leaning against the counter just out of sight from the kitchen. I straighten when a car pulls into the parking lot. The sun glares off the windshield, blinding me. Flinching, I slosh coffee down the front of my uniform and probably give my chest a first-degree burn. The curse that flies out of my mouth is enough to turn all heads in my direction. Lee's out front in a heartbeat, checking me over for blood or broken bones.

"The coffee's hot," I say and blot a bar rag to the brown stain down my front.

"You're supposed to drink coffee, not wear it, hon."

"Oh, so that's what I'm doing wrong?"

"Sarcasm is a good sign. You can't be dying if your comebacks are that quick." He cups both sides of my head and plants a kiss on my forehead. "Are you okay?"

Physically, yes. Emotionally, that's still up for debate. I nod to get him to back off. "I'm fine. It was an unpleasant surprise, but I'll live." Thankfully, the cream had cooled the coffee enough that it was only scalding and not melt-your-skin-off hot.

"I'm counting on it," he says.

With the damp fabric grating against my skin, I shoo Lee away to nurse my embarrassment in relative peace. Then the front door opens, adding insult to injury as a petite girl in all black walks inside. "Shay." Her name is out of my mouth before I can stop it.

Shay balls her hands at her sides and steps up to the counter in front of me. There's nothing bright about her now. Her heartbreak bursts like a rain cloud, shrouding her in shades of copper and teal. "Gotta admit I'm a bit shocked you're not pretending not to know who I am." Her expression tightens, her lips sharpening like daggers.

"What are you doing here?"

"My mom brought me," she says, pointing to the car that made me spill my coffee. "I wanted to be able to say this to your face."

My lungs remember how to work after a few seconds, though they burn with the effort. Whatever she has to say, I already know I don't want to hear it. But I want everyone else to hear it even less. I have to get her out of here as quickly as possible. "Maybe we should go outside." I take a few steps toward the door, but she crosses her arms over her chest, feet cemented to the spot.

"I'm good here." Shay checks to make sure she has an audience from the surrounding tables, then says, "There is seriously something wrong with you, you know that? What kind of a person pretends to date someone who, one, already has a girlfriend, and two, doesn't even know you're using him to make everyone think you're God knows what?"

Her words are like a grenade, pin pulled free. They come

at me, and all I can do is wait for the explosion. There is no outrunning it. No deflecting. No diving for cover.

Three.

Two.

One.

Kaboom.

Ren's table is a few feet away. Well within earshot, though I doubt there's a person in the restaurant who didn't hear Shay's damning accusation.

He stops eating midbite. His eyes lock on me, confusion and betrayal crinkling his forehead. "Who is she, and what is she talking about?"

"I'm August's *real* girlfriend," Shay says while I'm busy piecing myself back together. "Or I was until last weekend when he broke up with me because of Imogen. And I'm talking about how Imogen never dated August. That she made it all up. Their entire relationship was fake."

"But he was here for spring break. He was trying to talk to her about the breakup literally right there," Ren says, pointing to a spot a little farther away.

"Yeah, because he found out what she was doing," Shay says.

Defending myself is not an option, even if I wanted to. There's nothing to defend myself with. No way to justify what I did, and now everyone will know. But I won't go down without a fight a second time. I check over my shoulder for Lee, who is, thankfully, nowhere to be seen. If I can get her out of here, maybe I can contain the fallout. "You don't know the whole story. I'll tell you everything, but not in here."

Rolling her eyes toward Ren, she chews on her lip, like she senses he's the key to my destruction. "Only if he comes too. I need a witness to keep you honest."

"He doesn't know anything," I say. I'm desperate to keep it that way, but what choice do I have?

"He's about to," she counters. "If you want me to leave."

Ren's already pushing out of the booth, but I don't know if he's agreeing to her terms to help me or simply to learn the truth. "Mo?"

I nod, not trusting my voice to contain the panic trying to claw its way out of me. Shaking, I lead them outside.

"So let's hear it. What's this excuse you don't want to say in front of everyone inside?" Shay asks.

I hate myself for taking August down with me, but he's not innocent in this either. If the truth is coming out, I want it to be the *whole* truth. "August already knew."

Shay stares at me, her eyes all wrath and destruction. "Excuse me?"

"He knew about being my fake boyfriend for months. He only confronted me about it when I ended it."

Ren forms a T with his hands for a time-out. "I'm so lost. Did you or didn't you date August?"

"I didn't," I say. My voice is simultaneously a whisper and a wail. All the secrets I've been holding in, all the lies I've told, amplify my admission tenfold.

"So she's right about you making it all up? All the posts and the romantic surprises and everything? That was all you?" Ren asks, recoiling a step like I've slapped him.

Hugging my arms over my chest, I try to hold myself together. But the cracks are too big, the damage too extensive to keep the truth from pouring out. "None of it was real. I mean, August is real, and I do know him. But he was never my boyfriend. I made it all up."

"Why?"

Shay makes a strangled sound and shoves the sleeves of her hoodie up past her elbows. Faded black marker that looks suspiciously like a poem circles one forearm. "It doesn't matter why. She did it. And because of her, August dumped me."

"I had nothing do with your breakup. He wasn't happy. He said you weren't happy either," I say. He said so much more. About their relationship and how she'd made him feel like he wasn't enough. About how I had felt more real to him than she did. Was that all a lie? "But when I saw you with him the other day, you both seemed like you were back together and things were good. You were kissing."

"We weren't *back together* because we hadn't broken up yet. What you interrupted was him in the actual act of breaking up with me because he fucking *likes* you."

My brain spins, trying to make sense of what she's saying. I mentally flip back through everything August said to me about Shay. It's all fragments. Half-truths. He said as little as possible and let me fill in the details. "No, he made it seem like y'all broke up months ago."

"Looks like you're not the only liar then," she says.

If they only broke up this week, then August was still dating her when he was here. When he kissed me.

Love rule twenty-three: Following the whims of your heart when the feelings are fleeting will only end in pain.

Ren, who's been quiet since he asked me why, breaks his silence. "What the hell, Mo? Is that why you kissed me out of the blue? Because you saw her with August and wanted to get back at him?"

"No, it wasn't like that." Except it was exactly like that. Even if I didn't consciously mean for it to be. Turning my back on Shay, I give Ren my full attention. I have to make him hear me. Believe me. "I told you I've liked you for a long time. That was true. I do like you. When you and Lana broke up, I thought I might finally have the chance to show you that you could like me back. August was never supposed to be more than a ghost in my life. Something people believed existed but never actually encountered."

"But he's more than that," he says.

"Are you even listening to yourself?" Shay demands. "How can you possibly justify faking a relationship with someone, let alone using him as an excuse when you get caught?"

"I'm sorry. For all of it," I say, spinning back to face her. "I didn't know he had a girlfriend, and then when he came here over spring break and I found out about you, he said it was over. I honestly thought you were broken up, or I would never have started anything with him."

"Apology not accepted."

"Then what do you want?" I ask.

"I want everyone to know what kind of person you are. That you're a liar and a manipulator and a really shitty person with no respect for other people's relationships. With the way you've been recruiting recently dumped people for your photography project, I think that's something they should know before you fuck with their lives too. I wouldn't put it past you to have orchestrated a few of those breakups so you had more people willing to take part." She turns to Ren, who's digging his keys out of his pocket to leave. "Looks like at least one person is smart enough to see the light."

"Ren, that's not true. About my project, I mean. I would never purposely ruin someone's relationship."

He looks me up and down, as if he's trying to find some small piece of me he recognizes. His eyes are cold when they meet mine. "Maybe not, but you sure as hell took advantage of it. Of me. What is wrong with you?"

I reach for him but stop short of touching him. Whatever friendship we formed is broken along with the rest of me. "I'm sorry. I didn't mean for any of this to happen."

"It doesn't matter what you meant to do. What matters is what you *did* do. That's what shows what kind of person you are. And you are not a good person, Imogen," Shay says.

As much as I don't want it to be true, I think she may be right.

Chapter TWENTY-FIVE

Love Rule #1: True love doesn't break hearts.

"What was all that?" Lee asks when I come back inside. Half the diner's watching me, all pretense of eating gone in favor of a spectacle. "Everything okay?"

"I'm sorry," is all I can say in response.

After a fierce hug, he sends me on break. He says it's so I can go take care of myself, but he probably just doesn't want me crying in front of the customers I haven't run off yet. It's bad for business. Then again, so is having all my worst secrets exposed to diners over their breakfast.

I'm shaking when I get out to my car. Despite the relative privacy of the parking lot, I struggle to get my breathing under control. The air in the car is sun warmed and stuffy and not at all helpful. Cracking the windows, I let in a small breeze. Maybe it's the heat. Or the rush of adrenaline slowly fading from my system after my encounter with Shay. Or maybe I just need an excuse—any excuse—to vent my frustration onto someone else. I grab my phone and shoot off a message to August.

MoGlows: I met Shay today. Our conversation was very enlightening.

TheRealAugust: Shit.

TheRealAugust: What did she say?

TheRealAugust: Actually, I don't care. I just want to tell you my side.

TheRealAugust: I'm going to call.

TheRealAugust: Please pick up.

I'm so used to the way August messages now, I don't bother trying to respond until multiple messages come through. This time I wait too long. My phone's ringing, and I stare at his picture filling the screen.

"I don't want to hear your side," I say when I answer.

"Hi," he says. It's relief and surprise and something I can't quite place.

"Don't do that."

"Do what? All I said was 'hi.'"

The tears I've been holding off sense my weakness and make a play for domination. Pinching my eyes shut, I press a finger and thumb to the inner corners to keep from losing this battle. When I'm sure my voice is steady, I say, "Don't make me regret picking up."

"Why did you?" He sounds so normal. So *August*. Like

everything we felt for each other when we kissed is still there. Unchanged.

He's such a good liar, even he believes what he's saying.

But not me. Not anymore.

"Because I'm really pissed, and it will be so much easier to say all this than to type it," I say.

"I'm sorry. About Shay. For what you saw when you were here and for her messaging you. I don't know what she told you—"

"She didn't message me. She showed up at my work today and proceeded to tell me and anyone within earshot about what a psycho she thinks I am and how you were still together this whole time even though you let me believe it's been over for a while. And suddenly things started to make sense. Like how Owen stopped himself from saying her name when I was around. Or why your heartbreak wasn't that strong when you talked about her. Was that payback for me lying about us dating?"

"No. Of course not," he says, panic making his words run together. "Everything I told you about Shay was true, except that we hadn't technically broken up. But the relationship was done. We'd barely seen each other in weeks."

"But you were still with her," I say.

"I didn't want to be."

"Then why were you?"

"Because I didn't want to have to tell her I was falling for someone else. Or that the girl I was falling for had made up some fictional version of me that felt more real than the me I was with Shay." August goes quiet. I don't fill the silence. He wanted to tell his side of things, and I'm not going to make it easy on him. Not after what I just went through with Shay. Eventually, he says, "I did tell her though. That's what I was doing the day you came up. And the kiss you saw, she caught me off guard, that's all. She was trying to get me to change my mind, but I don't want to be with her."

I want to believe him. If I were anyone else, I probably would. But I'm not. And I can't forget what I saw. "You do though. When you were with her, I could see how much you love her. Present tense. She lights you up even if you don't realize it."

"No, that wasn't because of Shay. It was you. I told her everything. About meeting you two years ago and about spending spring break with you and realizing the way you and I are together is the relationship I want. It's what I was always chasing with her, but I was never going to get it because she's not you."

"Why did you lie to me then? Why not tell me you were still with Shay so I wouldn't kiss you?" *Or fall for your cheating ass.*

Mom may think you can love two people at the same time, but she wouldn't have her love rules if that were true.

And if August didn't want to be with Shay—with or without me in his life—he should have been brave enough to end things before starting anything with me.

"I didn't plan to lie to you. I knew things with Shay weren't working, but I didn't know if it was something I could fix. Or something I wanted to fix. So when you came to apologize and I told you about her, you assumed Shay and I were broken up because you could see how sad she made me. I let you think that because I wanted to know what you thought I should do without anything other than my emotions guiding you. Then we started talking, and I didn't want to stop. So being a part of your project seemed like a good way to do that. I know I should have told you the truth, but being with you was so easy, I forgot it wasn't real."

I have no right to be mad at him after what I've done. But I am. Thanks to him I'm the type of girl I never wanted to be. The type who ruins love for someone else just so I can be happy. It doesn't matter that I didn't do it on purpose. Shay still blames me.

I still blame me.

"That doesn't make it okay to cheat on your girlfriend. Or to make me complicit in said cheating," I say. The tears finally win, spilling out faster than I can wipe them away. My words follow suit. "And now everyone's going to know that not only did I lie about dating you, I've also screwed over your real girlfriend in the process. Her mom drove her all the way here just so she could confront me in person and make sure she told as many people as possible. Ren was sitting right there. Now he knows the only reason I kissed him was because I saw you kissing Shay, and he's pissed."

August sucks in a breath like I've punched him. "You kissed Ren?"

"That's what you're taking away from all that?"

"You just told me you willfully kissed another guy two weeks after I kissed you. How am I supposed to ignore that?"

He cheats on his girlfriend, yet somehow me kissing another guy is a problem? Fuck that. I don't owe him anything. "Because the girl *you* kissed is trying to ruin my life."

"I kinda think you did that all on your own, Mo."

"If that's what you think, then I guess whatever this was is officially over. You can tell Shay you're all hers."

I hang up before he can respond. I can't let August's feelings sway me. Not again.

I thought Gemma would have reached out after everything went down with Shay this morning, but it's been radio silence. Enough is enough. I need my best friend, even if she doesn't want me. After punching in my code into the electronic door lock on her front door, I let myself into the house. The McCallie family's nineteen-year-old Norwegian forest cat, Sir Stewart Wallace, opens one eye to glare at me for interrupting his sleep. But when I stop to scritch under his chin, he rolls over to offer me his belly. I bury my face in the fluffy gray fur.

"Why are you the only one who can do that without him clawing your face off?" Gemma asks, coming into the living room.

I straighten, tears springing to my eyes at the sound of her voice. She's in the tie-dye coveralls she always sculpts in, and her hair is in two messy knots on either side of her head. Looks like I interrupted her too. "I know you're still mad at me, but can I just stay here tonight? You don't even have to talk to me."

"Of course you can. And I'm not still mad." Gemma opens her arms for a hug then reconsiders, brushing at the flecks of bark, mud, and sand caked on her clothes.

At least I think that's why she backs off from physical contact. "Really? Because you have a funny way of showing it. You've been avoiding me all week."

"I've just been working on this piece I really want to finish so I can include it in my portfolio. It's consumed me for days. That's why I haven't been at work. It has nothing to do with you. I promise."

"I thought your dads were just saying that so you didn't have to be around me," I say.

"That's the stupidest thing I've ever heard." She pokes my forehead as if she's trying to knock the stupid out.

I swat her hand away, fighting a laugh. "Well, it's not like you've tried to get in touch since our fight."

"Arting, remember? And you haven't exactly been lighting up my phone either."

"Because you were mad at me. I was giving you space to calm down."

Unzipping the front of her coveralls, she strips down to

her tank top underneath, leaving the bottom half in place. She drapes a blanket over the couch and throws herself down onto it. I take my usual spot on the other sofa across from her. Her dads moved in two chairs years ago so they had a place to sit when we took over the couches with pillows and blankets and buckets of popcorn for our frequent movie nights.

"So what made you come over here tonight?" she asks, turning her head to look at me.

How is it possible she doesn't know? Didn't Lee tell her what happened when he got home? "Are you building your sculpture underground?"

"I take it I missed something."

"You could say that. Shay—August's Shay—came into the café today and told Ren and everyone else there that I lied about August. Now Ren hates me. And I got into a fight with August, and we're done. Like, that bridge is now just a smoking pile of ash. Which is a nice metaphor for my entire life, really."

She sits up so fast, she rolls off the edge of her couch. Kneeling on the floor with the blanket tangled around her head, she says, "Why the hell didn't you tell me? Even if I were still mad at you, I would have happily redirected my anger at any one of them."

I should've come to her days ago. It wouldn't have stopped Shay from showing up and telling everyone I'm a big fat liar, but at least I would've had my best friend by my side while it happened. I lean over the edge of the couch and stretch to grip her hand across the coffee table.

"It's not Shay's fault. Don't get me wrong, I'm not happy she came and blew up my life, but apparently August lied to me about her, so when I saw them kissing, he was in the process of breaking up with her. And he told her all about me and that he was breaking up with her to be with me. So she kind of has every right to hate me."

"Okay, that's a lot to unpack." Climbing back onto the sofa, Gemma lays it all out to make sure she's following, and then says, "So your secret's finally out in the open, your dream boy says he wants to date you, and you still managed to find some reason to turn him down?"

There's no use arguing with her. I don't come out looking good in any scenario. "Basically. But I have good reason not to date him. Did you skip the part of the story where he kissed me when he was still dating Shay?"

"No, I heard you. Still processing it all. I seriously can't believe I missed all this."

"At least you'll have a portfolio to submit by the deadline," I say, grabbing on to any subject change. I came here to get away from reminders of everything that's going wrong, not sink further in.

"Yeah, I guess setting your life on fire makes it hard to focus on your photos."

"Hey, maybe I could burn them, in an artistic way, and turn my portfolio into a physical embodiment of that life-on-fire metaphor. Do you think Mrs. Clemente would go for that, or is it still too safe?"

"You are not burning your photos. Though it would look sick." With her legs crossed underneath her, she props her elbows on her knees and steeples her fingers under her chin, studying me. "Now that I'm mostly caught up, I can start dumping water on whatever fires you need me to."

"I hope you have a lot of buckets," I say. But there might not be enough water in the world to contain the wildfire I've started.

Chapter TWENTY-SIX

Love Rule #11: Love should fill you up, not consume you.

I've spent most of the day Sunday staring at Ren's photo, trying to get up the nerve to paint his heartbreak. I don't know if it's because I chose his photo as my experiment or if it's just that I have no desire to test this ridiculous theory, but I can't make myself pick up the paintbrush.

It doesn't help that I keep looking at August's latest poem, wishing things were different between us.

I took a screenshot of it in case he can somehow track every time I view one of his posts. It's by far the most viewed photo on my phone. I don't want to think about what that says about me. Nothing good, I imagine.

emptiness
dark
And
heavy
filling
me
up

After flicking the paintbrush across the table, I lean over and beat my head against the cool wood.

It takes me a minute to realize the knocking sound that continues once I've stopped is someone at the studio door trying to get my attention.

Great, now I have an audience for my existential crisis.

Mom leans in the open door, concern pinching her forehead. "It's going that badly, huh?"

"The photos or my life? Because either one applies here," I say.

"I meant the photos, but if you're ready to talk about everything else, I'm good with that too."

Lee called Mom about Shay before I left the parking lot. She was waiting for me at home for the full download when I eventually left Gemma's. As word spread through town over the weekend about what I'd done, my Instagram flooded with comments calling me a liar and a fake and a hypocrite. I set my account to private and deleted the comments, but the damage was already done. Mom's been checking on me multiple times a day, like she doesn't want to be too far away in case I break and she needs to pick up the pieces.

"What's there to talk about?" I ask. "It's not like what everyone's saying about me isn't true. I screwed up, and now I'm living with the consequences."

She sits on the sofa, patting the cushion next to her for me to join her. When I do, she curls her arm around me. "I know you didn't mean to hurt anyone. And it's good that you're taking responsibility for your actions. It'll take some time for people to trust you again, but they'll see you're sorry, and you'll be able to move past this."

The only person I'm worried about not forgiving me is Ren. My romantic feelings for him may be gone, but I still care about him as a friend. And I don't want him to hate me. Tipping my head onto her shoulder, I let my worry spill out. "What if they can't? What if I've ruined everything?"

"The people who really care about you will give you another chance even when you don't think you deserve it." A cloud of teal manifests around her, pulsing with regret. She rubs at her chest as if to dispel it.

"Maybe you should take your own advice," I say.

"About what?"

"About second chances and Alex. That's who you were just thinking about, isn't it? I can see how much it hurts you not to let yourself be with him. You can't help who you fall in love with, remember?"

Mom goes rigid next to me, and I lift my head to look at

her. Pulling away, she stands, like she can't bear the thought of touching me. "Don't try to use my rules against me, Imogen. You see what you want to see. I know I push love on my clients like it's the ultimate achievement in life, but that's because it's what they come to me for. I thought I raised you to have a better sense of the world than that. To see there's more to life than romance because that can be taken away in an instant."

Is she serious right now? I wait a beat for her to backtrack or clarify what she means. When she does neither, I say, "How could I possibly think anything is more important than love? It's all you've ever made me believe. Made me *want*. You can't try and walk it back now just because you're scared to find love again."

Mom walks out of the studio without responding. Not even a goodbye. Which is fine with me. If that's how she really feels about love, I have nothing left to say to her anyway.

I overhear Mom on the phone with Alex after she thinks I've gone to bed. He had a date with Delaney last night that ended without dessert or the promise of breakfast in bed tomorrow. From my mom's side of the conversation, it sounds like he finally told Mom how he feels about her. I catch phrases like "we can't do this again" and "no, I can't say it was a mistake, but it was wrong." Then: "Imogen already thinks there's something between us. It's best if we end things here."

Whatever happened between them, Mom is determined to keep it from me. But why?

The next morning, Mom's in back-to-back meetings with clients, which means I have a small window to get to Alex and find out what she's not telling me before school alerts her to my absence. Thankfully, he's staying at the same B and B as his past few trips, so he's not hard to find. It's early enough that he's still eating breakfast in the dining room. I say hi to Mrs. Wareham and accept the cup of coffee she offers when I say I'm there to see Alex.

Alex looks up from his plate of scrambled eggs and toast, a bite of egg and sourdough speared on his fork. We haven't officially met, but it's clear from the way he's staring at me, all wide-eyed and cautious, that he knows who I am. "Does your mom know you're here?"

"No. She's not very happy with me right now." Understatement of the year. I hesitate in the doorway of the dining room, trying to gauge if he blames me for Mom cutting ties. He hasn't thrown his breakfast plate at my head or called Mrs. Wareham to escort me out, so I take a step inside. "Can we talk?"

"Of course. Come sit." He scoots out the chair next to him. The table's large enough to seat ten, though he's the only guest here this morning.

I watch the tendrils of steam curling off my coffee, unsure where to start. How do you ask someone if they're in love with your mother? Short answer, you don't. Not straight off anyway. That's something you ease into. Or come at sideways so they're caught off guard enough to answer honestly.

"I'm sorry about my mom," I say. Good manners always put grown-ups at ease. "We've been arguing about a lot of things lately, and I think she's taking it out on you."

"This isn't your fault. If I'd stayed out of your lives, I wouldn't have dredged up a lot of old feelings she thought were behind her. She has every right to be upset with me."

Not true. All he's done is confess his feelings for my mom. Mom's the one making this into a big deal by refusing to acknowledge her own. I wrap my hands around the coffee mug, wishing the heat could burn away the unease Mom's words last night—both to me and to Alex—churned up. "Why did you ask my mom to help you find love? I overheard you talking to her during your first match meeting, and it seemed like maybe you came here for a different reason."

Alex clears his throat, then seems to think better of answering me. "I think that's something you should discuss with your mom."

"I've tried," I say. It's all lies and deflection when I try to get a straight answer about Alex. "She refuses to admit there's anything between you two, but I can see it. It's so obvious, she has to see it. To *feel* it. I just want to know why she's lying to me."

"I don't think she's lying to you. Not on purpose."

"The result is the same."

"True. But that doesn't cancel the intent," he says, his tone firm but not unkind. His heartbreak aura is so faint, I almost miss it. The watery teal is shot through with copper and rose gold like stubborn bits of glitter, catching the light and demanding attention. "Your mom is just trying to protect you."

No, she's trying to protect herself. But since he's taking her side, I appeal to the part of him that's still in love with her. "From what? Seeing her happy? Because I can't think of any reason why her being in love with someone for the first time since my dad died is a bad thing."

"You're right. That's not a bad thing. But being in love with me isn't easy for your mom. And I'm not sure it will make her happy."

"That doesn't make any sense," I say.

He leans back, the wooden chair creaking beneath him as if the weight of his sadness is becoming too much to bear. "I was your dad's friend."

That's one of the few things Mom did tell me about him. "Which means he cared about you. That makes you a better option for my mom, not a worse one."

"Your mom doesn't see it that way."

I roll my eyes. I come by my stubbornness naturally. "Why not? He's gone. It's not like she's cheating on him with you."

Alex chokes on his coffee. Thumping a fist to his chest, he coughs, and his heartbreak deepens, chasing away all traces of love. He hangs his head as if ashamed as the dark teal hue riots around him.

There's only one reason the idea of them cheating would cause that visceral of a reaction.

"Wait. She didn't cheat on my dad, right? You two were just friends. That's what she said. She *loved* my dad."

"She did love him. So did I." He leans forward, clasping his hands on the table. Praying for mercy or begging for forgiveness, I can't tell. "We didn't mean for anything to happen between us, but it did. And then your dad died, and she was convinced it was her fault. That it was her punishment for how we felt about each other, and she ended things. God, I shouldn't be telling you this." He slumps back in the chair again, dragging both hands through his hair.

What.

The.

Fuck?

Suddenly, Mom's reluctance to admit her feelings for Alex makes sense. She's not afraid of falling in love with him. She's scared she never *stopped* loving him. Is that why she told me it was possible to love two people at once? Because she loved my dad *and* Alex?

In this moment it doesn't matter. She cheated on my dad and spent every day since he died making me believe her love for him is what got her through the pain of losing him. Such a liar. I guess I take after her in that too.

"No, you shouldn't have slept with my mother. Period. Full stop."

"I know. I tell myself that every day, but I've never loved anyone the way I loved her. I know that doesn't make it right, but I need you to know that. It wasn't a casual, careless thing between us."

"Is that why you came here? To convince her to give you another chance?"

"I hoped enough time had passed that we could both let go of our guilt and see if our feelings were there. I knew mine were—I never stopped loving her—but she was so angry with me, with us, that there was a chance she'd never forgive me. I needed to know definitively if I'm holding out hope for something that'll never happen." Defeat hangs heavy on him, drags the words down until there's nothing left.

I get the feeling he's already told me as much as he's going to, so most of the questions burning holes in my internal organs will stay there smoldering until they die out. But there's one that licks higher than the rest, desperate for air. "Did he know?" I ask.

"Your dad? No, I don't think so."

"I guess the universe did him a favor by killing him before he found out."

"Imogen—" he warns. His sense of duty to my dad is alive and well despite its convenient disappearance where my mom is concerned.

I shove back from the table, sending his breakfast plate—the food still half-eaten—and our coffee mugs clattering against the wood. "It's awful, but it's true. Finding out about your affair would have broken his heart."

It also explains why Mom's heart didn't break when Dad died. It's not that hearts don't break when it's true love. It's that she'd already given it to someone else.

Chapter TWENTY-SEVEN

Love Rule #3: Finding true love requires taking risks.

I've missed first period. If I head to school right now, I have a good shot at convincing them it was just car trouble. But going to school today would be one long lesson in torture now that I know the truth.

I trip over Mom's yoga mat that she left by the back door when I come inside the house, catching myself on the washing machine. The metal groans under my weight. So much for the element of surprise.

"Mo, is that you?" she calls from the kitchen.

"I thought you had meetings this morning." I brandish the mat like a shield, a barrier to keep Mom from getting too close.

"After the first one, I decided to push the second one so I could go to a class and center myself again." She finishes filling her water bottle at the fridge door and tucks it into the tote bag on the counter with her towel. Like it's any other day. Any other conversation we've had a million times. If she's holding a grudge from our fight last night, she's hiding it well. "Speaking of class, shouldn't you be in school right now?"

"Are we really going to pretend like everything's fine?"

"No, but the whole point of me doing yoga is to calm down and let go of all the negativity surrounding me right now. I don't see a point in winding myself up right before I go."

Any other day, I'd hold my tongue, let her get in a better frame of mind before dumping my shit on her. Not today. Not after learning she's been lying to me most of my life. "I talked to Alex," I say. The words fall like bombs, exploding one after another in rapid succession. I let loose a second wave. "I know about your affair."

She drops the bag to the counter, all the fight draining from her. When she looks at me, her eyes are wet. "I'm so sorry, sweetie. I didn't want you to find out that way."

"No, you didn't want me to find out at all."

"You're right. I never wanted you to know about that part of my life. I was so ashamed of what I'd done, of how I felt about Alex. And then to lose your dad..."

All the heartache and pain that's been building inside me breaks free. It lashes out, desperate to make her feel the same. "All your rules about love, were they a way to rewrite history? To make yourself believe you loved Dad?"

"I did love your dad. So much."

"Not enough if you fell in love with someone else," I say, unable to stop myself. Or maybe I just don't want to hold back. We've both been lying for so long, it feels good to finally tell the truth. Say what I'm actually feeling.

Mom's face flushes. Sinking to a stool, she drops her head in her hands and takes a few deep breaths before responding. "Love isn't that simple. Sometimes you can love someone, really love them with everything you have, and it's not enough. Your heart still wants more. If you find the person who fills you and satisfies your heart after you've already committed to someone else, you have a tough choice to make. Unfortunately, there's no right answer in that situation. Someone always gets hurt. I didn't set out to hurt your dad or to break my vows to him, but what I felt for Alex was too strong to ignore. I wish I was stronger back then. I wish I could have fought harder for your dad and for our marriage and for you to have two parents who loved each other as much as they loved you. But I wasn't. And I didn't." Her voice gives out under the pressure of so much truth. The tears she's held back for so long spill over and race over her cheeks. She wipes them away as if they've betrayed her.

"You were supposed to be with Alex the night Dad died, weren't you? When you danced me around the living room? That's why you were glowing. It wasn't for Dad. It was because you were in love with Alex and he was coming over." As soon as I say it, I know it's true. And I hate her for it. "My whole life, that's the image I clung to about what real love looked like, and it was all a lie. You made me think love was the most important thing in the world. That your love for him made you strong enough to carry on when he died. But it was never him. Did you even care that he died, or were you happy because then you didn't have to make the choice to leave him?"

My anger ignites hers, her sadness burning up until there's not even a trace left. When she lifts her head to look at me, her expression is so dark, I almost don't recognize her. "Don't you ever say that again. From the second I got the call that your dad had been in an accident, I was devastated. I would have given anything to save him, to have him back with us."

She doesn't get to say that. Not after she chose another guy over him. I drop her yoga mat. It unspools between us, all words of forgiveness rolling out of my grasp with it. "It's a shame you didn't feel that way before he died."

It's cruel and unfair. But I can't make myself care. I can't take it back or say I'm sorry. I can't see her side. Not when Dad's gone and she's still in love with someone else.

"I understand you're upset, but I am still your mother, and that kind of attitude is not going to cut it." Mom's voice is sharp enough to rip a hole in the atmosphere. But the flash of teal aura softens her anger. "There's not a day that goes by when I don't regret what I did. If I could go back in time and change things, I would. But I can't, so I've had to find a way to move on and make a life for both of us."

"You say you'd change things, but if that were true, you wouldn't still be in love with Alex."

Mom reaches for me, but I step back, holding my hands up to ward off more attempts. She says, "I learned the hard way that just because your heart wants something doesn't mean you have to give in to it."

"You are such a hypocrite, Mom. You spout all these rules for finding true love, but you turned your back on it. Don't you get how that makes it even worse? You cheated on Dad with one of his friends, and it was all for nothing. You didn't love him enough *not* to cheat on him, but you also didn't love the other guy enough to make it worth ruining multiple lives. At least if you'd been willing to own up to it and fight for Alex, I might still have some respect for you. You tell your clients to believe in love. You *make* them believe in it. But it's all a lie because the kind of love you sell isn't real. You don't even know what that looks like anymore."

Now neither do I. Maybe I never did.

Skipping school is one thing, but I can't bail on my evening shift at Yeastie Boys. Emotional identity crisis be damned.

It's a slow night, but I'll do anything to keep from having to go home and face Mom. The café closes for a day in the spring and again in the fall every year for a deep clean. We're only a month out from the most recent cleaning day, so there's not much grime accumulated yet for me to work out my aggression on. Not that this stops me from trying. There's got to be some hidden grease buildup in the kitchen that I can tackle. If not, I'm not above creating a mess just so I have something to focus on that's not my life.

As I dig in the supply closet for cleaners, I accidentally knock half a dozen sleeves of to-go cups to the floor. The shelves are crammed so full, I can't fit them back into place without jostling something else loose.

Hello, distraction.

I drop the cups back to the floor and start pulling everything else from the closet too. There's so much crap piling around me that any attempt at sorting it is moot within minutes. At this rate, I'll be here all night. But I'll have plenty of time to figure out how to organize it while I'm fitting it all back in. It'll also delay me having to go home.

Only about half the closet is emptied when Gabe calls my name from down the hall. It's a mix of exasperation and pity. Like he can't fully commit to being annoyed with me because he knows how pathetic I am. I step over the stacks I've made, careful not to send anything toppling, and join him.

Gabe pulls me into a half hug. "Don't think your initiative isn't appreciated, but blocking the path to the restrooms is probably something better done when we don't have customers in house."

I scan the cluttered hallway, mentally calculating how fast I can clean it up. Not fast enough. "Sorry. My organizing got a little out of hand."

"This is what you call organizing?" He nudges a pile with his foot, and it wobbles, threatening to crash.

His teasing is well founded. There is nothing orderly about this. "I'll get it cleaned up," I assure him.

"Want to talk about it?"

"About what?"

"Your recent life choices that sent you on this emotional cleaning spiral," he says.

I'm sure he's heard enough of what I've done to piece together something resembling the truth. But I appreciate him not pointing it all out in detail. Especially since *my* choices are not at fault for once. "Not really." Gabe knew my dad. Which means there's also a good chance he knew about my mom's affair. And that, like her, he's been lying to me this whole time. If that's the case, I don't want to know. There are only so many hits I can take before I'm down for good. "Thanks for the offer though."

He presses a kiss to my hair like he's done my whole life. Like I'm his bonus daughter. And the tears I've been running from all day finally catch up to me. I swipe at my eyes, a useless attempt to stem the flow, and hold my breath until my lungs burn. When forced to choose between breathing and crying, the human body will always side with survival. It takes me another few deep breaths to get myself under control. Only a few customers notice. Gabe doesn't try to move me to a less public area, but he does turn so he's blocking their view of my meltdown. It's not even a question that he's doing it to protect me, not the café.

"You go on home. I'll finish things here," he says, releasing me.

"I'm okay. Really," I lie.

"No, you're *really* not."

I glare at him, but with my tear-streaked face, I doubt

its effectiveness. "Well, I was okay until you came out and fathered me." I nudge him with my elbow and scrub my cheeks with the heels of my hands to remove the lingering traces of salt drying on my skin.

"This ill-fated organization attempt, if it can even be called an attempt, says otherwise."

"I wasn't crying before you interrupted."

"Maybe you should have been." With his hands on my shoulders, Gabe steers me into the kitchen and sits me on the stool in the corner. "Seems like you're in need of a good cry. And a shortcake."

Strawberry shortcake is what he always made Gemma and me when we were little to cheer us up. Scraped knee? Shortcake. Bad grade? Shortcake.

Realizing your life is a lie? Shortcake.

"I wouldn't say no to that," I say. I even manage a small smile.

He boxes up one of the jumbo biscuits and spoons heaps of macerated strawberries into a separate container so it's not all soggy by the time I get it home. It makes it as far as the car. I take a few bites while still in the parking lot, hoping its comforting flavors will get a head start on regulating my emotions. By the time I get home ten minutes later, I'm calm. My nerves finally relent enough that I can think clearly. I still sneak in through the side gate to avoid my mom in the house though.

It's going to take more than shortcake to fix what's wrong with us.

I curl into the corner of the couch in the studio. The cushions are worn, conforming to my body like a hug. I break out my partially eaten biscuit and dump the strawberries over them. After forking up a bite, I dip it in the container of whipped cream and send up a silent thank-you to Gabe for knowing I needed this. The strawberries are a sweet burst of flavor on my tongue. The biscuit is so fluffy and buttery, it practically melts in my mouth. It's impossible to be in a bad mood when eating shortcake.

The reprieve doesn't last long. My phone buzzes with a notification, reminding me I can't hide from the world forever.

TheRealAugust: Are you okay?

TheRealAugust: Your mom called my mom. I guess she thought I could help you.

TheRealAugust: Sounded like some shit went down with y'all.

TheRealAugust: I know we're fighting, but I'm worried about you.

TheRealAugust: Please just let me know you're okay.

I'm still raw from my argument with Mom and not in the mood to rehash it with August of all people.

MoGlows: Turns out I'm surrounded by cheaters. Compared to my mom, your offense isn't that bad. Congratulations!

TheRealAugust: Shit. So not okay, then.

TheRealAugust: What can I do?

MoGlows: Nothing. There's nothing anyone can do.

TheRealAugust: I'm calling.

MoGlows: I'm not picking up.

TheRealAugust: Yes, you are.

TheRealAugust: If you didn't want to talk to me you wouldn't have messaged me back.

He's got me there. I *do* want to talk to him. There's something about the way August sees the world that brings things into focus. Getting his perspective on this might help me figure out what to do. How to move forward when everything I thought about love is a lie.

When the phone rings, I answer. "Don't think this means we're good," I say.

August laughs, and it's like a cooling salve on my hot skin. "I wouldn't dream of it. But seriously, how are you? That stuff with your mom—the cheating—that sounds shitty."

A sharp laugh escapes me. "'Shitty' is a mild way of putting it. She was having an affair when my dad died. The *day* he died. But it gets better because she was sleeping with his best friend, who's now back in her life, and they're still in love with each other. Like my dad dying was an inconvenient thirteen-year interruption to their happiness."

"Wow. Okay, that is not what I was expecting. And you

needing to talk to someone about it, even if it is me, makes much more sense."

"How am I supposed to forgive her?" How am I supposed to believe anything she's said about love when she's broken every one of her rules?

"You're going to have to see it from her perspective. Do you think she loved your dad?"

A few days ago, I would have emphatically said yes. Or, more likely, I would have gone all Hulk smash on whoever had asked that for even implying anything to the contrary. Now there's too much doubt. "I think so. So yes?"

"And do you think she purposely set out to hurt him by falling in love with someone else?"

"No," I say. My mom made a seriously bad decision, but she's not a bad person.

He sighs like he's a little annoyed he has to direct me through these questions and answers that seem so obvious. "Do you think she regrets it? Being with this other guy, knowing what it would do to your dad?"

We could just as easily be talking about August. I shove the rest of my shortcake away, my stomach too twisted to finish it. "Yeah, I do. But that doesn't change that it happened. Or that she's still in love with Alex, whether she wants to be or not."

"So maybe you forgive her because people can't help who they love. It sounds like she tried. And it didn't work. Now she just needs to accept it, and so do you," he says. His voice is so quiet, almost pleading. Like the fate of the world hinges on my answer.

Buckling under the pressure, I ask, "What if I can't?"

"Then, for someone so focused on revealing love to the world, you don't really understand it at all," he says.

Maybe he's right. Because being able to see love is not the same as knowing what it looks like.

Or what it feels like.

I wish I could say August is wrong. That of the two of us, he's the one who doesn't understand love. How could he when he kissed someone who wasn't his girlfriend? But he's at least been in a serious, (mostly) committed relationship. He has practical experience being in love. I have a heart full of fantasies.

Which is why my portfolio is lackluster. I don't know what it feels like. Not real love. Not real heartbreak. And until I open myself up to both, I'll never achieve the kind of connection I want people to have with my photography. Not to mention with my heart.

I leave all the lights in the studio dark except one so Mom doesn't see me out here. I'm not ready to talk to her yet. Despite August's logic where she's concerned, I don't know if I can forgive her. Maybe giving myself over to love will help me find a way to do that too. Grabbing the jars of sample paint, I sit in the small circle of light at the table and look, really look, at Ren's portrait. The photo is static, but his heartbreak pulses around him. Half a dozen shades of teal, from an oily dark green to the most delicate seafoam. Streaks of copper and rose gold peek through in places, his love for Lana holding strong in the maelstrom. I mix the various paints, trying to get as close to the colors as I can. Then I paint.

And I paint.

And I paint.

Until every photo in my portfolio is as vibrant and chaotic as the love or heartbreak I can see.

And I guess that's the point of art: not to create something perfect but something that reflects what you feel so deep inside, no one can see it until you've set it free.

Now I just have to hope it's good enough.

Chapter TWENTY-EIGHT

Love Rule #13: There is no problem love can't conquer if you're committed to working it out.

Mom's lies about her relationship with Alex and her asinine rules about love really screwed with my head. And in turn, I unintentionally screwed with others. Now it's up to me to fix it.

If I can.

Yeastie Boys is neutral territory, so when I ask Ren and Lana to meet me there Wednesday after school, they both agree. Reluctantly. I'm not working tonight, so I'll be able to sit with them for as long as it takes.

"Does your mom know you're gunning for her job?" Gemma asks.

"Oh, no. I'm not in the matchmaking business. This is just righting a wrong."

"If it works, you'll be two for two."

I glance at her, my face crinkling in confusion. "What are you talking about? I haven't set anyone else up."

Gemma just smiles as a warm rosy glow builds around her.

"Holy shit. You and Greer? When did that happen? Why am I just hearing about this now?"

"Last week. You've had a lot going on. I didn't want to rub my happy all in your sad," she says.

Throwing my arms around her, I dance us from side to side. "This is the best news! Don't you dare ever keep happy news from me because you think I can't handle my shit. I will always celebrate with you. No matter what."

"I know you will." She squeezes me hard, then breaks free of my hold. "I'll tell you all about it later. Right now, you need to go deal with that."

I follow her gaze toward the front door, where Ren enters. Relief floods me. Of the two, I half expected Ren to bail after our last conversation, while I thought Lana would show up just to watch me squirm. Not that I blame her. I was so blinded by what I thought love was supposed to be, I missed it when it was staring me right in the face. They may not accept my apology, but I have to try.

Nerves bubble in my stomach like activated yeast. Tightening my core like Mom's yoga instructor is always on her about, I walk to meet him. "Hey. I'm glad you came."

Ren barely acknowledges me, keeping his eyes on the checkered floor. "It sounded important."

"It is. Are you hungry? I'm buying."

"I wouldn't say no to some food." He dares a quick glance at me then. "Can I get it to go?"

I take a deep breath to force the guilt down as well. I'm

doing this for his own good. If it works, he'll thank me for not letting him leave. "Nope. Sorry. Lana's joining us." I nod to the door as it opens, letting Lana inside.

"What are you doing, Mo?" he asks.

"Just give me a few minutes, okay? If you don't want to stay after you've heard what I have to say, I won't try to stop you from leaving," I say.

Lana notices us a few steps in and swears. "You've got to be kidding me."

Gemma runs interference, blocking the door before Lana can walk right back out again. "I'm sorry, this exit is currently unavailable. Please try again later," she says.

I mouth a thank-you to her. To Lana, I say, "You may as well come sit because she's not letting you out of here until you listen to me."

"This is kidnapping," Lana says.

"It's more holding you against your will," Ren says.

Lana shoots him a look. The corner of her mouth twitches like she wants to smile, but she pinches her lips closed, refusing to give him even that. "Either way, it's illegal."

"I'm trying to make things right. So, please, just let me do that." I point to an empty table that offers as much privacy as we're going to get.

Ren is the first to move, sliding into his normal side of the booth. It takes Lana another ten seconds or so to follow.

"Ugh. Fine. Let's just get this over with." She sits across from Ren in the middle of the seat. Leaning back, she crosses her arms and legs, effectively closing herself off from any willing participation in this conversation.

She's going to make this as awkward as possible, I see. That's *so* nice of her. I sit next to Ren, careful not to touch him. "I want to start by saying I'm sorry for lying to you. Well, to everyone. But especially to you. What I did—faking my relationship with August—was never supposed to get so out of hand. I wanted what you two had, and in the process, I ruined things for you. For that I am truly sorry."

"So you admit it then?" Lana asks, vindication ringing in her voice. "That you purposely broke us up so you could date Ren?"

Ren rests his arms on the table, a more relaxed version of Lana. He cuts his eyes to me, waiting for my answer.

"I didn't. I swear. The things I did in August's name were solely to make *me* feel less alone. Did I go over the top? Yes. There are only so many times a person can be used like a love-themed Magic 8 Ball before they break. But I didn't purposely do anything to come between you two."

Lana's foot kicks against the table leg, rattling the salt and pepper shakers in their caddy. "Didn't stop you from swooping in the second he was available."

"If it wasn't me, it would have been someone else," I say.

"Can you both stop talking about me like I'm not here?" Ren says, tapping his fingers on the table. His only sign of nerves.

I turn in the seat so I can see both him and Lana at the

same time. “Absolutely. How many girls have asked you out since you and Lana broke up?”

Turning his tapping into something constructive, he counts them out. “Four.”

“And how many have you gone out with?” I ask.

“One. But that was under duress.”

“Not true,” Lana says. “You took Mo to watch our meteor shower.”

“There were like twenty people there. It was *not* a date,” he says.

I try not to be offended by the vehemence in his voice. Our ice-cream-for-dinner night was a solo outing and as close to a date as you can get without technically being one. But bringing it up now would be counterproductive. “It wasn’t. But the point is that Ren had multiple options to date someone else, and he didn’t. Because he’s still in love with you, Lana. And you’re still in love with him.”

“People might stop treating you like a Magic 8 Ball if you stopped acting like one,” Lana says.

Ignoring the dig, I continue as if she hadn’t spoken, “I was raised to believe that if a relationship left you heartbroken, it wasn’t true love. That even when awful things happened, love would protect your heart so you could keep going. So when you broke up and all I could see was complete heartbreak from both of you, I thought maybe it was a good thing it was over. Not just because I thought I wanted to date Ren, but because then you were both free to go out and find your soulmates. But due to some recent events, I've realized that life lesson is utter crap."

Ren looks at Lana, his heartbreak aura pulsing to life. There are threads of copper and rose gold burning bright at the center as his love fights for a resurgence. "If it's crap, what's the truth?"

"I think your heartbreak is proof you loved Lana. That you still love her. It's the same intensity as your love for her, just a different color. Like you're so wrapped up in it, you can't feel anything else."

Lana flicks her gaze to him and, unable to see what I do, rolls her eyes. "We don't need you to tell us we loved each other. We lived it. We know."

"Really? I thought the whole reason you broke up with him was because you didn't think he loved you?" I ask.

"Yeah, because you and your perfect fake relationship made me want something that doesn't exist," she says.

"That's the thing though. I watched you two together long enough to know what real love looked like. When I needed romantic things for August to do for me, I thought about what Ren would do. What he had done for you over the years. I don't know if he stopped doing those things or if you stopped noticing because they were so much a part of your daily life, but I was so desperate to have what you had that I made up an entire relationship to get it."

I thought I wanted Ren. That he was the ideal guy—good looks, equally good personality, even better heart. And while he does have all those things, it's what they represent that I want. Not him specifically.

"And that's supposed to make it okay?" Ren asks. His voice is still razor-sharp, but his expression is softening. Like he wants to trust me to make this right.

Folding my hands in my lap, I roll my shoulders forward to take up as little space as possible. "No. I know I can't take back what I did. Trusting me again is going to take time. But I need you both to believe me when I say your love deserves a second chance."

Lana leans forward, her legs knocking into Ren's under the table. Their eyes meet, and the longing on both sides is strong enough to set the whole place ablaze. She looks away first. Her expression is still fiery when she turns it on me, but now it feels villainous. "Why should we believe you? You've never even had a boyfriend."

"That doesn't mean I don't know what love looks like." It comes out harsher than I mean it to, my residual anger with my mom tainting everything. Snapping at Lana and Ren will only keep their defenses up. I roll my shoulders to release the tension and attempt a smile. "And no, I've never had a boyfriend, but my idea of love was enough to make you want it. So I do know what I'm talking about." At least when it comes to other people. My own love life is a totally different story.

Ren's eyes go all wide and hopeful. He may be mad at me, but he wants to believe me more. To Lana, he says, "Mo told me you're sad about our breakup too. Is that true?"

"Did she tell you that before or after you kissed her?"

"Before. And that kiss was a complete surprise. She and I talked about you and August and how neither of us was ready to start something new because we were still in love with you. I mean, I'm still in love with you, and I thought she was still in love with August, but since they never dated, she can't *still* be in love with him, but there are definitely some strong feelings going on there, and none of them were directed at me. Right, Mo? You even apologized for kissing me after, so that proves it didn't mean anything."

Lana sits with the explanation a moment, chewing on her lip as she decides if she's going to let his admission sway her. "Okay, fine. You didn't mean to kiss her. Can we back up to the part where you still love me?"

He fights a smile. Slouching back into the booth, his demeanor flips. Jaw tight and hands fisted on the table, he says, "Not if you're going to tell me I didn't ever love you—that's a lie and you know it. You breaking up with me is the worst pain I've gone through in my life. Like having my heart cut out of my chest while it's still beating."

I would think he was exaggerating if I hadn't seen his heartbreak for myself. "I can show you what he felt like."

They both ask, "How?" at the same time. Two halves of a whole.

"The picture I took. The one for my broken-hearts project."

"I don't see how that will help here," Ren says. "It's just a picture. No offense."

"That's because you haven't seen the final version. I edited it so your heartbreak over Lana is incorporated into the portrait, if you both want to see it."

"Why do you care?" Lana asks. But she leans forward, her eagerness to see it on full display.

I retrieve my bag from under the table. "I don't want to be the reason you two broke up. Not even a small part of it. Whatever issues you have, that's on y'all to work out. But I'd like to try and make up for skewing your relationship expectations. Making sure you know how much he loves you is the only way I know how."

After pulling the portrait from my bag, I slide it across the table to her. Lana sucks in an awed breath, somewhere between reverence and disbelief. Ren stiffens beside me.

"The colors are a little cheerful for heartbreak, don't you think?" she asks. But she can't tear her eyes away from it. "I would have thought you'd go with black or something more depressing."

"Are you seriously critiquing the color right now? Because I didn't randomly pick these colors. That's what actual heartbreak looks like. All that rose and copper you see swirling in there, that's his love for you that hasn't turned to teal yet."

"So the teal is love I felt that's gone?" Ren asks.

"No, not gone. Just changed into heartbreak," I say.

"Can it change back?" Lana asks.

His hand stretches across the table toward Lana. An invitation. A plea. "Do you want it to?"

She shakes her head. Her braids fall across her face, and she brushes them back, keeping her hands occupied. Out of reach. "I don't want to be responsible for doing *that* to you. And if all that color was once love, then you really did love me. Like, a lot."

"Yeah. More than anything," Ren says. "But I don't want you to be with me because you feel guilty."

"I don't think I want to have this conversation with Mo sitting with us, do you?" Lana says, not taking her eyes off him.

"Good call." Ren nudges my leg under the table with his knee. "Mind giving us some privacy?"

I still don't know if my portraits will be good enough for Kinsey, but renewing their hope in love—and each other—may be even better.

"Of course," I say, smiling at Lana, who is tracing the curls of color with her fingers. "You can keep the picture if you want."

She wouldn't give it back even if I wanted her to.

That night, Mom makes fried chicken and waffles. The ultimate breakfast-for-dinner meal. She's the only person outside the Yeastie Boys staff that Lee and Gabe shared their sriracha and maple syrup recipe with. If she's breaking it out tonight to make my favorite dinner, she's up to something. The only way to know if it's a good something or a bad something is to face her.

"Smells like a cease-fire in here," I say.

With a pair of tongs, she lifts one golden-brown chicken breast from the oil and sets it on a stack of paper towels. The second piece follows, and she moves the pan from the hot burner. Then she settles onto one of the stools at the island, patting the one next to her. "Come sit. We need to talk."

I set my bag on the counter but don't take a seat. Sitting implies forgiveness. It says I'm willing to trust what she says despite all her previous lies. I'm not ready for that yet. "I don't want to fight with you."

"I don't want that either. So let's have an honest but calm conversation. I'll go first." Mom twists the stem of a half-empty glass of white wine. Sighing, she looks at me, her eyes tired. "What you said was incredibly hurtful and out of line. I understand you're upset by what I did, and I didn't handle things with your dad the way I should have. But I've done everything I could to give you a happy life. Even if you're mad at me, I still expect you to treat me with respect. Understood?"

"Understood." Whatever goodwill I earned with Ren and Lana doesn't extend to the situation with my mom. The shame burns as I swallow it.

"Good. Now, I am so sorry for keeping the truth from you. My relationship with Alex is not something I'm proud of, and I didn't want you knowing I had messed up our lives so completely. I couldn't stand the idea that you would be ashamed of me too. There's nothing I can do to make up for what I did to your dad. Or to you. I never meant to skew your view of love. You were wrong when you asked if I created my rules to try and change the past. I never planned to tell you about Alex and me, but the rules were my way of ensuring you understood what true love was like. So you'd understand the difference and not make the same mistakes I did."

"Was Dad the mistake or Alex?"

"Neither. Or both. I'm not sure anymore."

I don't agree with what she did, but I can try to understand. To forgive. To ask for forgiveness.

Sitting next to her, I lay my head on her shoulder. "You said you would do things differently if you could. What would you change?"

She smooths my hair back from my forehead and kisses it the way she did when I was little. "I don't think I can answer that. I didn't love your dad the way a wife should. Don't misunderstand, I *did* love him. He was a wonderful man, but as much as I wanted to be in love with him, I wasn't."

"Not the way you were with Alex."

"No, not the way I loved Alex," Mom admits, her voice soft with regret. "Falling in love with Alex was simultaneously the best and worst experience of my life. I've spent years wishing that I never met him. If I hadn't, I may never have known what that kind of love felt like. But maybe I would have been happy with the choice I'd already made."

"Were you really that unhappy with the life you had with Dad and me?" I ask.

"No, absolutely not. Since the day I knew I was having you, you've been the most important thing in the world to me. I would never want to change what I had with your dad because I would never want to change a second of being your mom."

She turns, easing my head from her shoulder. When I meet her eyes, she grips both my hands and pulls them into her lap. "We all go about our lives thinking we've reached some invisible limit on how much we can love, and then someone enters our lives and opens a whole new level of love we never knew existed. I didn't know how much I could love another person until you. Alex did that for me too. In a different way, of course, but something about him called to something in me and made me realize there was more out there. And once I saw it, it was impossible not to want it."

That's how it was with August and me too. Not that I'm in love with him, but I could be.

So easily.

And what I had with him is so much bigger than anything I've felt before. I couldn't go back to something less than that, not when I know that kind of love is waiting if I'm not scared to look for it. Mom shouldn't have had to either.

"Why did you end things if you loved him so much? When I talked to Alex, he said you felt guilty for Dad's death."

"I did feel guilty for a long time. It's still there now, especially since Alex came back into my life. Why did I deserve to find love and be happy when your dad didn't have that chance? Giving Alex up was my penance for not loving your dad the way I should have," she says.

"You get how ridiculous that sounds, right? Punishing

yourself for loving someone else when Dad was already gone didn't fix anything."

"You're right. But it only hurt Alex and me, not you. I never wanted you to feel like I was replacing your dad or that he was anything but my first choice."

"I get that you wanted to protect me when I was little. But you clearly still have feelings for Alex. I don't like that you cheated on Dad with him or that you lied to me about it for my whole life, but you deserve to find love," I say, squeezing her fingers so she knows I mean it.

She releases my hands and reaches for her wine. "I can't be with him."

"Why not? If I'm saying it's okay, then what's stopping you?"

"I can't do that to your dad. Not again."

But that's just an excuse. She's scared of getting hurt. I can see her fear in the creases around her eyes and the tight set of her mouth.

I won't let her get away with that. Shaking my head, I say, "Dad's not here. I'm not saying he'd understand, but I do think he'd want you to be happy. More importantly, *I* want you to be happy. From what I've seen, Alex does that. You owe it to each other to try. Love rule number three, remember?"

"Finding true love requires taking risks," she says. "Maybe I'll see if he wants to get coffee this weekend."

"Maybe you should."

And maybe if Mom has the courage to tell Alex how she feels, I can muster up enough to tell August too.

Chapter TWENTY-NINE

Love Rule #12: When you know, you know.

Two days. That's all that's standing between me and my Kinsey application being submitted on Friday. Well, that and the fact it's still not done. The photo collages are all finished, and I have a meeting with Mrs. Clemente tomorrow to (fingers crossed) get her approval, but I still need to finish my essay. Not that I'm letting anyone outside the submission panel read it.

I started out writing a generic essay about love, but the second August's name appeared on the screen, it detoured so far off the map, I had to scrap it and start again. And somehow my essay on photography and art and why I want to attend the summer arts program turned into a confessional on love and heartbreak. And how I had gotten it all so very wrong.

Gemma keeps trying to sneak peeks at my computer to read over my shoulder. My handprint is going to be permanently etched on her face from the number of times I've had to shove her away. She finished her essay a week ago. A fact she reminds me about every time she fails to catch more than a word or two. I thought having Greer here would keep her distracted. At least long enough for me to knock this out. But the only one distracted by the two of them is me.

"If you keep glowing like that, I'm going to put *you* in my portfolio," I say.

Smug as ever, Gemma just goes on shining, her smile adding to the vibrancy. "You're one to talk."

"One, I'm not glowing. And two, even if I were, you couldn't see it."

"You could show me. Or more accurately, you could show August how you feel. Tell him you want to be with him instead of sitting around pining for him."

Not that she's close enough to see, but I tilt my computer screen in case this is another ploy. "I'm not pining."

Greer looks up from their book. They're snuggled into Gemma's side of the studio couch and not as absorbed in their book as I thought if they're following our conversation. "I don't quite know my role here yet, but am I allowed to disagree?"

"No," I say at the same time Gemma says, "Hell yes."

When Gemma leans over and kisses Greer, the room explodes with silent fireworks. I shield my eyes for dramatic effect—and a little bit because I don't want to damage my eyesight. Gemma lobs a pillow across the room at me. Greer hides their pink-stained cheeks behind their book again.

Back to the problem at hand, I say, "What would I even say to him? *Sorry for calling you a cheater and a liar, but I do actually want to date you, so do you think you can forgive me?*"

"Sounds good to me," Gemma says.

"You know I can't actually say that, right?"

Extricating herself from Greer's side, she comes to join me at the table. "I don't think it matters what you say as long as you say something. Because if you don't, you're both going to sit there waiting for the other to make the first move, and you'll still be sitting there when you're dead."

I finally put voice to the doubt swirling in my head. "What if he's not waiting?"

"He is."

"And you know this how?" I ask.

Gemma rolls her eyes. "Just because you're not talking to him doesn't mean *I'm* not."

My hand flies out to grab her before she can drop that bomb and flee. "I'm sorry, what?"

"He's been worried about you, but he's also trying to respect your boundaries."

"I'm pretty sure talking to my best friend behind my back is a few steps over those boundaries." And exactly the kind of thing August and Gemma would do. I'm an idiot for not expecting it.

"Don't even pretend to be mad. I've been very clear that I am Team August from the start. And since you are too, we're on the same side here," she says.

Greer waves their book in the air to interject into the conversation again. "Plus, she had to tell him off for being such a dumbass and almost killing his chances with you." Their smile is timid, like they're not sure they should be divulging that information.

The smile I send back is full of encouragement and gratitude. "Well, *that* I'm on board with."

While I'm distracted, Gemma gets her hand under my screen and raises it. "It was more of a warning to get his shit together before it's too late."

"How'd that work out?" I ask, dragging the laptop into the safety of my lap.

"Seeing as how you're still into him, he's got time to figure it out."

Maybe by the time he does, I'll know how to tell him how I feel. Until then, I need to put him out of my mind. My submission for Kinsey isn't going to finish itself. "Unlike me and my Kinsey application."

"I thought you were happy with it," Greer says.

"Mo's too much of a perfectionist to be happy with it for long," Gemma says. There's no trace of meanness in her words, only tough love. "Even when it's flawless."

"It just feels unfinished somehow. Like something's missing." Like *I'm* missing. The collection shows everyone how I see love, but that's only part of the story I'm trying to communicate. Because seeing love and experiencing it are very different things. "I'm thinking I might add a selfie to show both sides of my perspective."

"Do it. Do it. Do it," Gemma chants.

Greer sets their book down, obviously realizing that trying

to read around the two of us is too fraught with interruptions to continue. “Whoa. Calm down there. Adding it to her portfolio is not the same as sending it to August.” They give me a pointed look. It’s the most direct and confident they’ve been around me.

Message received.

“Maybe not,” Gemma says, missing both the look and my acceptance of it. “But it proves she has feelings for him, and I’m one sneaky click away from sending it to him when she’s not looking.”

Tightening my grip on my computer, I say, “Keep talking like that and the picture will never happen.”

“Liar,” she says.

“Um, yeah. Everyone knows I’m a liar, remember?” I blow her a kiss so she knows I’m teasing. “But you’re right. I’ll still do the photo—you’ll just never see it.”

August though? He deserves to know how I feel about him. But I can’t think about that yet. Right now, I have to focus on my Kinsey application.

I hesitate outside Mrs. Clemente’s office. If she says my work is still not good enough, I don’t have time to do anything else. Either I’ve done enough to earn my place in the summer arts program, or Kinsey is off the table. Not just for this summer but for good.

When Ren calls my name from farther down the hall, I wonder if this is the universe’s way of telling me it’s a lost cause and I should give up now before all my dreams are crushed. Attempting to shake off the doubts, I paste on a smile for him.

"Have a minute?" he asks when I meet him halfway.

"Yeah. Sure."

He hikes the strap of his backpack higher on his shoulder. "About the other day—"

"I'm sorry. Again." It feels like all I do is apologize to Ren. But I'd rather get it out of the way first and save him the trouble of telling me how badly I fucked up. "I know I overstepped with you and Lana, but I swear I was trying to make things better."

"No, it was good. That's what I wanted to tell you. We talked after you left, like, a lot. More than we've talked in months. About serious stuff anyway. And I was wondering if you could do one of those pictures of Lana? It really helped to be able to literally see my feelings for her and talk about how we felt, and we thought maybe having one of her would get us back on the same page."

He may have forgiven me, but Lana's the type to hold a grudge. Like, forever. I'd rather not have to look over my shoulder for the rest of my life, waiting for retaliation. Though maybe wrecking my own life is satisfaction enough for her. "I don't think Lana wants me anywhere near your relationship."

"She's more on your side than you think after that picture. You're not responsible for our breakup, and Lana knows that. Even if she's not ready to admit it yet. A lot of it's on me, but some of it's on her for not telling me how unhappy she was so

I could do something to fix it. *You* brought us back together and got us talking."

I'm also the only girl he's kissed in the past three years who isn't Lana. But I'm smart enough not to remind him of that right now. "If you can convince Lana to let me take her picture, I'm happy to try." It's the least I can do for him. He may not blame me for the current state of his relationship, but I do.

Ren bumps my shoulder, leaving his arm warm against mine for a few extra seconds. "Leave Lana to me."

"That's the plan," I say, smiling for real this time.

"Yeah, I guess it is." The air around him goes all warm and rose gold. The faint teal streaks of his heartbreak are still there if I look really hard, like cracks running through a sheet of thawing ice. Before long, they'll be gone. Not a trace left behind. "If I can offer some advice, you should talk to August. Just hash things out with him and see where you both stand at the end. Who knows? Maybe you'll realize you want to be together."

I don't need to talk to August to know he's the one I want. I'm pretty sure he wants to be with me too, but after the way I've treated him, I'm going to have to really put my heart out there to prove I'm all in. The picture I made last night will be a good start. If Mrs. Clemente thinks it's good.

"I'm working on it. But there are a few things I have to do first. One of which is talking to Mrs. Clemente before lunch ends."

"Your application's due soon, right?" he asks.

"Tomorrow."

"Good luck with that. And with August." He pulls me in for a hug that's so aggressively happy, he lifts me off the floor for a few seconds before releasing me.

Laughing, I wave him off as he heads back down the hall. Then I make my way to Mrs. Clemente's office, every echo of hesitation gone.

"You're cutting it awfully close," Mrs. Clemente says when I enter. Her expression is neutral, probably to keep from unloading her disappointment on me so early in the meeting. "I thought maybe you were actually giving up."

I shake my head, giving her a tentative smile. "I had some personal things to deal with."

"Sometimes personal struggle makes for the best art."

"You might rethink that after you've seen these." I set my bag on the chair and remove the portrait paintings, each kept safe in a separate plastic sleeve Greer gave me from their comic book collection.

There's nothing neutral about Mrs. Clemente now. She presses a hand to her mouth, which is open in awe. Her eyes widen as she takes in the colors and patterns, the love and heartbreak pulsing from each one. "Oh, Imogen. They're wonderful."

"They're not too similar? Too one-note now that they're all the same style again?" I ask. The worry that they're still not enough churns in my stomach like acid.

"Definitely not. Each one is unique in how you mixed the color palette with varying shades and movement patterns. They complement each other beautifully but have distinct points of view. A message you as the artist are trying to convey. You really have captured the feelings of love and heartbreak here. Now the question is what do *you* think?"

I look at them critically. Try to see them as an objective party. "I thought I would hate it. I mean, if I can't show what I want in the photo itself, then how good of a photographer can I be?" I frown. She *tsks*.

Before she can launch into a lecture about how wrong I am, I continue, "But you were right. These portraits needed something to make them stand out that would also let the world see what I do. Now that I've painted them, I can't imagine them as standard portraits anymore."

"Does that mean you're going to submit them?"

"Yes, now that I have your stamp of approval. Though I added one last night that I'm on the fence about including." After taking my self-portrait from the bag, I hold it out to her.

"That's a very brave choice," she says, a half smile playing on her lips.

"Good brave or bad brave?" I ask.

Mrs. Clemente passes the photo back to me, closing her hands around mine. "I don't think there is such a thing as bad brave when talking about art. As long as you're staying true to yourself and putting out work you're proud of, you can't go wrong. That doesn't mean everyone will love it or even understand it, but you should never hold yourself back when it comes to your art. If your whole heart isn't in it, people will see it. But this, Imogen, is quite literally your heart laid bare, and it is your best work yet."

My body goes hot. The rush of gratitude and pride swells inside me so fast, I wouldn't be surprised if I started to float. "So that's a yes on including it?"

"That's a yes." She releases me but doesn't move away. Her eyes hold mine, a gravity settling over her that brings me back down as well. "On a personal note, I've heard some things about your love life. I try not to believe any of the rumors that go around this school, but looking at this picture of you, whoever this boy is who lights you up like this, he would have to be an idiot not to love you back."

"That's him. August," I say, tapping his photo on the table. If she's heard the rumors, then she knows we've both made some idiotic decisions already.

"Oh, he very much looks like a smart boy," she says.

I guess there's only one way to find out.

I've put it off long enough. With my application for Kinsey's summer art program officially submitted as of ten minutes ago, I have no excuse. Or at least none I can justify. August may not feel the same, or he may have decided I'm too much drama and a relationship with me isn't worth it. But I have to try.

I have to give him the opportunity to say yes.

After opening my Insta, I select the self-portrait I created for my portfolio. Thin tendrils of copper and teal are woven through the rose gold cascading around me in wispy waves. The colors are light, delicate. Like I'm merely dreaming of love, and the second I wake up, the colors will vanish like fog on a sunny morning. But there's a bright spot of gold over my heart. If I stare at it long enough, I can see it pulsing, pumping love and those tiny moments of doubt out into the atmosphere. Getting stronger and surer of itself as time goes on.

It's a picture of a girl unmistakably falling in love.

I could post the picture without a caption, but I don't want there to be any question in August's mind about what it means.

> Imogen's Love Rule (unnumbered because there's only one rule that matters): Trust your heart.
>
> I have a confession to make. No, not that one. Everyone already knows that one. What you don't know is that I've never been in love. I've done a bang-up job of faking it this past year, tricking even myself into believing I knew what love was. But I was wrong. I couldn't even see it when @TheRealAugust was right in front of my face this whole time. So this is me, eyes wide open, ready to trust my heart and the boy who quite literally makes Mo glow. #mostloved

I post it before I can change my mind. Now it's up to fate.

Chapter THIRTY

Imogen's Love Rule: Trust your heart.

Turns out, I'm not good at waiting. And thanks to my rash decision to tell August how I feel, I'm now waiting on two responses that hold my future in the balance. I'll be okay if one of the decisions comes back a no. But both? That kind of crushing disappointment might be enough to keep me down for good.

I won't hear from Kinsey for another month. August though? He's never taken more than a few minutes to respond. I'm trying not to read too much into the fact my post has been up for over an hour now and there's nothing. No reply. No DM. No call. At this rate, I'll drain my phone battery just from keeping the screen on so I don't miss a notification.

I can't even blame August for leaving me in limbo.

The last thing he said to me was that I didn't have a clue about love. And he was right. I didn't.

But I want to.

A fact I made very clear in my post.

My post he's *ignoring*.

If this is what love does to a person, maybe I'm better off without it.

When my phone finally chimes with a new notification, I'm so conflicted that I throw it onto the carpet out of reach. Then I practically fall out of bed to retrieve it. Mom yells from her office to make sure I'm okay, but I'm too busy laugh-crying at my current state to respond. Not bothering to get up in case it's a false alarm and I need to prolong my despondency, I lie on the floor and…wait. Phone in hand, finger hovering over the screen. All it will take is a tap. A press of a button. And I'll know if August has replied. Good or bad, a response is better than silence.

I scan the sky outside my window, all ink and glitter now that the sun's gone down. Where is a shooting star now that I have a wish to make? Waking my phone up with a quick tap of my thumb, I whisper what I want to the universe anyway.

"Please be August. Please let him want this too."

I don't think I've ever clicked on a notification so fast.

TheRealAugust: Was that post from you or Gemma?

TheRealAugust: I'm trying not to get my hopes up here.

TheRealAugust: You know what? Don't tell me. I'm just gonna assume it was you and that you meant it.

MoGlows: It was me. And I did mean it.

TheRealAugust: That's what Gemma would say too.

MoGlows: Then pick up.

The phone barely rings before he's answering.

"You swear it was you?" he asks, his voice edged in desperation.

I laugh, my nerves bubbling out of me at the sound of his voice. "I swear."

"And you meant it? You want to be with me? Despite everything with Shay and how much of an asshole I am for hurting you?"

"Do I wish you had broken up with her before kissing me? Yes. Do I understand why you lied to me about her? I'm trying to." Mom's relationship with Alex is proof enough that good people can make bad decisions when their hearts are involved. It doesn't matter how many rules there are, love will always find a way. There's no use fighting it. So I'm not. "Am I going to let any of that stop you from kissing me again? Absolutely not."

August's relieved exhale crackles through the phone. "It would be a shame to let these lips go to waste."

"We wouldn't want that," I say.

"So we're doing this for real? A proper relationship?"

Climbing back to my bed, I smile at the snapshots of August's poems taped to the wall next to me. I've spent the past year coming up with every romantic idea imaginable. None of them even come close to this. To him. "Dates may be a bit more complicated seeing as how you live four hours away, but I'm up for the challenge if you are."

"And here I thought you were an optimist," he says. "There just so happens to be a rest area halfway between us. If we each drive two hours, it's not so bad."

"Tell me when and I'll be there."

"Now?"

It takes all my willpower not to say yes. Not to grab my keys and be in the car before he can say he was joking. "As much as I would love that, we should maybe—"

August lets loose a buzzer sound, signaling a wrong answer on my part. "I won. My date, my rules, remember?"

Mom catches me trying to sneak out of the house. She lets me message August so he knows I'm not coming, and then she confiscates my phone. I'm so keyed up with a potent mix of anticipation and disappointment that I'm as twitchy as a live wire all day Friday. While she holds my phone hostage, I borrow Gemma's to talk to August.

I only get my phone back on Saturday morning before work because she's going to meet Alex and won't be home until late in the afternoon. It also comes with the stipulation that I will under no circumstances leave town.

She's explicit with her wording.

If Mom had told me not to drive to see him, I'd ride shotgun in Gemma's car.

So our first date is just going to have to wait a little longer.

There's a blackout poem taped to my front door when I get home from work. Once I'm close enough to read it, I realize it's not a poem at all. Just three words.

go out back

I cut through the house, dropping everything except my phone so I can call August and thank him for whatever he roped Gemma into setting up for me to find. A charcoal-gray blanket is spread on the end of the dock. A trail of ranunculus flowers leads down to it. These are a mix of pale blush, deep peach, and white—as close to rose gold as a flower can get. I pluck one from the ground as I pass, brushing my finger over the ruffly petals. The variation of shades in this one flower could rival the brightest love glow.

I've posted enough photos of ranunculus that it's not surprising he picked them. This color combination couldn't have been easy to track down though. There's no way it was a coincidence.

A Taylor Swift song starts up from somewhere in the studio, flowing out the open door. Soft and dreamlike. I turn as August follows the music out and have to pinch myself to make sure he's really here and not some fever dream brought on by so many days of just wishing he were. He walks toward me, his smile unfurling with each step. And I know he's real. Not even my love-obsessed brain could conjure a moment this perfect.

And instead of running to him and kissing him, I ruin the moment by asking, "What are you doing here?" It's not that I don't want him here. I do. But the shock of him being unexpectedly here in person is so much like that first day at the café that my brain short-circuits.

"If you can't come to the date, the date will come to you," he says. He keeps smiling, unfazed by my lukewarm reception.

He picks up the flower closest to him and hands it to me. Our fingers twine together around the stem, sending a spark of warmth buzzing along my skin. It's enough to take the fight right out of me. My body remembers the last time we were this close and leans into him, muscle memory taking over. Hands in his hair. Lips claiming and being claimed. Breaths desperate and fast.

He takes his time with the kiss, as if my lips are something to savor. A favorite flavor he can't get enough of.

"Best date ever," I say against his mouth, unwilling to get too far from him.

"Just wait. It's barely even started."

"Nope. You're here. That's all I need."

Pulling back, August shakes his head. "I'm pretty sure you're gonna like the rest of it too. Wait right here." He doesn't wait for a response. Just turns and heads back into the studio to collect whatever the *rest* is.

He comes back a few minutes later with a small cooler

swinging from one hand and a wireless speaker in the other. With a nod, he sends me ahead of him. I pause at the first flower I come to. The longer they're out of water, the faster they'll wilt. But it's all so beautiful. So romantic. Everything I tried so hard to fabricate to show everyone how epic my love story was. Now it's here for real.

"You want to take a picture of it, don't you?" he asks, dropping his chin on my shoulder from behind. His laugh is warm on my neck.

"Maybe later," I say. Because for once, I don't. This date isn't for everyone else. It's just for us. I turn my head, pressing a kiss to his cheek. "I can't believe you did all this."

"I have a lot to live up to. Fake me set the bar for romantic gestures pretty high."

My post professing my feelings for him should have removed all his doubts. But he still thinks he's not enough. That he has to try to prove he's worthy of being loved. I spin to face him, needing to let him know he's wrong. That he's *everything*. "August—"

"No, don't look at me like that. I meant it as a good thing. I *want* to be that guy for you. The kind of boyfriend who will do anything to make sure you know how he feels. So you never have to question it."

That's the thing. I don't need some grand gesture to know he's falling in love with me. All I have to do is look at him to see the rose-gold glow lighting him up. "You don't have to try to be that guy. You're already everything that I want."

Read on for a peek at

The Holloway Girls

1

Nothing holds more potential than a blank page. Especially a page from the Book of Luck. The leather-bound notebook is a family heirloom. It chronicles the name of every Holloway girl and a short account of the luck their magic has bestowed on the people they've kissed.

After being raised on stories of other Holloway girls, it's finally my turn to start writing my own. It's a rite of passage. But also, it's something I've looked forward to my whole life. And with a few quick strokes, I sign my name across the top of the paper, binding myself to the magic of the kissing season.

Remy Reed Holloway

My great-great-great-times-infinity grandmother was the first Holloway girl to experience the season. With just one little kiss, she gave some love-struck boy a gift of good luck.

And just like that, all the women in my family were imbued with magic.

We became love goddesses.

Good-luck charms.

Before the ink's even dry, I can feel the magic claiming me for the coming year. It's a lightness in my chest, a buzzing in my blood. A promise that the charmed future I've always dreamed of—one with true love and a faint luster of luck clinging to my skin like glitter—is just one kiss away.

My season doesn't officially start for five and a half more hours. But there's no way I'd be able to sleep, despite it being almost midnight, if I didn't do this first. I do my best attempt at a happy dance with my sister, Maggie, squeezed onto my twin bed, hugging me from behind. It's basically off-kilter bouncing accompanied by jazz hands. But it serves its purpose.

"You're going to have so many boys lining up to kiss you that you won't be able to get their names on the page fast enough." She squeezes me tight, as if she doesn't mind that her season ends tomorrow when mine begins.

Which, to be fair, she probably doesn't. My sister's kissed more boys in the past year than I'll probably kiss in my lifetime.

Maggie subscribes to the kiss-any-boy-who-strikes-her-fancy philosophy. It's what all the boys hope for during the kissing season—equal opportunity and all that—but also Maggie just really enjoys kissing. I, on the other hand, lean toward a different school of thought. When I kiss someone this year, I want to know it means something. For both of us.

"Let's not go wild, Mags." I nudge an elbow into her ribs, eliciting a laugh. "I'd be happy with just one who wants to be with me more than he wants the luck."

Holloway girls have zero control over who falls for us during the season. But if I could choose, that someone would be Isaac Fuller. I can't even think his name without a smile curving onto my lips. It's like a flashing neon sign that says *kiss me* every damn time I see him. If things go my way, I might get him to do just that.

Isaac and I aren't friends, exactly, but we're friendly thanks to a few mutual classes and a few more mutual friends. Our lockers are practically next to each other—just three people between us—and somehow last year we'd gotten into this ritual of Isaac knocking on my locker door as he passed every morning before first period and saying, *There she is,* and me replying *Here I am*, and him saying, *Now my day can begin.* He had a girlfriend then, so he didn't mean anything by it. But that hadn't stopped my heart from tripping all over itself every day. When he broke up with Hannah at the end of the school year, I'd finally let myself hope that maybe our morning ritual had started to mean something more to him too.

Reaching for the book, Maggie flips the cover closed. Then she falls back onto the mattress, taking me down with her. She presses our foreheads together, her eyelashes whispering against mine, as if the contact will give her direct access to my thoughts. This close, the light smattering of freckles high on her cheeks makes an appearance, as opposed to mine, which are dark and abundant and cover both cheeks down to the curve of my jaw and up the bridge of my nose.

Tucking a hand under her jaw to protect my pillowcase from her raspberry-colored lip stain, aptly named *Girl About Town*, she says, "I get that the season makes it hard to know which feelings are real and which are fueled by a desire for the luck. Just remember that kissing people you have true feelings for trumps all."

It's a version of something Mom has said to us our whole lives. Like a Holloway motto. If we had a family crest it would be the cheesiest one around: *True love trumps all.*

I want to tell Maggie about Isaac. How I want to kiss him and no one else. But I know my sister—almost better than I know myself—and I'm not in the mood for a lecture about the rules and how I can't kiss Isaac if he's still in love with Hannah. So I just say, "That's the plan," and smile like I haven't already narrowed my choices down to one.

Nana always said kissing someone who's already given away their heart was one of the worst sins against the season, right up there with refusing to kiss anyone at all. But there's nothing in the Book of Luck about what happens if a Holloway girl breaks the rules. I can only remember hearing one or two stories about girls in my family who never found love. And even then, those were just whispers.

I push the worry away, refusing to let it spoil this milestone moment. As long as Isaac's pulled under the season's spell tomorrow, that means his feelings for me are real. And there's nothing to stop me from kissing him the first chance I get.

There's a piece of paper taped to my bedroom window when we wake, both still in my bed. Maggie—ever vigilant where I'm concerned—spots it before me and falls out of bed, her foot tangling in the sheets in her haste to see what it says. Pressing the back of one hand to my mouth to stifle my laughter, I extend the other to help her off the floor. She glares at me, but our fingers twine together as we examine the message facing us through the glass. The paper's been torn from a spiral notebook, the edges ripped and uneven. The words, written in a messy scrawl that slants down to the right despite the paper's faint blue lines, read: *Making you smile is the best part of my day.*

It's not exactly a love letter, but it's as close to one as I've ever gotten. Usually, Maggie's the one garnering all the attention—even before her kissing season started. Knowing that someone's choosing me over my sister for once is a serious hit of serotonin. I run my fingers over the glass, tracing the outline of the words one at a time.

"Who's it from?" Maggie leans closer, trying to locate a signature. "And how did he get it up here without us hearing him?"

"I don't know." But I do. I've seen hundreds of these types of love notes on Hannah's locker over the years. They were Isaac's way of letting her—and everyone who walked by—know that she had his heart. Maybe this is his way of saying that I do now.

"It's really sweet. And also accurate. Whoever he is, he should definitely be on your list."

"Why does there have to be a list? What if I like *him*?" I don't mean to ask it, but my heart refuses to comply.

She lifts our joined hands and taps on my chest like she can knock some sense into my heart. "It's called the kissing season for a reason, Rem. If we were supposed to kiss just one person, it wouldn't last all year. Or the magic would only work on one person."

"Yeah, but there's no rule that says we *have* to kiss more than one. Just that we can if we want to." Sliding the window open, I reach up to dislodge the tape. The paper flaps in the wind when I free it, almost ripping from my hold like it wants to blow away and spread its message all over town. I slip the note into the top drawer of my nightstand so Maggie doesn't sense how much it means to me.

"Oh, you'll want to," she insists. "Just give the season time to work its magic, and you'll see."

2

There's a party at Firelight Falls tonight to usher in the start of summer—and a second kissing season.

People say they can tell the season is coming because the air smells sweeter, like it's been sprinkled with sugar. Or, on days when the humidity is so thick you can barely breathe, they claim it's like the air's been dipped in honey. Really, that's just their way of romanticizing the whole thing. The summer solstice is what triggers the magic in a Holloway girl's blood.

The magic's been building inside me all day. When it reaches full strength tonight, it's with a gust of hot air pushing in through the open car windows that tickles my skin and leaves the town smelling faintly of vanilla buttercream. But that could just be the dozens of whoopie pies in two of Mom's Wild Flour Bake Stop tote bags on the back seat. There's something about these small cake-and-frosting sandwiches specifically that all the boys in town love. Maybe it's just the name, which they usually say in low, suggestive tones, or maybe it's because they're easily portable and so fan-freakin'-tastic that you want a second one before the flavor of the first one has even left your mouth.

Either way, our mom's s'mores-flavored whoopie pie—fluffy marshmallow filling and a dollop of chocolate ganache layered between round puffs of graham cracker cake—is a staple at gatherings up at the falls. No matter how many we bring, we always run out.

The parking lot at the trail's entrance is overflowing with cars. They spill onto the street, blocking half of a lane and begging to have the cops called to raid the woods for underage drinking. Maggie parks at the Lookout Bed & Breakfast next to the trailhead. Mrs. Chastain has signs posted warning against doing exactly that, but since all her afternoon tea sweets are baked by my mom and me, she won't have us towed.

Maggie and I heft the tote bags from the car and follow the path from the lot as it gradually descends into the trees. The dense thicket of branches above us blocks most of the early-evening sun so only a little light filters down through the leaves. It also stifles the breeze. My dress clings to the sweat beading on my ribs and stomach. I pluck at the thin fabric so it won't be marred by dark, wet patches when we reach the falls—and Isaac. I want everything to be perfect if our first kiss happens tonight.

The whole way down the trail, Maggie keeps tossing

smiles over her shoulder at me. Her eyes catch on mine for the briefest second, the glint of excitement setting the air between us on fire. And because I know my sister as well as she knows me, I'm certain she plans on kissing one last person tonight before the season's magic leaves her for good.

The past few weeks, she's been on her phone nonstop. Though she's barely contributed more than a passing comment or two in the group chat we have going with our best friend, Laurel. At first I thought her mystery crush was Theo, the hot barista from Pour House who's been writing flirty messages on Maggie's cup every time we go in. But she has no reason to hide that from me, and she's definitely been cagey about whoever's messages make her bite her lip to keep from smiling too hard. But since I haven't told Maggie about Isaac, I can't exactly be mad at her for keeping this from me.

So, I just smile back at my sister, hoping we both get the kisses we want tonight.

The woods give way to an expanse of sand and rocks and moss-covered logs bordering the pool at the bottom of the waterfall. I scan the faces, taking stock of who's here and who's not. I find Isaac without trying. Like I've been living in a real-life version of *Where's Waldo?* for the past few months and I've trained my eyes to skip over everything that doesn't fit what I'm looking for.

He's knee-deep in the water, one hand shielding his eyes from the sun as he watches one of his friends leap from the top of the waterfall. His dirty-blond hair is slicked back with water, and his eyes, so murky green they're almost hazel, squint just a bit, causing a dimple in his left cheek. He splays his fingers to indicate a score of seven to the jumper. The two guys on his right, his best friends Ethan Wells and Seth Anders, give a seven and a nine respectively. They're all on the diving team at school, but Isaac almost always wins these impromptu competitions, so he's made himself a permanent judge so others can win too.

Isaac notices me a few seconds after Felix Vega splashes out of the shallows, already heading toward me. Last summer, I made out with Felix at Paige's midsummer party. That was before he'd realized kissing me wouldn't bring him even an inkling of luck since it wasn't my kissing season yet, but he'd just laughed when I broke it to him, then he'd kissed me again. He was a pretty good kisser. If I didn't already have my heart set on Isaac, I might have given him another shot.

Maggie slides the tote from my shoulder and whispers, "It doesn't have to happen tonight."

The magic in my blood surges in disagreement, and I turn to tell her I have no reason to wait, but she's already moving toward the cluster of people circling the firepit, whoopie pies lifted in offering. Paige and Audrey, who fill out the rest of our close friend group, wave to us from the far side of the fire, where they've already laid claim to a prime spot. They didn't save space for us to join them. Probably Hannah's doing. Since Hannah's dad married Paige's mom last year, Paige has been slowly going over to the dark side. Laurel immediately gives up her seat on one of the logs behind them to join my sister. Her smile rivals those of the guys' vying for Maggie's attention.

But before I can work through what that might mean, Isaac shouts, "There she is."

It's only been a few weeks since school let out, but hearing his greeting is like a favorite song randomly playing on the radio. "Here I am," I say.

All he has to do now is come and get me.

"Y'all are still doing that?" Felix asks, shaking his head to fling off excess water. He smiles at me, only a glimmer of disappointment lingering in his eyes.

I duck my head to keep my smile from giving away everything I feel for Isaac. "It's kind of our thing." My voice doesn't get the memo and comes out all moony and velvet soft.

Catching up, Isaac cuts between us and slings an arm over my shoulder. "Now my *night* can begin." His lips graze my ear just long enough to send a shiver racing across my skin.

We're basically the same height, so I know he had to tilt his head down just a fraction to make contact with my ear. The thought sends a wave of tingles coursing through my body. I can't look at him for a sign that he did it on purpose without positioning my mouth directly in kissing range. But judging from the huskiness of his voice, I'm guessing he did.

Acknowledgments

There will never be enough thank yous for my editor Annie Berger and the whole Sourcebooks Fire team. Annie, you saw to the heart of this story and knew exactly what it needed to make it shine. Extra thanks to Liz Dresner for the perfect cover and Laura Boren for the gorgeous design inside; Manu Velasco and Aimee Alker for the thorough and fabulous copy editing and proofreading; Thea Voutiritsas for keeping everything moving smoothly in production; Rebecca Atkinson and Madison Nankervis for your marketing and publicity expertise; Jenny Lopez and Gabriell Calabrese for all the behind-the-scenes support; and Dana SanMar, for the cover art of my dreams!

Thank you to my amazing agent, Jenny Bent, for loving my stories and finding the best homes for them. Here's to many more!

All the hearts and eternal gratitude to my critique partners, Jessica Fonseca, Zoë Harris, and Courtney Howell. Our little

Writing Committee is the whole reason this book got written. Thank you for the check-ins, Zoom calls, cheerleading, support, and especially your brilliant feedback along the way.

Writer friends, I am so lucky to know you all. Special shout out to Megan McGee, Kerry Rea, Roselle Lim, Waverly Night, and Alexandra Kiley for your excitement and friendship. Tall Poppy Writers, you ladies inspire me every day. And to everyone at the Dalnaglar Castle retreat, led by Maggie Stiefvater, Anna Bright, and Sarah Batista-Pereira, (especially House Banshee!) our week in Scotland was magical and exactly the creative recharge I needed after turning in this book—let's burn some shit.

Hugs and massive thanks to Krysti Adams, Thalia Scott, Lindsay Smith, and Erin Williams for your friendship and willingness to read early (and sometimes messy) drafts of my books. Suzanne Junered, Sarah Southern, and Ashley Williams, despite the miles between us you are always in my heart. <3

So much love to my family: Dad & Susan, Mom, Karen, Art, Car, Nicholas, Chamberlain, Skip, Holly, Skylar, and Blayden; the Crispell crew—Gary, Pat, Pete, Liz, Dave, Amber, Asher, and Zeke; and JoAn Shaw, the Potters, and the Ledbetters, thanks for the coffee dates and years of friendship.

And always, thank you to Mark for believing in me—even when I don't. I'm so grateful for you and our kitties and this wonderful life we have (wherever we may be living by the time this book comes out!).

To every reader who picks this one up, thank you from the bottom of my heart.

About the Author

Susan Bishop Crispell earned a BFA in creative writing from the University of North Carolina at Wilmington. Born and raised in the mountains of Tennessee, she now lives twenty minutes from the beach in North Carolina with her husband and their two cats, Whisky and Orkney. She is very fond of baked goods and is always on the lookout for hints of magic in the real world. Her other books include *The Holloway Girls*, *The Secret Ingredient of Wishes*, and *Dreaming in Chocolate*.